nerve

LITERATE SMUT

Fiction, Essays, and Photographs
from Some of Today's Most Provocative Writers and Artists

nerve°
LITERATE SMUT

Genevieve Field and Rufus Griscom,

founders of the celebrated Webzine, *Nerve*

BROADWAY BOOKS   NEW YORK

BROADWAY

Broadway Books titles may be purchased for business or promotional use or for special sales. For information, please write to: Special Markets Department, Bantam Doubleday Dell Publishing Group, Inc., 1540 Broadway, New York, NY 10036.

BROADWAY BOOKS and its logo, a letter B bisected on the diagonal, are trademarks of Broadway Books, a division of Bantam Doubleday Dell Publishing Group, Inc.

Library of Congress Cataloging-in-Publication Data
Nerve : literate smut.
   p. cm.
  Selections compiled by Genevieve Field and Rufus Griscom from the Internet website Nerve.
  ISBN 0-7679-0257-2 (paper)
  1. Erotic literature, American. I. Field, Genevieve. II. Griscom, Rufus.
III. Nerve (Computer file)
PS509.E7N47 1998
818'.54080803538—dc21   98-15141
                                     CIP

FIRST EDITION

Designed by Lee Fukui

98 99 00 01 02 10 9 8 7 6 5 4 3 2 1

Contents

Habits 113

Debauchery 137

Reportage 187

Love Stories 211

Acknowledgments

Rufus and Genevieve

Numerous accomplices were necessary to inspire, shepherd, and sustain *Nerve* and its founders from the first "wouldn't it be great if . . ." conversation through the creation of this book.

Leif, Bruce, John P., Isabelle, Noel, KT, Amanda, Bronson, David, Marisa, Alex, and Megan nodded when *Nerve* was folly, smiled when it was madness, and pried us out of our desk chairs when it was the entirety of our lives. For this they are each due our eternal gratitude and an undistracted meal.

Steven, Stefanie, Marisa, Mark, and Andy unwittingly offered their example, camaraderie, and like-minded prodigal optimism. We look forward to sharing more of the same in the coming years.

Our beloved partners in crime—Joey, Lorelei, and Jack—thanks for your invaluable contributions to this volume, and for your friendship, music mutinies, and real doll jokes. They sustained us. Dr. Morningspam, we are better for your good humor, clarity of vision, and firm, decisive pen. So is this book.

Paul, John, and Peggy, we are grateful for your faith in us back when faith required squinting.

To our parents, and to Catherine and Marty, thank you for your unyielding support under duress.

And most of all, to every author and photographer who contributed to nerve.com and this book, we are grateful for your trust, iconoclasm, and common belief that human sentience must be celebrated with all possible lucidity.

Richard Kern

Introduction

Rufus and Genevieve, April 14, 1998

About a year ago, we set out to publish a magazine about sex. Not a magazine of porn or erotica—genres primarily dedicated to producing arousal—nor another glossy proffering tips on sex and romance, but rather a forthright magazine *about* sex. We were less interested in sexual technique or fantasy and more interested in the subtleties of real sexual experience. As clear as these distinctions were to us, they were lost on some of the journalists who wrote about *Nerve*, for whom sexual content necessarily fell in the preexisting porn–erotica–self-help continuum.

It's no accident that most writing on the subject falls in these categories; it's far more difficult to write outside of them. Describing the experience of sex—not just the positions—presents a challenge similar to that of describing color: language does not yet have much purchase on these perceptual realms. Describing the mechanics of sex presents the opposite problem: the process has been described too many times with the same constellation of words. Too many lovers have "warmed to the touch," then "purred like kittens," and eventually "switched into high gear," and finally "thought they were going to explode"; too many of these were "religious experiences" followed by obligatory cigarettes. Only the best writers are capable of discarding the Lego sets of sexual cliché in favor of describing sex and sexuality from scratch.

Even for those writers, there is a second challenge: Sex is a subject trip-wired with insecurities and conflicts—a subject that people lie about as a matter of course. Excavating one's desires requires bravery and an appetite for honesty that can overwhelm the gag-reflex of psychological discomfort.

Even when authors achieve this honesty, it may be confusing to readers who are used to focusing on how to *improve* their sex lives. We are a nation of improvers, forever looking for ways to increase efficiency and productivity, forever trying to fix things. Aging bothers us, so we try to fix it with plastic surgery and the latest miracle moisturizer; sex challenges us, so we deploy armies of sex therapists, erect bulwarks of self-help books. Popular magazines pitch in by recycling the same ten ways to improve our sex lives year in and year out. The assumption seems to be that once we are all operating at peak efficiency, having orgasms on command, undistracted by embarrassment and guilt, the sex "problem" will be solved, and there will be nothing more to talk about.

Nerve stands in stark contrast to this mentality: We don't want to fix sex, we want to examine it. We don't want to achieve perfect sex, we want to savor imperfect sex. The obsession with fixing things, in our opinion, can be a way of avoiding them. The best writers and artists have long suggested this alternative to the self-help ethos: Relish life's complications. Don't do away with them, record them. Do this first because the result is often beautiful and second because the process helps us better understand each other, helps us bridge the gulfs between our insular skulls.

When we first concluded that we had no choice but to create this magazine, we immediately assembled a list of our favorite sixty writers in the world. We then spent several months writing heartfelt letters to the ones we could track down, which we sent along with a copy of our mission statement ("What Are We Thinking?" which you'll find on page xiv). We knew at the time that this was the whole game: lacking significant money or name recognition, we needed to compel a critical mass of talented writers and photographers with our idea and the strength of our conviction.

The response to *Nerve* from writers, and subsequently from the media and public, wildly exceeded our expectations. On June 27, 1997, the morning after we launched the magazine quietly from our cramped New York apartment, the phone rang. An hour later we were live on CNN; a week later, we were in *Newsweek*. Since then, millions of readers have been through the Web site, and our lives have been a frenzied blur of ink-smattered manuscripts, half-eaten Chinese food, and strobing computer screens.

Many of the writers and photographers whose work appears in the pages that follow responded to that first series of letters; most of them are people whose work we've admired from a distance for years, though a few were unpublished writers we discovered through word of mouth. The book is divided into seven chapters that reflect some of the different sensitivities and themes that we looked for in submissions. Each chapter begins with an introduction by one or both of us: We figured that after many months of encouraging writers to bare themselves on the page, it was only appropriate that we do the same.

What Are We Thinking?

Rufus and Genevieve

We are a couple of garden-variety sex enthusiasts, much like the rest of you mammals. On a good night we call out to the heavens and thrash about like hooked bass, clamoring after those precious few seconds of blindness. As the bed comes to a quiet stop and the last picture falls off the wall, the recent commotion can be hard to explain—it all made sense a few moments ago and now we are just sticky and naked and looking for our clothes.

We've created *Nerve* (nerve.com) because we think that sex is beautiful and absurd, remarkably fun and reliably trauma-inducing. In short, it is a subject in need of a fearless, intelligent forum for both genders. We believe that women (men too, but especially women) have waited long enough for a smart, honest magazine on sex, with cuntsure (and cocksure) prose and fiction as well as striking photographs of naked people that capture more than their flesh.

Nerve has set out to be more graphic, forthright, and topical than "erotica," but less blockheadedly masculine than "pornography." It's about sexual literature, art, and politics as well as about getting off—and we realize that these interests sometimes conflict. Erotica does not always understand this—that once our desire reaches a certain clip, attempts at artistry become annoying obstacles in the path of the nouns and verbs (or precious pixels) that deliver the goods. We find ourselves hunting for the naked details in erotica like rushed shoppers in a crowded store. *Nerve* intends to be direct with both word and image, whether the result is flushed faces, genitals, or perhaps just reflective thought.

This is why we decided the subject of sex deserved a magazine of its own: less to celebrate the gymnastics of sex than to appreciate the way it humbles us, renders us blushing teenagers. Our bodies are fickle, oblivious to convention, and not always beautiful. But we think shame (in small doses) is to be cherished—it makes us honest and human and trims our paunchy egos. It is also lush terrain for good writers; after all, rarely is honesty as difficult and memorable as it is in bed. We both still have a smelly-fingered fascination with our shame and desire and have spent the last year encouraging others to unveil theirs in the stories and personal essays gathered here.

Just as we individuals are not sure whether to be embarrassed or thrilled by our libidinous flights, our society as a whole suffers a similar schizophrenia, at once sex-obsessed and puritanical. *Nerve* is dedicated to shedding light on some of these cultural ironies. Sex, after all, is more than a popular sport and marketing tool: It is a truth-telling vehicle. Sex calls our bluff—it makes us want to lie, sermonize on the weather, spill our beer. We think this is good reason to look a little closer, examine our discomfort, maybe finish the drink.

Finally, we would like to make plain that although we believe in sexual freedom and obvious political rights, we are not on some fix-eyed mission to rally the forces of sexual revolution. Though some would dispose of taboos entirely, we prefer to gnaw on them like squeaky dog toys. Of course it's not lost on us that a world without taboos would be a little less in need of *Nerve*.

Shame
Shame

Lyle Ashton Harris

Shame, like orgasm, can be fleeting. It sends its message as swiftly as a hornet underfoot, stinging me for sharpening my tongue on someone softer than myself or for letting down a good friend in some small but significant way. But I am forgiven or I forgive myself and move on, hopefully noting the incident for future reference. I can count on one hand the things I'm ashamed of at this very moment, and my sexuality is not one of them...at this very moment.

I spend my days editing personal essays and stories about sex—born as painfully, sometimes, as children—and what I've learned is that sexual shame is hard to shake. Slump-shouldered from the weight, we carry it with us until we stop noticing the burden. Of course, there are the rare few who see all sex as good sex, who've never cringed at the sight of themselves flagrantly fawning over a hot prospect, never regretted following a capricious sexual impulse, never worried about their reputation. But for most of us, shame is to lust as a mother is to a teenager: a dampener, a voice of temperance that persists until it is heard.

For years, shame did my libido a significant disservice. I've spent considerable mental energy and some money tracing its origins and pondering why it grew even as things got good in bed. Here's a fact that several former boyfriends don't know: I had my first orgasm at twenty-five. (There you have it, boys, in print.) I wouldn't blame them for being surprised, for I was a good faker. No *When Harry Met Sally* melodrama was necessary; a few adoring sighs did the trick, or should I say, got me off the hook. I do, however, have a small bone to pick with one of them: for almost a decade, my voice of shame spoke not in a mother's hushed tones but in the jocular, California-drawl of my first love.

I was a shy, bookish teenager, brimming with fantasies of some black-eyed artist with paint-stained nails who'd hand me my sexuality like a perfect red rose. The rebellious artist never materialized. If he had, who knows? Perhaps he'd have nurtured my inner beast, rather than teaching it to watch its mouth and sit and stay until it was called upon. Anyway, just when I was beginning to believe I was invisible to the opposite sex, the captain of the basketball team plucked me from obscurity with a kiss, gave me his letterman's jacket (yes, really), and then his devotion—with some qualifications.

Sex was boring, but that wasn't the point. The point was that I was finally having it, and I'd done everything right—insisting we wait a year, securing birth control well prior to the fact, etcetera. It became as regular as the commute from my country house to his mom's apartment in town. Then one night, we split a bottle of wine out on the golf course where the grass was soft and the stars bright, and when he pushed himself inside me I forgot about *his* pleasure, for once. Maybe it was the wine, but behind my closed eyes, where the scrim was usually black, I projected the entire varsity basketball team. Fresh from post-game showers, they stood around us in a circle, fondling themselves. I reached down and rubbed myself in the place that felt the best. I made feral noises in the back of my throat and wiggled for the team. "Fuck me!" I cried gleefully, and not surprisingly, he did, for about three more seconds, before collapsing on top of me.

The next morning he came to my house, wearing an expression I'd last seen on my father when I was caught cheating on my Chemistry final. He drove me to a remote cul-de-sac and asked me if I remembered what I'd said the night before. I did, because it was the first time I'd ever spoken that way, but I hedged my bets and said I didn't.

"Maybe I misheard you," he said, "because we were both drunk. But I thought I heard you say..." He turned away, unrolled the window and breathed deeply of the crisp winter air.

"You must have misheard," I said.

"Yes," he said, relieved. "Thank goodness. It's still you."

But I knew the truth: I wasn't still me. Overnight, I'd spawned an evil twin—a slut, a shameless hussy—and if I wanted to keep the letterman's jacket, I'd better keep her quiet.

To be fair, the blame for my years of so-called frigidity cannot rest on one Puritanical high school boy. I was too high strung about sex: every absent-minded thrust, every windowward gaze or half-hearted stroke was a sign of my lover's greater discontent, even disgust, with me and my body in its various states. Where had I learned to be so insecure? And why?

I tried to blame my proper mother for all of it: the guilt, the boredom, the insecurity in bed. "Nonsense," she said, clearly stung. It *was* nonsense. Blaming her was about as useful as blaming the media—tempting, but missing the larger point that (with some horrible exceptions) a woman's body and mind are accountable only to each other.

Eventually, I had my first orgasm, but I'm going to skip *that* story. I will say that it happened only after I stopped giving myself such a hard time, realizing that shame was a natural by-product of an active imagination and an analytical mind. I'll even argue that shame makes sex more interesting, raises the stakes between two people who must coach each other through their insecurities to that hyperreal moment when they can finally let go.

That's why we can devote an entire chapter to shame without fear of depressing our readers—far from gloomy, the stories here are wise and often funny. Al Goldstein, founding father of raunchier-than-thou *Screw* magazine, remembers his first lover, a prostitute, who told him, "Anything you do is fine," and, with those words, set him free. In "Autobiography of a Body," Lucy Grealy reflects on the years she spent punishing herself for being "ugly" by sleeping with the wrong men and rejecting the ones who could see beyond her physical scars. Thom Jones describes a teenage boy's public humiliation—one that he can see no way to undo save subjecting himself to a much more complex degradation. Debra Boxer shares her pride and embarrassment as a twenty-eight-year-old virgin. And though John Perry Barlow declares himself a shameless ladies' man, the attentive reader will detect that he's no stranger to shame. Indeed, after submitting the essay that follows, Barlow got cold feet and gave us a version in which his brashness was dampened considerably. We liked the first version better, believing that readers would finally appreciate his impolitic honesty even if they didn't agree with his personal philosophy. Why do all of these writers embrace their most intimate weaknesses? They may have learned that in moments of shame, humanity is at its most human.   —*GF*

Autobiography of a Body

Lucy Grealy

I began my seductions incognito, as a boy. With hair shorter than my brothers' had ever been and my thin body almost breastless, the only thing which might have given away my true sex was my rather curvy (though at the time I would only describe them as "too big") hips. This problem was solved by wearing huge shirts and baggy pants, clothes usually bought in the boys' or men's departments of the local thrift store. At one point, at the age of twenty or twenty-one, I was denied entrance to a PG-13 movie because the ticket seller was convinced I was a twelve-year-old boy. A degree of pride deepened my voice when I told my friends about the incident.

A few other times men approached me in the bars I haunted with my friends. I could see them eyeing me from across the room, and I'd watch them slowly but surely work their way through the crowd towards me.

"What are you drinking?" "I haven't seen you here before." "You look just like someone I know. What's your name?" The lines were ancient and predictable. And just as predictable was the gallant quickness with which these men would scramble away as soon as they heard my high, undeniably female voice. These were, after all, homosexual bars.

I told my friends about these comic scenes too, but I left out crucial elements to the story. I left out how secretly thrilling it was to have these men desire me, even if for only a minute, even if only by mistake. I left out how safe I felt, knowing that I could "pretend" to be attractive, yet without challenging my deeply ingrained habits of fear. I was afraid, no, make that sure, that I was ugly, that no one would ever want me, that I would die an unloved virgin. My chin and jaw were scarred and distorted from childhood jaw cancer, and the words "scarred" and "distorted" were, without a doubt, synonymous with "ugly," which was synonymous with "unlovable."

Being "ugly" was the cause of all my life's despair, of this I was sure. It was true I had many friends who loved me, but the fact that I didn't have a lover, even by the time I graduated from college, was proof that I would never be a card-carrying member of the sexual world. Beauty was the key to all happiness and the only way I would ever find love; without it, I was meaningless.

Sex became a litmus test; if I could get someone to have sex with me, that would prove that I was lovable. I overlooked the fact that all the men I knew were gay, and that I made no attempt whatsoever to find a lover—no, my virginity, my unhappiness, my sense of self, and my face all grew so intertwined that I became unable to respond "I'm depressed" when someone asked me how I felt. All I could say, believing this said it all, was, "I'm ugly."

During my first year of teaching, I asked my English Composition students to write a paper about a time when they were truly afraid. To my surprise, every single one of them wrote about either a ride on a roller coaster, or a horror film they had seen. Though I had no doubt that they'd experienced real fear in the course of their lives, it struck me as sad and foreboding that they could only recognize it clearly when it happened vicariously. No fear that originated within them was acknowledgeable.

I had a similar blindness to the nature of my relationships with gay men. Gay men, especially the kind that frequent particular clubs in lower Manhattan, structure their personalities around the grammar of sex. My friends throbbed and sweated and grinded around me, spoke constantly in overt innuendos; yet there I was, poor little old me, secretly learning about sex by osmosis, pretending that none of this had anything to do with me.

Even at the age of twenty-one, sex was still a murky thing—I wasn't entirely sure how people could bear to look at each other afterwards. All those legions of friends who adored me and who told me I was beautiful and lovable meant nothing in the face of such an event; only actual intercourse would convince me I was worth anything at all.

A week after moving to Iowa to attend the Writers' Workshop, far away from the safe male homosexual world of college, I lost my virginity. Looking back, I have no doubt I was an easy mark for Jude, the man who had the honors. He was tall, broadly built, and extremely chivalrous. We met when I asked him the time at a local auction, where I was buying furniture for my barren apartment. I must have glowed with naïveté and I know now that this was precisely what attracted him to me, for Jude was without a doubt an opportunist and, in many respects, a bastard. He was seventeen years older than me and deep in the throes of a rather unoriginal midlife crisis which demanded he drive imported sports cars and seduce young virgins. Of course, I did not see it this way at the time.

In my mind, Jude was the most dashing thing going, and I could not believe someone as worldly and as handsome as he would want me. Jude was obsessed with sex. Fortunately, he was experienced and taught me both the basics and the exotics: the precise place on a man's penis that was most sensitive; how, while sitting on top of a man, I could vary the speed and depth of the thrusts; that if I hummed as gutturally as possible while performing oral sex it had a noticeable effect. He taught me all this openly, even academically, standing or lying there stark naked in his living room, speaking as evenly as if he were teaching me how to drive a stick shift. "You'll drive men wild for the rest of your life," he told me. The thought filled me with power, yes, but also hope: someone might one day love me.

Unfortunately, I began to assume some of his philosophies about sex. If before I had confused sex and love, now I was slowly becoming exactly the kind of person I'd never quite understood before: someone who could use sex as a weapon, someone who could distance herself from a lover through sex. This hit me one day while listening to a Leonard Cohen song in the car—a song about a man leaving a woman. My whole life, up until that point, I'd always identified with the lovelorn woman; suddenly, I realized I identified with the man who just wanted to be free.

It was not only for his immediate sexual pleasure that Jude taught me things. Jude, who had been raised in an orphanage, was deeply unable to commit to any one woman, yet, at the same time, was desperate to mean

Taryn Simon

something special to women. Jude wanted me to go out and sleep with other men, but he wanted me to always think of him when I did so. A dedicated emotional manipulator of women himself, he told me how to manipulate men sexually. He taught me how to choose and then perform a specific yet nonsexual act during sex, such as a certain way of stroking a man's forearm, or tapping his elbow. Do this often enough and the act becomes sexualized, so that, in public (and it was important that it be in public), all I would have to do was tap my man's elbow and immediately he would get a hard on. This kind of power astounded me—astounded me that it was *me* who had it, and astounded me that anyone could be that easily manipulated. Once more, I felt unloved, no longer because a person *wouldn't* have sex with me, but because mere calculation could steer them towards desiring me.

Jude also taught me about the complicated relationship most men have to their anuses; how sexually charged yet humiliating this arousal is for them; how, if I could break that barrier with them subtly and correctly, they would become dependent upon me to provide that secret pleasure. Now I could not only convince men to have sex with me, and then resent them for it, but, if I used their desires against them, cause them to resent *me* for it. Jude's world was all about emotional dominance and manipulation, about tricking people into becoming obsessed with you, and, ultimately, about the total absence of love. I had come full circle.

But I'm getting ahead of myself here. In one year I went from dressing like a boy to becoming a seductress—quite a swing of the pendulum. Once Jude had me under his sexual wing, he started instructing me in how to dress. Short leather skirts, high heels, garter belts. These were items I'd never have considered wearing only a short time ago, but the simple fact that Jude was "willing" to sleep with me gave him power over me. And even though I still hated my face, I had to admit I had a good body. Yet the scant clothing I wore became just as much a costume as my asexual garb had been previously: it hid me from myself, from my own fears. I became dependent upon the clothes to the point where I could not even go to the grocery store without dressing up.

Before I'd ever had sex, I saw it only as a way to prove that I was not ugly, and therefore lovable. Yet because the sex-equals-love equation didn't bear out, I continued to feel ugly and concluded I was not having *enough* sex, or *good-enough* sex. This was, after all, easier than reconsidering the basic truth of the equation itself. Despite the fact that all I really wanted was for one special person to love me, I persisted in believing I could only conjure this person by being as sexual with as many people as possible.

At Jude's urging, and even long after we had our final split, I went out and seduced men whenever and wherever I could. I vaguely reasoned that each man I slept with brought me five to six inches closer to the man who would ultimately love me. Bent on proving I was desirable, I worked my way through a series of affairs that always ended, I was absolutely certain, because I wasn't beautiful enough. Convinced that anyone who might actually want to have a relationship with me was someone I didn't want, I began hurting people, though of course I never saw this. If they regretted my leaving (my favorite ploy was simply to move to another city or even another country), I simply refused to believe I could matter that much. I felt I had only tricked them into loving me, and therefore their love could never be genuine. In retrospect, I see my lovers dropped me many hints that it was more than this, but at the time I thought I had to hedge my bets by investing my energies in quantity.

There was no easy way to climb out of this cycle, which cavorted on for years. Each man offered some type of power: I slept with a friend's boyfriend because it made me feel sexier than her, I slept with a plastic surgeon in his examining room because it made me feel less like a patient, and I slept with numerous married men because, perversely, I wanted to be married. I slept with sleazeballs because I thought it would prove I didn't care, I slept with drunks because I was drunk, and I slept with men I hated because I thought it would prove I would do anything for love.

Though often sorrowful throughout the years of my sexual rabidness, I do not want this to stand as a parable on the virtues of monogamy. What caused my sadness and my deep-seated insatiableness was not a moral breakdown on my part (as conservative cultural watchdogs would have us believe) but rather my credulousness in believing beauty equals worthiness. I had not yet recognized all the subtle clues that beauty is only an easy label for a complex set of emotions: feelings of safety and grace and well-being.

Most important to my blindness, I think, was my belief that I was in this alone, that I was the only one who had these doubts. Though very subtly, without my ever knowing it consciously, my sexual and emotional lives were slowly forming some kind of underground harmony. Consciously, however, I still did not recognize sex as a shared experience: I saw it as a contest, two people in different rooms trying to push various buttons, despite all the hints that Fate was dropping me.

I remember, once, having sex inside a wax museum in Berlin with one of the curators. He was a very handsome curator—a bit like Paul Newman, but with bad teeth. We were behind the Franz Liszt display: a dusty Liszt in a yellow brocaded coat seated on a bench mechanically and repeatedly bent forward and sat up in front of a piano that was playing the same solo over and over again. My lover and I fruitlessly rubbed against each other. Museum patrons kept clopping past us, hidden from view by a fake wall.

"I think this I can't do," he finally told me in his heavy accent, sitting up. "Too many people. And, I keep thinking how I could lose my job."

"But you do think I'm attractive, don't you?" I asked him, worried again.

He looked at me quizzically for a long moment, the piano starting again at the beginning of its loop. "Of course," he said, and paused again, a line of deep and serious concern on his face. "We both are. It is the music that makes us so."

Das ewig weibliche zieht uns hinan.
The eternally feminine leads us forward.
Goethe

He who binds himself to a joy does the winged life destroy,
But he who kisses the joy as it flies lives in Eternity's sunrise.
William Blake

Only connect.
E. M. Forster

A Ladies' Man
and Shameless

John Perry Barlow

I'm finally ready to declare myself. I am a ladies' man. A womanizer. A libertine. A rake. A rogue. A roué. A goddamn running loose dog. I'd admit to being a lecher, but that word implies a solipsistic predation that I hope never applies to any of my relations with the mysterious sex. This is about something more sacred than anything a drooling wanker could appreciate.

This is about worship. From the time the testosterone kicked in, I have knelt at the altar of that which is female in this world. I love women. What I love in them is something that moves and must be free to do so. I love their smells, their textures, their complexities, the inexhaustible variety of their psychic weather patterns. I love to flirt with them, dance with them, and to discourse with them endlessly on the differences between men and women. I love to make love.

The sexual fires have always burned bright in my brainstem. Priapically preoccupied, I've written poetry by the ream, stormed police lines, ridden broncs, thrown punches, and generally embarrassed myself on countless occasions. (Actually, I suspect that history consists largely of foolish things men have done to show off for women.)

There are probably twenty-five or thirty women—I certainly don't count them—for whom I feel an abiding and deep emotional attachment. They're scattered all over the planet. They range in age from less than half to almost twice my own. Most of these relationships are not actively sexual. Some were at one time. More never will be. But most of them feel as if they could become so. I love the feel of that tension, the delicious gravity of possibilities.

I must also admit that for me this gravity generally increases with novelty. The New, the fresh and unknown expanses of the emotional frontier, hold a fascination for me that I wish they did not. This breeds superficiality and the appearance of a hunger for conquest. But, unfortunately, I love the voltage, the charged gap between two people that can draw across itself such huge flows of information from so many parts of us. I love the feel of human bandwidth—intercourse on all channels—and there is so much more to exchange when nothing is yet known.

Despite many clear and cosmic messages that women (and death) were meant to be the curricula of my life—my dharma—and that practically everything I've done has been about trying to understand them, I resisted formal matriculation into this perilous course of study until well past the age when most men have already given up and settled into monogamies as comfortable and unquestioned as their football loyalties.

And now, late in my forties, I doubt I'll ever be monogamous again. For reasons I'll explain, I feel strangely exiled into a condition of emotional wandering. I think my heart will travel widely. I want to know as many more women as time and their indulgence will permit me.

Even so, I also want to go on loving the women I love now—and I do love them—for the rest of my life. These are relationships that have already lasted much longer than most marriages, even though some of them had to endure the hiatus of my own previous monogamies, one imposed by society, the other by what felt like an act of God.

The Road to Hell

I tried monogamy despite feeling from the get-go that being monogamous made as much sense as declaring that I liked, say, mashed potatoes and gravy so darned much that I would resolve to eat nothing else for the rest of my life.

So I got married and stayed that way for seventeen years, attempting with some grim success to impose fidelity on myself. It was, I figured, the price I had to pay in return for a good place to raise kids. And though I loved my ex-wife, and still do, I wasn't in love with her. Didn't believe in it, actually. I thought being in love was a myth people had invented to punish themselves for lacking it.

Fidelity always felt like work: an act of will rather than nature. As time passed, nature gradually gained the upper hand, as she almost always does. I was never quite able to stop flirting—a form of exchange that has always felt holy to me—nor was I able to disguise from my wife my undiminished appreciation of other women. This led to sexual distance between us, and I started to get hungry. There began to be incidents of what is called, in rock 'n' roll, "offshore drilling." Not realizing that women hate deceit even more than they hate infidelity—and they *always* know—I turned into a sneak and a liar. I became someone I couldn't respect, and so I left my marriage.

Not long after that, I experienced the miracle of *voluntary* monogamy for one brief and blissful period, during which, at the age of forty-six, I did fall in love for the first time in my life. During the year that followed, it was as though there were no other women except in the most abstract sense. I still delighted in the presence of pulchritude, but it was an appreciation as sublime in its detachment as my enjoyment of nature's other wonders. I didn't want to *do* anything about these beauties, any more than I would want to *do* something about sunsets or Bach fugues. Cynthia was the only woman. But two days before we were to be married, I put her on a plane in Los Angeles and somewhere between there and New York the virus that had been secretly consuming her stopped her heart.

The most important consequence of losing Cynthia is that I now believe in the human soul. I had to see it and, once seen, it became obvious to me. No longer did I dismiss it as a biological artifact, a kind of software that arises in the electrochemical sputterings of the squishyware and cannot run otherwise. Rather I can feel the soul as an independent though immaterial identity that wears bodies like a costume.

I finally had the answer to a question I'd been asked shortly before I met her. I'd been speaking to a bunch of kids at the New York University film school about virtual reality when I got the usual question about virtual sex.

This was such a predictable question that I had a mental tape I always ran in response to it that went something like: "I don't get the fascination with virtual sex. Sex is about bodies, and being in VR is like having had your body amputated. What could be less sexy?"

At this point, a very embodied young woman in the front row raised her beautiful hand. "But don't you

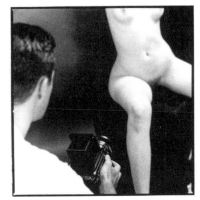

Barbara Vaughn

think," she asked, "that when it comes to sex, the body is just a prosthesis?"

My tape stopped running. "A prosthesis for what?"

"That's the interesting question, isn't it," she smiled, all sphinxy.

Yeah. That was the interesting question alright, and Cynthia, in both the way she inhabited her body and the way she remained after leaving it, answered it for me. There is, indeed, a hand that moves the hand.

At that point I decided that, whatever the pressures of society or the propensity of most women to insist on it, I wouldn't attempt monogamy again unless and until I encountered someone who induced it in me as naturally as she had. And I like to believe that nothing would make me happier than to have that happen. To fall in love. To be singularly devoted again.

(But I have to confess to aspects of my current behavior pattern that are subconsciously designed to prevent this very thing from happening. If just once in your life you've put all of your emotional eggs in one basket, only to have that basket smashed almost immediately, it inclines you toward more distributed systems of emotional support.)

There is a central woman in my life, a luminous Swede who lives in San Francisco. She is the person I always call when I feel bad in the middle of the night. She is beautiful and funny, as game on an adventure as Indiana Jones; she is a sexual poet, and I love her.

That she is not the only woman in my life pains her—as will this piece—and I wish to cause her no pain. But I learned from my marriage what suffering can be inflicted by someone who tries unsuccessfully to contain himself in the service of someone else's feelings.

And scrupulous honesty, though it requires courage on both sides, is a lot more practical than most men believe it to be. The fact that I don't lie to her about these other encounters brings us closer rather than separating us. And sin, as Nietzsche said (and I often quote), is that which separates.

A Pariah's Advantages

While I've been honest about all this to my girlfriend and the other objects of my affection, I haven't come clean in public until now. It's an odd omission. I've tried to write as candidly as possible about my other deviations from standard American morality. I'm in the lucky position of being so deinstitutionalized that I can say whatever I like without fear of adverse economic consequences. Indeed, lunatic candor seems to be my primary product these days. Like Hunter S. Thompson, the badder I get, the better I get paid.

A bad reputation can set you free. After all, if you've already declared yourself to be a pot-smoking, acid-addled slut, your opponents are forced to oppose your ideas on their merits, rather than strategically revealing your hidden depravities. Shame is no weapon against the shameless.

In fact, part of what motivates this public revelation is a belief that I am behaving morally, despite following a course that society would generally condemn. My conscience is clear, a fact that is not simply due to poor memory or an unwillingness to examine it carefully.

These admissions are also related to the fact that I find myself a few gray hair-breadths away from turning fifty, an age beyond which surreptitious ladies' men become pathetic in direct proportion to the uneasiness they feel with their own lascivious impulses.

The phrase "dirty old man" begins to haunt me, especially as I continue to find my pot-bellied old self attracted to the same youthful feminine specifications that put steel in my poker when I was twenty-five.

Yet that's not all there is to it: for me, it is the combination of the two beauties, the inner and the outer, that draws me most compellingly. There are plenty of perfectly formed surfaces that have no light within them and they don't do much for me. At the same time, there are beautiful souls within bodies that are the female equivalent of my own, and while some of these are close friends, they lack the sexual spice that really fuels most discourse between the sexes.

I thus remain convinced that there is something holy about beauty, whether attached to a woman or a waterfall, and I have the entire history of art—at least until the twentieth century—to back me up on this. I don't think of beauty as being something that is part of a woman, but rather something like a mist that gathers around her that becomes more beautiful if illuminated brightly from within. The real beauty, the part that lasts, is in the soul and not the skin.

Though even when one is seeking sex between souls, the "prostheses" they wear are not irrelevant.

King Dick Meets My Inner Lesbian

But ironically enough, a lot of being sexy means getting past the root-level sex drive. One of the great moments in my sexual education came some years back when Dick Cavett was interviewing Raquel Welch at the height of her va-va-voomishness. "Tell me, Raquel," he leered, "what's your favorite erogenous zone?"

She paused, gave him a level look that completely revised my opinion of her intelligence, and said crisply, "My mind, Dick."

The mind, I have since discovered, is just about every woman's favorite erogenous zone, but it is mystical terrain and must be explored with care and time. The dick, in its youthful phase, is not big on care or time. It is the very definition of urgency. It makes nonnegotiable demands of its bearer that are related to the inner nature of its target only to the extent that some knowledge of her has strategic value in getting her into bed.

Now my formerly dictatorial appendage is more like an old sidekick. A fellow veteran. It doesn't have the same reload rate of old, but there's no *ejaculatio praecox* to worry about either. The old soldier can pace itself. And if it can't spit five shots in quick succession, it's no longer calling my shots as it once did. Into the vacuum of its diminished authority has risen my heretofore undiscovered inner lesbian.

My inner lesbian is a wonderful accomplice, since she knows a lot about what turns women on, is more attuned to sensuality than the old in-out, and believes strongly that the journey is the reward. This doesn't mean that she is not interested in orgasms, but she knows that one great thing about being a woman is that if you can come at all—which a lamentably high percentage cannot—you can usually come a lot and in a variety of ways. She makes it a lot easier to get away from my own sexual objectives and into the multifarious delights of the joint critter, the one Shakespeare called "the beast with two backs."

And creating that larger organism, making the Other into the Self, merging the Self into the Other is, after all, what sex is ultimately about. And of course, the point is not to have a self at all. To be Everything.

The Infinity of Love

All said, you're probably wondering why any woman would want to become emotionally or physically involved with a man whose promiscuity is so freely confessed. Of course, many of them don't. I eliminate a lot of opportunity by wearing my Don Juan warning placard so visibly (even then, the hesitant don't leave me entirely bereft).

But most of the resistance to becoming involved with a self-admitted playboy has to do with that all-important female perception of being *special*. It is hard to feel that knowing there are others out there. But there is an answer to this, and finding it has enabled me to feel a deeper sense of connection not only with women but with all the rest of my species.

The answer is that everyone *is* special. So also is every relationship. The creature that forms between any one person and another is like no other creature in the world. It is theirs and theirs alone. Furthermore, while time and space and attention may be painfully finite, love is not. Love has no quantity to exhaust. It is a quality, a living thing, that grows stronger the more it is felt. The vigorous practice of love expands the heart and opens its apertures to the world.

In other words, to love a lot of women, you have to love them, without a trace of bullshit, one woman at a time. You have to bring each of them with you into the perfectly present, creating there a private zone of space and time that can be filled with that particular love. You won't have any of the comforting (though generally broken) social conventions to assure you that your vulnerability is safe. There are no assurances at all except for those that come directly from the feeling of connection you can make together. You are, in effect, beating back the darkness with the light you generate yourselves.

When I judge myself, there is one question I ask: Would I want my daughters to encounter a man like me? And because I want them to be brave in their love, because I want their faith to be annealed by experience on the edge, I hope they find a few of my kind. But I hope they don't bring too many of us home.

I Love You,
Sophie Western

Thom Jones

Frankie Dell tried to get a fix on the bathroom mirror. He was jangled and wired still from an acid trip on Saturday night and had a wicked case of double vision. The surface of his arms and legs tingled and deep down in these extremities he felt his very bones buzz. All shook up. Yeah, shook up and with his electric bones, Frankie was moving around the bathroom only partly sure of what he was doing, partly sure of what was going down. Barely had a clue. Getting ready for school? So it seemed.

Fifteen seconds after Frankie dropped the acid, he knew he had made a grave error. Now, he was drawing blanks. He couldn't remember diddly. He would never know the whole truth. Funny he wasn't back in the nuthouse. Funny, he was in his own bathroom. Like, funny-ha. He opened a medicine vial, shook out two lithium tablets and dry-swallowed the pills. Horse-chokers.

There was a pimple in the crease of Frankie's nostril. He took a drag on his Marlboro and studied it. Of all the damn things. It was a hot one, too.

He felt like callin' the old lady in and have her take a look at it. Call a dermatologist or sumthin'.

Frankie dabbed some Clearasil on the pimple. Needed another tube. Well, you better put it on the pharmacy list, slim. And you better fuckin' hurry up. What time is it, anyhow? He could hear his mother bustling around in the kitchen.

Frankie draped a cigarette in the corner of his mouth and did his cool look *with cigarette*. It was definitely better *with cigarette*—too bad you couldn't smoke at school. He frowned at the thought and it made his hooded black eyes look cruel. Bushy eyebrows, snake-dead eyes. From the front-and-center mugshot view and from the profile, it was such a bad look he scared his own fuckin' self.

"Frankie, I'm late. I gotta go," his mother said through the door. "Don't forget to take your lithium. You were up prowling all night. If you start another cycle, I'm gonna lay down and die, Frankie. Lay down and die."

The Monday morning homeroom scene was dismal, but Darlene D'Arcel was there, and that was unusual for a Monday. Her neck was full of hickies and Darlene seemed proud of them. In spite of all the skin flicks Frankie knew by heart, sex was still a mystery. God, he wanted some of that fine stuff and Darlene D'Arcel knew it. "Hey, Frankie, whatcha doin'? Checkin' out my hickies ain't ya? Caught ya, ha ha. You wan' some nookie, doncha? Ha ha. Eatcha heart out kid."

Darlene spread her legs and flashed a little white thigh meat before she gathered up her books and twitched her hot little ass out into the hall...ssst ssst *boom*. Patent leather Mary Jane's, lace-fringed anklets, slender legs, and nice, firm breasts. Humongo! Frankie flashed his cool look as he slung his books under his arm and moved out behind her.

Darlene D'Arcel couldn't have been more than fifteen but Frankie regarded her as a grown woman. She had those kind of moves. He knew she went out with some real bad testosterone motherfucker who drove a jet black 'Vette, with the rear license plate framed in blue neon. It went without saying that she was putting out. Frankie wanted to stab himself in the heart with a dull spoon.

Following Darlene through the hall he was so entranced that Jesse Stillman hit him like a freight train. It happened way too fast. Stillman got right up in his face, his horny finger thumping Frankie in the chest, a deep basso voice. "I'll see you after school!" And then—gone!

Shit! Frankie came down from the pink panty cloud in a hurry. Man, why did he have to run off his mouth so much behind Stillman's back? He doubted that Stillman knew Frankie had flattened his tires. He hadn't told anyone that. He hadn't told Altman on LSD last night. Or had he? God!

Second period math, and Mr. Harding called Frankie to the board to do a geometry problem. Frankie glowed red as he fumbled with the chalk, knowing he couldn't solve the problem if he had a year. And Harding didn't let him off as usual.

"I can't do it," Frankie said, his body shifting from pose to pose. He couldn't do the problem but at least he could show a little attitude. *So hip. So cool. So tough. Such a bad motherfucker!* Then he thought of the pimple. He wondered if it was popping through the blotch of Clearasil. He crinkled his nose and a little white dust settled on his lips. Christ, if he was standing there with a Rudolph-the-red-nose pimple he was a double fucking loser. He said, "Ya know, Mr. Harding. I don't get it, man." Frankie gave a short, chesty laugh. Embarrassment up-the-ass.

"Obviously you don't get it, Mr. Dell," Harding said with an air of shrill amusement. "Perhaps tomorrow you can redeem yourself a bit by expounding on Heisenburg's uncertainty principle."

"On what?"

"Heisenburg, sir. Go to the library and check it out or you're going to fail, my little friend."

Half the class tittered, but a girl in the second row didn't. She gave him a conspiratorial wink. She was on his side. Or was she? There was definitely eye contact, but he was so damn paranoid and hungover he didn't know how to interpret the look. He had never even spoken to her before. Was it a look of compassion or of mockery and disdain? The more he thought about it the more paranoid he got. Ever since he got out of bed his whole life had become a ludicrous cartoon. Frankie went to third period hall monitor station feeling weak all over. He was shot. Couldn't someone call an ambulance? Jesus Christ!

Once the halls cleared Frankie walked into the boys' toilet and torched a Marlboro. The smoke calmed him a little and after he flushed the butt he stepped up to a urinal. With visions of Darlene D'Arcel's glossy thigh meat and her pink panties dancing through his brain, he just had to commit an act of self abuse. It was tension reduction, pure and simple. Get it over with and try to reestablish contact with reality. He was so strung out, he didn't know if that was possible.

As soon as he had his pleasure, the door to the boys' rest room bounced open. Frankie quickly stuffed his dissolving erection back into his blue jeans. He tried to compose himself and casually stepped away from the urinal as though he had just taken an everyday piss. To an astute observer the truth would be obvious. Fortunately it was only the janitor, a fat guy with a ton of grease in his hair.

"You feel okay?"

"Yeah, why?"

"You're all red there, short man."

"Naw, I'm all right. It's hot is all."

Frankie's English class was studying *Great Expectations*. Frankie had read it and liked it. While he was terrible at math, he was a speed reader with something close to a photographic memory. When he was in the nuthouse, in spite of the Haldol and lithium, Frankie could burn through thick books, a couple a day—they were like excursions to different worlds. Options, new possibilities for his own life occurred to him when he read good books. But back at home, in spite of his resolves he quickly fell into the old, bad habits as if he were in the very grip of the devil. It seemed that he lived only to masturbate. Five times a day? No problem. Seven? Hey, a piece of cake. How about twenty, try that one on for size. Twenty times! Once, twenty-two! Twenty-two times in a single day and still no peace—only monumental Catholic guilt. Twenty-two times!

After class Frankie remembered Stillman's threat and managed to collect his jacket and notebooks and take them to P.E. so he wouldn't get caught at his locker after school. When class ended, he made a clean getaway and went to Booker's Pool Hall to kill the couple of hours before work. After a dozen games of eight ball he stopped in at the Red & Black Spot for french fries and a Coke and then walked down the hill to his job at the movie theater.

It was "Old Oscar Week" at the Tivoli and there were only twenty-eight people at the seven o'clock showing of *Alfie*. Some kind of 1960s shit. Frankie gave the rest rooms a preliminary cleaning and then went out into the lobby to jaw with Donna Wilcox, the popcorn girl. He loved the refreshment stand where the boxed candies were neatly arranged under the immaculately clean plate glass of the dark oak display counter. The Tivoli sold the everyday cheap junk that you could get at any theater, but also hard-to-get stuff the bohemian types liked: Holloway Suckers, Slo Poke's Walnetto's, Necco Wafers, and Juji Fruits. The centerpiece of the refreshment oasis was a vintage corn popper inside a glass display case bordered with narrow strips of green, blue, and yellow stained glass. There was a "Fresh Popcorn" sign hand-painted in bright red with a yellow border on the front of the popper and just beneath it was a cardboard placard painted by Wesley, the projectionist. "Our popcorn, the finest available in the world, is organically grown in Amana, Iowa, exclusively for the Tivoli Theater. Choose between our iodine-free coarse sea salt, harvested from the crystal shores of Northern Morocco, or from the familiar Morton's in the classic 'When it rains, it pours!' boxes. Farmfresh, hot creamery butter is available upon request."

This was all a lie. The storeroom was stacked with sacks of generic salt and shiny aluminum tubs of thick white coconut oil and rancid margarine. Earl, the Tivoli's manager, approved of the deception and jacked up the price of a family bucket from three bucks to five after Wesley produced the sign.

Like Frankie, Donna Wilcox wore a uniform reminiscent of bygone times. She looked like a candy striper at a hospital. As she sliced a wedge of congealed coconut oil and dumped it into the corn popper, she smiled at Frankie and said, "So what's it like inside a nuthouse, Frankie? Or is this the nuthouse, this life we have here?"

"Nuthouses are boring," Frankie said. "Give me a box of Juji's."

Donna reached under the counter and Frankie saw a little cleavage. Donna's cotton uniform showed her figure off to a good advantage. She had pretty skin, full lips; at certain angles she almost looked okay. Donna handed Frankie a box of candy. "They'll rot your teeth, but here," she said pushing a box of candy over the glass case. "You don't look like a nutcase. You look like a normal guy. A cute guy."

Frankie began to launch Juji's up towards the ceiling and catch them in his mouth. He got to feeling cocky. Then he winced and raised his hand to his jaw. He flipped the box back on the counter. "Jesus! These are too hard, man. They been aged too long. Gimme a box of Black Crows."

He got another peek at Donna's cleavage and caught a faint whiff of perfume. Frankie ripped open the box of Black Crows and began catching them with his mouth. He flipped one up for Donna and she caught it. He popped a few more up and they made a game of vying for them. Frankie arched a long one up near the ceiling and after he caught it, he and Donna fell together. She planted her mouth on his and kissed him deeply pressing her soft bosom against his chest. Frankie's cheeks got hot and he sprung an instant boner. Donna kissed him again and then suddenly pushed away. "Oh shit!" she said. "Here comes Earl."

Donna quickly dumped another chunk of grease into the corn popper and Frankie swept around the concessions stand. By then it was time to take tickets for the second show, *Tom Jones*. There was the usual bunch of bohemian types, people with whom he felt an odd kinship. Earl relieved him at the ticket stand and as soon as Frankie completed cleaning the bathrooms, he got lost in the upper balcony. He turned to leave and there she was, triple life-sized and Panavisioned up on the silver screen, the beatific vision of his life, Susannah York in the role of Sophie Western. With one look Frankie knew his life had been changed irrevocably. Sophie Western, angel, the antithesis of everything he had known. She was radiance, a melodic birdsong on a soft summer morning. She was life.

What a great world, how unlike his own, and, oh, Jesus, God, if ever there was a more beautiful woman than Sophie Western—well, there just couldn't be. Frankie walked home in a trance. What was that poem they had done in English?

> *Whenas in silks my Julia goes*
> *Then, then (methinks) how sweetly flows*
> *That...*

Liquid something. Sophie was like that poem. Refined. And that's what Frankie would aspire to. Culture and refinement. He had imagined there was time, that he could reform at his leisure, but that time never seemed to come along. It was like, wake-up, motherfucker—the time is now! The movie was the signal he had been waiting for. He needed to change and he knew he could do it. A photographic memory was a gift, a terrible thing to waste. He needed to put it to good use.

After work, Frankie followed the tracks past school and on home. He would apply himself, learn something, find himself. Forget the old bullshit, it was definitely time to show or to go.

Frankie had a bowl of cereal and just after midnight, he went to bed with Fielding's novel. By dawn he was penciling out a book report at the kitchen table when his mother crawled out of bed and staggered into the kitchen for coffee. Frankie had plugged in the pot and had everything ready for her. He had not taken his lithium, but for homework that was allowed. He felt great.

This was certainly a better way to begin the day than coming down from an acid trip. He was afraid his mother would start nagging at him for staying up all night, but when she saw him so absorbed with his homework, she did little more than chirp a CW tune as she started breakfast. Frankie finished the paper, redotting the i's with a final flourish, and then began to eat. He complimented his mother's greasy eggs and ate her oatmeal in spite of the fact that she had run out of milk. "It's no problem, Mom. I should have gotten it myself. I should be helping you around the house more."

Frankie thought of Sophie on the way to school. Sweet Sophie. Things were going to be different now, there were resolutions. He tossed a pack of Marlboros into the bushes along with his Zippo. Smoking was over. So was jacking-off. It was nothing but sordidness and negativity. It's over, God, I quit! What else? What else? It would all come to him. He whistled as he walked. It was a merry tune from the movie. He was taking the long route to school. He paused to smell a lilac bush. The odor was so glorious it made his eyes water. The breeze shimmering through the scented bush sounded like a freight train—but this was not an acid flashback—this was how it really was.

Suddenly Frankie found himself walking next to the girl from geometry class, Suzie Trowbridge. He was saying witty, clever wonderful things, things he didn't know he was capable of saying. Her eyes were like Sophie's, and her hair, too. She was laughing with him and he seemed to get funnier as he went along. His rap was inspired and it just came rolling out with no forethought. He was telling her how he was going to be a great actor some day, after he won the middleweight title. Hell, he might even play second base for the Mets in between fights. He could do it, too. Susan appeared to be convinced of it. The way it was all coming out was incredible. Frankie couldn't wait for her to ask the next question, so boss were his answers. Yeah!

When he asked her to the Saturday night school dance and she said yes, he had to turn his face away. He felt like hiding it in his jacket and dashing away from her but she took his hand, the hand-of-a-thousand-jerk-jobs-that-would-never-jerk-again. Numb with ecstasy, Frankie recited the capper:

> *Whenas in silks my "Susan" goes*
> *Then, then (methinks) how sweetly flows*
> *That liquefaction of her clothes.*
>
> *Next, when I cast mine eyes and see*
> *That brave vibration each way free;*
> *O how that glittering taketh me!*

She kissed him on the side of the mouth as they rounded the corner and neared school. "Christ, you know Shakespeare by heart," she said.

"That's Robert Herrick, not Shakespeare."

"You gotta monster zit by your nose," she said.

Frankie's face blazed red. He was suddenly so embarrassed that he found it almost impossible to move, to put one foot in front of the other. Yet they walked together silently for a moment and then it seemed that Susan had picked up the pace as if to get away from him. He had to hustle to keep up with her. As they turned the corner near the Red & Black Spot Frankie spotted Stillman and a bunch of the school wrestlers. Suzie waved at Stillman and Frankie waved, too, a limp passive wave, hoping Stillman would wave back. Instead, Stillman threw his Mets cap on the ground and charged.

Frankie was paralyzed with fear and disconcerted by an already large, forming crowd. Only at the last second was he able to move. Side-stepping Stillman's rush, Frankie cuffed him hard on the ear with a right, then turned, planted his feet and pumped a doublejab in Stillman's face coming over the top with a right hand. The speed and placement of Frankie's punches stopped Stillman cold and caused his eyes to glaze over with a milky white film. The right connected to Stillman's chin like a heat-seeking missile, and the jabs busted Stillman's lip. Frankie kicked Stillman in the balls, doubling him over, and then kneed him in the face. Frankie lashed an elbow out with such ferocity that he lost his balance and fell to the ground. He quickly scrambled back to his feet and stood in front of Stillman hardly able to breathe. There was just enough time to pick up a rock, inflict a disabling blow and win, but as the tenor of the crowd shifted into Frankie's favor, he was undone by it. He stood there like a wooden Indian frozen with indecision, as a strong and familiar born-to-lose vibe pulsed through his soul. And then it was too late.

The glaze cleared from Stillman's eyes and he felt his bloody lip, laughing. "Hey there, friends and citizens, we got us a live one he-yuh," Stillman said. An excited crowd huddled around the two fighters. Stillman bashed Frankie in the face with one short punch, breaking his nose. A small geyser of blood spurted on Stillman's jacket, and he began to bash Frankie's face until his hands began to hurt.

Susan Trowbridge tossed a forelock of hair away from her eyes. "Leave him alone, Jess, you big asshole, you're sixty pounds bigger than him; he's just a kid."

"Fuck you," Stillman said. "How could you be seen with a fool like this? How could ya possibly walk with this snakey motherfucker?"

"I needed help with my English."

"You want help with yer English? See me," Stillman said leaning back, easing off.

The blood from Frankie's nose was running down his throat, choking him. Stillman turned to him and elbowed the broken nose one final time. "That'll teach you to let the air out of my tires, goddamn it."

The crowd began to chant, "Pants him! Pants him!" Frankie went crazy trying to get away, but Stillman still got a fresh hold on him. Then in one quick jerk, he pulled Frankie's pants off and then the size 28 Jockey Classic Briefs. Wriggling free, Frankie cupped his genitals with both hands and tried to bull his way through the crowd. As he did, he saw a big grin on Susan Trowbridge's face. He saw her blonde hair spilling down the front of her navy blue car coat. It was the most beautiful hair. The next moment she shook her head back, flipping her hair over her shoulders like the slut that she was.

Frankie punched through the circle and ran until everyone was out of sight. He ran all the way home naked from the waist down.

The old lady had left for work, thank God for that. Frankie took a long shower and bawled. Jesus Christ, Susan had laughed right along with the rest of them! After he dried off, Frankie snagged a handful of the old lady's Darvon and headed for the pool hall.

That night at work, high on Darvon and a quart of Bud, Frankie burst into the projectionist's booth and confessed the whole scene to Wesley Lame Duck. He had to tell someone.

In rambling, slurred speech, Frankie told him all about falling in love with Sophie Western, about the poem and the lilac bush and the sound of the freight train. Frankie told him how much he loved Susan Trowbridge and Wesley said, "Stop it right there," and gave him a lecture about how that sick-in-love, kicked-in-the-stomach feeling would max out in three days and totally peter out in two weeks. It was all brain chemicals.

Alfie had the right idea, he said. Hadn't he seen *Alfie* last night? No? "Then you watched the wrong fuckin' movie, Jim."

Wesley told Frankie that he should save some money for the down-stroke on a Mustang, get a ragtop in midnight blue. The adolescent female wasn't looking for the real person inside—all that mattered to them were clothes, hot cars, and so on. Also, you had to radiate confidence and self-esteem. "Show them some shit, pachuco. Hey, man!"

Wesley was in an uncommonly vulgar mood. It was as if some new demonic personality had emerged. He suggested that Frankie could quit school and get a full-time job in a factory and keep his night gig at the Tivoli. "Are you listening to me, Frankie, or are you completely fucked up on pills? I must say this crybaby routine is a definite turnoff for me."

Then Wesley suggested the car would be there all the quicker if Frankie went down on him. He started stroking Frankie's thigh. "It's plain and simple. No big deal at all," Wesley said, peeling off a pair of crisp fifties— "A hundred bucks, Ace, deal?" And Frankie, half ready to puke, stared blankly into space. Everything was just sort of spinning around; but one thing led to another and pretty soon he found himself with his face in Wesley's lap, staring at a fish of a dick.

The part of him that was outside of himself watched curiously as he took Wesley's cock and stuck it in his mouth. It didn't really have a taste to it although there was a smell. He worked the organ up and down to get it over with and forgotten as soon as possible. Wesley sharply corrected Frankie's essential failings and was soon choreographing a fairly sophisticated blow job. It was a paradox, Wesley said, giving a guy a gobble job so you can score some pussy, but life was like that.

Wesley closed his eyes, let his head loll back, and began to grind his soft, wide hips as Frankie mechanically worked his mouth up and down.

The screen flashed brightly and the thwack/crackle of the old movie snapped Frankie back into awareness. He could hear his precious Sophie on the sound system and started to look up to her but Wesley yanked his head down hard. "You can forget that shit, Susannah York has got to be pushin' sixty by now."

Bleary-eyed, like a man climbing out of a well, Frankie raised up to Sophie. But Wesley slapped Frankie across the face and pulled his head back down. "You took the money and now I'm going to fuck your face, Mister."

He grabbed Frankie's hair with one hand and the front of Frankie's uniform with the other as he bucked up. His semi-erect penis slid in and out of Frankie's mouth, stabbing him in and about the face.

"Watch your teeth! Quit that slobbering!" Wesley continued to bark instructions until the very last, when his pecker engorged fully, his head fell back, and he came in the back of the young man's mouth. As he pulled out, Wesley slapped Frankie so hard it snapped him sober. "Cop the load, damn it! Or you're not getting paid."

Frankie looked up at Wesley with sheep eyes and swallowed.

Innocence in Extremis

Debra Boxer

I am twenty-eight years old and I am a virgin. People assume a series of decisions led to this. They guess that I'm a closet lesbian, or too picky, or clinging to a religious ideal. "You don't look, talk, or act like a virgin," they say. For lack of a better explanation, I am pigeonholed as a prude or an unfortunate. If it's so hard to believe, I want to say, then imagine how hard it is for me to live with.

I feel freakish and alien, an anomaly that belongs in a zoo. I walk around feeling like an impostor, not a woman at all. I bleed like other women, yet feel nothing like them, because I am missing this formative experience.

I won't deny that I have become attached to my innocence. If it defines me, who am I without it? Where will my drive come from and what will protect me from becoming as jaded as everyone else? I try to tell myself that innocence is more a state of mind than body. That giving myself to a man doesn't mean losing myself to a cynical world. That my innocence doesn't hang by a scrap of skin between my legs.

In college, girls I knew lost it out of impatience. At twenty-one, virginity became unhealthy, embarrassing—a female humiliation they could no longer be burdened by. Some didn't tell the boy. If there was blood they said it was their period. I cannot imagine. Some of those same boys thought it was appalling, years ago, that I was still a virgin. "I'll fuck you," they said. It sounded to me like, "I'll fix you," and I did not feel broken.

I don't believe I've consciously avoided sex. I am always on the verge of wholly giving myself away. I think emotionally, act intuitively. When I'm attracted to someone I don't hold back. But there have been only a handful of times when I would have gladly had sex. Each, for its own reason, did not happen. I am grateful to have learned so much in the waiting: patience, strength, and ease with solitude.

Do you know what conclusion I've come to? That there is no concrete explanation, and more importantly, there doesn't need to be one. How I got here seems less important to me than where I am.

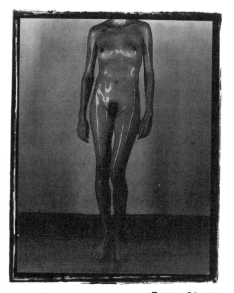

Taryn Simon

This is what is important. Desire. The circle of my desire widens each day, so that it's no longer contained inside me, but rather, it surrounds me in concentric circles.

Desire overrides everything and should be exploited to its fullest potential. It is the white-hot space between the words. I am desire unfulfilled. I hover over that fiery space feeling the heat without knowing the flames. I am a still-life dreaming of animation. I am a bell not allowed to chime. There is a deep stillness inside me. There is a void. A huge part of me is dead to the world no matter how hard I try to revive it with consoling words or my own brave hand.

I am sick of being sealed up like a grave. I want to be unearthed.

Do I have dreams about sex? Often. There is one recurring dream in which I can't see whole bodies at once. But I know which parts belong to my body. I know they're mine. I know, better than anyone, my curves, my markings, my sensitive places. If I close my eyes now, I can see this man's body. Thin, smooth, light-haired, limbs spreading and shifting over me like the sea. A small, brick-colored mouth opens and closes around the sphere of a nipple. Moist eyes, the color of darkest honey, roam up and down my spine. A sensation of breath across my belly induces the first wave of moisture between my legs. This reaction crosses the line into wakefulness, and I know when I awaken, the blanket will be twisted aside as if in pain. My skin itself will feel like a fiery blanket, and I will almost feel smothered by it.

Taryn Simon

In some versions of the dream I am on top and I can feel my pelvis rubbing against the man's body. Every part of my body is focused on the singular task of getting him inside me. I try and try and am so close, but my fate is that of Tantalus who was surrounded by water he could not drink. Thank God for masturbation.

My fingers know exactly how to act upon my skin—they have for over half my life now. There is no fear or hesitation. After, my hands shake as if I'd had an infusion of caffeine. I press my hand, palm down, in the vale between my breasts, and it feels as if my heart will burst through my hand. I love that feeling—knowing that I'm illimitably alive.

Though I've never had a man inside me, I have had many orgasms. I have talked with girls who not only can't have one with their lover but can't bring themselves to have one. I was shocked at first until I saw how common it was. And then I felt lucky. My first one scared me. At twelve, I did not expect such a reaction to my own touch; I thought I'd hurt myself. But it was such a curious feeling, such a lovely feeling, that I had to explore it further. I felt almost greedy. And, well, I got better at it until it was ridiculously easy. It is always easy.

I don't expect it to be so easy with a man. I've come to believe that sex is defined by affection, not orgasm. There is that need to be held that doesn't disappear when we learn to walk on our own. If anything, it intensifies.

I love being a girl. I think of my body as all scent and soft muscle. It is an imperfect body, but beautiful still, in its energy and in its potential. I love looking at my curves in the mirror. I love feeling them and admiring their craftsmanship. I love my hipbones—small, protruding mountains. Or maybe they are like sacred stones marking the entrance to a secret city. I trace the slope of my calf as if a slender tree trunk and I am amazed at how strong, yet vulnerable, the human body is. I have stared at my naked body in the mirror wondering what the first touch from a lover will feel like and where it will be.

Masturbation is pleasurable, but it cannot sustain a whole sexual life. It lacks that vital affection. I am left with the rituals, the mechanics of masturbation. I crash up against the same wall each time. It becomes boring and sad and does little to quell the need to be touched. I long to let go of my body's silent monologue and enter into a dialogue of skin, muscle, and bone.

There are sudden passions that form in my mind when I look at a man. Thoughts of things I want to do to him. I want to follow the veins of his wrists—blue like the heart of a candle flame. I want to lick the depression of his neck as if it were the bottom of a bowl. I want to see the death of my modesty in his eyes. Although I am swollen with romantic ideas, I am not naïve. I know it will not be ideal. Rather, it will be painful, awkward, damp, and dreadful—but that is always the way of birth. I want the pain in order to know that I am alive and real—to leave no doubt there has been a transformation.

I am powerfully attracted to the male body. I want to watch him undress. See him touch himself. I want his wildness in me—I want to touch his naked body and feel the strength of him. His sweat sliding down the slick surface of my skin until it pools in the crooks of my limbs. I imagine the rhythm of our sex like the slick, undulating motion of swimmers.

I want to hold him inside me like a deep breath. I want to leave kisses as markers on the sharp slices of his shoulder blades, then surrounding the oasis of his belly button. I want to slide him in my mouth like a first taste of wine.

I will hold my mouth to his ear, as if I were a polished seashell, so he can hear the sea inside me—welcoming him. I will pause and look at him—up into his face. I will steady myself in his gaze, catch the low sun of his cock between my smooth, white thighs, and explode into shine. I will look at him and think, I have spent this man's body and I have spent it well.

The Dawn of Screw

Al Goldstein

When I was a sixteen-year-old boy in Brooklyn in the 1950s, a good girl was someone who would let you kiss her, but would not let you put your tongue in her mouth. She would only let you touch her breasts from the outside of her sweater and massage her nipples for no more than a minute. Occasionally, if your hand was allowed inside her blouse, you could feel real flesh—you might actually feel a real nipple—and then she would chase your hand away. It was so exciting to actually touch a girl's breasts that it was customary among my friends to boast of the achievement by hollering "Nookie!" when we saw one another the next day.

I had begun to unravel the puzzle of sex at the age of thirteen with my friend Joe Berkowitz in our predominantly Hasidic neighborhood around Bedford Avenue in Williamsburg, Brooklyn. I looked at every girl and wondered if she had a pussy and what it would taste like. (Even then I was obsessed with food.) Joe and I would masturbate—not each other, but together—and I remember the first time I came. It felt so good. After hours of probing at my nerve endings I had a release of pleasure that was never equaled, not even by achieving fame or fortune. Other boys would occasionally join in; we would all masturbate and have contests to see who could ejaculate furthest. My world was playing with myself. My world was coming two or three times a day—by my own hand.

Three years later, in 1952, I was still living with my mother and father and attending Boy's High in Bedford-Stuyvesant—and I was still a virgin. Back then, no one ever talked about sex. Nobody had pussies or cocks. All the families were like the Brady Bunch. Thankfully I came from a lower-middle-class family in which the realities of daily life were given air, so our lies were less intense. We were not like some wealthy WASPs or smug suburbanites who lived in houses large enough to harbor secrets. I had secrets, of course, but they were closer to the surface. I felt as though my obsession with sex was so alien to the human condition, so different from those of other people who walked the streets, that I must be a monster. I felt like the cockroach in Franz Kafka's *Metamorphosis,* wrenched from the rest of civilization by some inexplicable force.

I kept from going insane by reading books that alerted me to others like me, a secret culture of people who wanted to feel and touch and be sexually alive. With the help of friends, I was able to smuggle copies of Henry Miller's classics that were still prohibited in the United States. I read *Lady Chatterley's Lover* and Frank Harris and I knew that there were men who looked at those mysterious creatures called women, bowed in front of them, tasted, nibbled, and licked what was between their legs and probed for that mysterious organ called the clitoris. What does it taste like, I wondered? Do all women have identical clitorises, or are they as distinct as fingerprints? God, I wanted to know. But I never would. At least this is what I believed: that women would always remain a mystery to me, always an unknown. My desperation felt like it would torment me forever. I now believe that most of my friends felt the same way. To us, women were unknowable, unattainable creatures who couldn't possibly be aware of the intensity of our desire.

The only real person in the banality of my adolescent life was my Uncle George. I only knew him as a guest at our seder table, but it was clear that he was the swinger in the family. He had been married three times. He did not live in Brooklyn or Long Island but in the Bryant Hotel in New York City. Uncle George would always give me his jazzman's riff on the world, which was much closer to the truth than those of the *New York Times* and

The New Yorker and all the elitists who didn't want to admit that sometimes when they pissed, a few drops fell on their underwear. George lived as close to the earth as anyone can in a city like New York. He may not have known any more than any other adult in my life at that time, but he wasn't ashamed to be honest about his take on the human condition.

During a conversation between my parents and Uncle George in my third-floor walk-up, it was decided that even though I had been bar mitzvahed three years earlier, I was still not a real man. At sixteen my mother and father felt that maybe it was time for little Alvin to have his first sexual experience. I owe that experience to my Uncle George; I owe him many thanks. He is the man who introduced me to pussy.

It was arranged that I would meet Uncle George at his hotel at 54th Street and Broadway. He took me out for a stiff drink, so I wouldn't be so frightened. I was in a frenzy, as if I were on some maiden voyage and about to get seasick. I was afraid I might throw up right in the middle of it. Should I take a barf bag with me? I didn't know. I hadn't even seen movies of people having sex. I had only seen the words of writers, and they left flaming images of what might happen. I yearned desperately for the sexual moment, for the blinding truth of climax.

After an hour of drinking I had difficulty standing up. I went up to my uncle's hotel room, knocked on the door, and walked into the darkness. A woman's voice said, "Come in." She told me to take off my clothing. When I did, it was as if I were in some delirium. I felt like Coleridge on an opium high. But this was real.

Standing there, I felt the light touch of a real woman, not just the fantasy of one. I felt a warm, soft female body. She said, "There is nothing wrong. Anything you do is fine." Then she blew in my ear and her lips pressed against mine. Her body rubbed against mine. I have no visual memories of that night, only tactile ones. Afterwards, every time I saw my Uncle George with a woman, I couldn't help but wonder if it was her. I don't know what she looks like to this day. I only remember that I felt the heat of flesh and then the fire of her lips around my cock and I was captured as surely as a fly in a spiderweb. I was a prisoner of the pleasures of the human body.

She pressed my head down between her legs and I felt hair against my cheek. I had trouble breathing; I thought I would die. I licked and I tasted and I didn't want to leave. It was a roller-coaster ride that may have lasted for days or years, but I was completely and utterly unaware of time. And then I was in some warm spot. My cock was someplace hot. There was movement, movement, movement—and then I came. I shot. I felt I had ejaculated so deeply from my own body that my head imploded; I thought when I next looked in a mirror I would see a headless person.

But I didn't care. I would sacrifice every part of my body for that feeling. I didn't care if I was left with nothing, if all that remained of me were a heap of broken bones on a dirty floor. An hour, two hours later—I can't say—I staggered out of the room and managed to look in a mirror. I seemed to be complete. I had my ears, my nose and all the other parts, but I didn't have my cherry. I had been with a woman. I met Uncle George downstairs at the bar and he welcomed me into the club of men.

Seventeen years later—on the day Richard M. Nixon was elected president—I published the first issue of *Screw* magazine. In the next two years I was arrested nineteen times—evidence of the relentless and futile battle the censors waged against sexual freedom. Today, twenty-eight years later, images that put me in handcuffs are now commonplace in popular magazines.

I have always felt that sexual freedom is less an issue of censorship and more of an issue of class. The wealthy can steal away to meet their mistresses in expensive hotel rooms, but poor people get busted for a twenty-dollar blow job. To understand what has happened to America's sexual landscape since 1968, you first must understand the puritanism of America in the 1950s.

I have been called the Guru of Gash, the Prince of Pussy, the Commissioner of Cunnilingus, the Baron of Blow Jobs and dozens of other goofy monikers, but finally I don't have any more answers about sex than the next guy. What I know is that sex is the greatest gift, and, even though I am an atheist, the pleasures of sex sometimes make me doubt my own lack of conviction. Perhaps there is a God, I think, and coming is a glimpse of her.

Fringes
Fringes
Fringes

Vivienne Maricevic

Much of the great literature of the last century has been preoccupied with the human fringe. Dostoyevsky, Beckett, Genet, Flannery O'Connor, and Cormac McCarthy, among others, have set out to plumb the depths of human experience, to call upon the insight of the dispossessed, the agonizing, and the suicidal. But readers reasonably ask, why mire ourselves in human misery? Reading, after all, is a recreation, not a duty. One answer is that if one can find inspiration in the bleakest of lives, if even the nadir of human experience contains a morsel of beauty, then we have damned good reason to relish our iced mochas. Another, of course, is that if we are students of life, exploring the breadth of the human experience, then through these authors we can explore the most remote regions—the ice-capped peaks, the deep-sea dives.

Literary interest in the fringe is often perceived as dangerous, however, because it neglects to make moral distinctions between priest and prostitute, senator and stripper—moral distinctions that help people make sense of the world and feel good about themselves. These distinctions, of course, help us function in a world of chaotic and unaccountable impulses, but there might be a lesson in the temporary suspension of morality that literature allows us to perform. Literature can help us remember the human circumstances that render us more similar to each other than we might like: We are born, struggle for approval, have desires we can't entirely control and can't entirely fulfill. And then we come to know that we will die, and be forgotten. Some of us sooner than others, but all of us eventually. Unless we are particularly embittered or delusional, we realize at some point along this road that we have more in common with all humanity, including those on the fringe, than we might have thought. We realize that we are all capable of beautiful and horrible things, acts of elegance and comedy and ineptitude. Nowhere is this more apparent, arguably, than in our sex lives.

Though the politics of sex can be divisive, the fact of sex joins us all at the groin—we all yearn for touch, for the moisture of sex, for the balm of each others' bodies. We touch the same, warm to touch the same, recoil from touching the same. We all have moments that are clumsy, embarrassing, earth-shaking, and beautiful. As we pant and wheeze and beg for more it might also occur to us that we are a lot like dogs, or chimps, or mice. We are big bundles of nerves, compulsively squeezing and contracting, always feeling, even in spite of ourselves.

The least we can do, it seems, with the riot of sensations that comprise each day, is savor them, take note of them, and maybe try to communicate them to others. This, anyway, is the conviction of the writers and artists featured in these pages. As my brother, a scientist, puts it, our job as sentient beings may not be so much to win as to feel deeply.

The pieces that follow are some of my favorite published in *Nerve*. They are indeed reports from the margins of society—accounts of a homeless man, a stripper, a prisoner, a male prostitute, and an irreverent photographer. What's most striking, in the end, is the familiarity of the human beings presented here and the challenge these accounts present to those who would rather not understand them.   —*RG*

Transient Sex

Lars Eighner

In 1988 I became homeless. Three years later, in a vacant building, I began typing up my experiences on an old upright Royal. This became the draft of *Travels with Lizbeth*. Some chapters of my draft that included sex scenes appeared in the *Threepenny Review*. When I edited those chapters out of the final book some people (including a reviewer for *The New Yorker*) thought St. Martin's had made me censor the manuscript.

Big publishers, of course, do not shy away from sex or homosexuality, but they do hesitate to issue 800-page first books from unknown authors. I had too much material for one book. Rather than cut good material that pertained directly to homelessness, I cut the few parts that were about sex. Indeed, Michael Denneny at St. Martin's encouraged me to put some of the sex scenes back in, and where they were essential to understanding other events, I did so.

Sex on the street is episodic, because life on the streets is episodic. For the homeless, sexual encounters, like all human encounters, tend to be spontaneous and fleeting—they don't lend themselves to a cohesive narrative. As it was, the story line of my book was criticized for being full of holes; I was told that interesting characters appeared out of nowhere and disappeared without explanation. This is the problem with a memoir: one is confined to the facts. While I believe sexual promiscuity requires neither apology nor excuse, for a homeless person all human relationships, even those having nothing to do with sex, are promiscuous.

Sex among transients is almost all masturbation or homosexuality. Since homeless people get gamy fairly quickly, many homosexual encounters consist of mutual masturbation. Orwell noticed the prevalence of homosexuality when he went around to the shelters in England as a counterfeit hobo. He blamed it—for when he wrote, hardly anyone questioned that homosexuality was blameworthy—on the shelters' rigorous segregation of the sexes. Today, in America, many times more men than women actually sleep on the streets. For most of the men it is homosexuality or no sexual society at all.

What may not be quite so obvious is that many men on the street are preferentially homosexual. Some are pushed out of families at a tender age, some cannot call upon families when a crisis occurs, and the same discrimination that may cause a white-collar worker to be passed over for a promotion may squeeze a dishwasher out of his job and his livelihood. Sexual revolution brought, for some people, a new kind of double standard: a superficial sexual liberation for the young, attractive, and affluent and an embarrassed silence surrounding the sexuality of the old, the less attractive, and the poor. If anything, the superficial sort of liberation is exaggerated in some parts of the gay community, where it is thought hot to play at being dirty desperadoes in greasy jockstraps but thought another thing to actually be one. For my part, as often as I had an object lesson in the futility of judging by appearances, I seemed never to learn the lesson; many times I discovered that companions of the moment whom I had assumed were straight had concealed their desires for fear that I would bash *them.*

At any rate, when sexually competent men who are not numbed to sleep by alcohol camp together, sex comes up. It came up even when I, for fear of being detected as a homosexual, tried to avoid the subject. It came up in groups camped near me who were unaware I could hear them. Sometimes one man jacked off while his neighbors, by unspoken agreement, pretended not to notice—but of course they did notice and invariably each man in the group would take his turn. Sometimes this led to open-circle jerks; other times group masturbation was planned, ostensibly to prevent wetting sleeping bags with nocturnal emissions or by attempts to conceal masturbation. Keeping the bedding dry also served as an excuse, when an excuse was wanted, for oral sex. And other times, it just happened.

An Excerpt from the First Draft of *Travels with Lizbeth*

When Lizbeth and I were camping in the very obscure Adams Park, once or twice a week we walked to a little gay bookstore where I sometimes received mail. The trip took most of a day. We would walk past fraternity row, and I would scrounge a picnic lunch from the rich Dumpsters. We would arrive at the very popular Pease Park just before noon and have our lunch in the shade. I would tie Lizbeth to a picnic table and go into the men's room for the occasional hand job and to wash up at the lavatory for my appearance at the bookstore.

I saw David for two or three weeks running when Lizbeth and I stopped for lunch. Hustling was uncommon in Pease Park because all types of men were available there for free. But I felt certain David was hustling, or trying to. I saw him turn down several attractive, athletic young men who would certainly have balked at paying, and I saw him go away almost immediately with a pair of well-dressed elderly gentlemen who had a nice, new, gray Oldsmobile. I thought David needed money, for one day I noticed someone—it could not have been anyone else—had pilfered the leftovers of our lunch from the wire wastebaskets by the picnic tables. What he got, if I was right in supposing it was he, was a large bag of banana chips, more banana chips than I could ever hope to eat, and I was amused that a Dumpster diver's refuse would in turn be scrounged from the wastebaskets in the park.

Then there was the matter of David's attire. He wore cowboy boots and cutoff jeans—not an unlikely combination for August in Texas. But the cutoffs were much too short and he rolled his red-and-white-striped T-shirt up into a bandeau. On a smaller, boyish type of about the same age the effect might not have seemed so strange, but David was big-boned and burly, muscular and hairy. Though he was young, he was a full-grown man and the costume was very unflattering. It was, I thought, what a straight boy who had decided to sell dick might wear in an attempt to look gay. At any rate the short, tight cutoffs showed off his main asset, which for its confinement

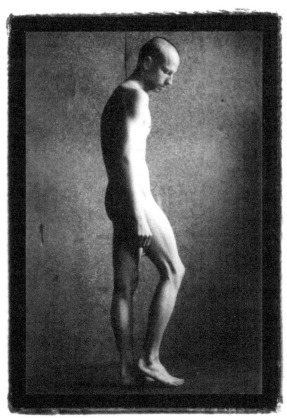

Vivienne Maricevic

needed adjustment at regular intervals, and I thought that could not have hurt his business much.

At last one afternoon—after Lizbeth and I returned from the bookstore and stopped to rest in the shade—David approached me. I had not found anyone in the men's room that morning and I was hoping someone in the afternoon crowd would favor me with a hand job. I was having a horny summer. I was beset with spontaneous erections in the daytime when there were no apparent stimuli. This sort of thing happened to me frequently enough in junior high school, but as an adult nearing forty I was finding the experience nearly as disconcerting as I had the first time around.

After David elicited many assurances that Lizbeth would not bite him, he came near enough to ask if I had seen a car of such-and-such description. I thought he wanted to talk because he had been in a better position to see the cars in the park than I had. Surely I had no better information about the car.

He did not want to talk. He had seen me in the park and in the men's room often enough to have some idea what I was about, but even so he was uncommonly frank. He told me he had a trick the night before who dropped him off this morning, unceremoniously, without any breakfast, but promised to come for him after work. I knew immediately that the john would not return. It was naïve of David ever to have thought otherwise.

"And he got out of paying you?" I asked.

"Paying me?"

David did not get paid. He never asked for money. The john was supposed to be wealthy, to keep several young men in apartments around town, and David had hoped to obtain a similar situation. Even secondhand these were transparent lies, but David believed them. Now he had no place to sleep for the night and the place where he kept his things was too ant-infested for him to sleep there.

I told David there were no ants in my camp and I would show him how to antproof a place if he came with me. This wasn't entirely a selfless proposition for up close I could see that David was even more muscular and attractive than I had thought. But I was not entirely selfish either. My camp was near a gay bar and a video arcade where David would almost certainly find more customers, many of whom would pay him in spite of himself—if only because they knew that a boy had to eat if they hoped to see him around again.

David wanted to wait in the park a little while longer. He was unwilling to give up the hope that his date had met some unforeseen delay. I began to suspect that David was not very bright. At last we went to the little bridge in the park to collect the things he had stashed there.

He was right about the fire ants. Lizbeth kept them at bay by eating them, but clearly no one could sleep here. David had an enormous duffel bag. He checked to see that it had not been disturbed. Then he turned to one of the pilings supporting the bridge and opened his fly. I realized that my bladder, too, was about to burst. But when I stood beside him and pulled out my cock, I discovered it was too hard to piss through.

David finished. He stared at me. I'm pee shy to begin with, and with my erection I hadn't got a drop out.

"Did I do that to you?" he asked. This seemed a guileless apology and not the tease it might have been.

"I was horny when I got to the park, but you didn't help matters."

David took this more to heart than I had counted on. I had meant only to tender him a roundabout compliment. He looked around. The creek was dry and the mud was hard as cement. "We can't fuck here. Too many ants. You want me to jack you off?"

"Yes." Well, I did. Since I was horny to begin with, near David, and out of public view, if he had not offered I might have done it myself, without any concern for his opinion.

"Then spit on my hands, 'cause I don't suck dick." He cupped his hands. I spit.

As soon as he put his hands on me I reached for his dick, which was large, but still floppy. He stopped to move my hands to his ass. And then I understood.

"I wish we had a dildo," he said.

As soon as I was able to think about it, it would seem a peculiar remark to me. But as it was I could only think of my hard dick and the condoms in my pocket—I always got a handful from the free basket when I went to the bookstore. When I offered to sheath myself, David explained, mercifully stroking me all the while, that a hard dick and a condom were not, to his way of thinking, an acceptable dildo substitute. Then he whispered, "You can kiss me," just in time. Though I tried to turn to the side, it wasn't what David wanted. He was much stronger than I was and managed to take most of my load on his belly; I guess it was fortunate that his shirt was still rolled up.

My hand had negotiated far down the back of his cutoffs and this had caused David's cock, which was still hanging out, to assume a half-hearted erection.

"I want to get you off too," I said. This was not a perfunctory remark. I was hungry for the animal strength I felt in him.

"Tomorrow," he said. "I've got a vibrator and a dildo stashed in a bag."

At last he let me go and I was able to piss. I offered him my bandanna to clean up with, but he only wiped his hands. He left the splotch on his belly. I don't know if that was meant to be flattering. I don't suspect David of having thought too deeply about not wiping his belly, but I did find it amusing to watch the splotch drying on his hard abdominal muscles as he hefted the forty-pound duffel bag onto his shoulder.

He had not wanted to come, he explained, because he still had some hope of seeing his date as we walked. He asked me if I would kiss him when we were not having sex. For a couple of hundred yards, we stopped to kiss every three or four paces, and the result of this was that I was as horny as I had been before, but this time there was nothing to be done for it.

To humor him we stopped at another cruisy parking area nearby to see if the john would drive by. We waited until the sun was setting, and David told me his story.

Aside from a little petting with a girlfriend in high school, he had been a virgin when he got out of the service in San Diego. (He was a marine—I should have guessed.) Thereafter, he met a much older man, a retired sailor, who was thoroughly impotent and who had introduced David to dildos. He did not pretend that high school experiences with girls qualified him as bisexual: he wanted men. Men with dildos.

What I understood when David moved my hand to his ass was that he was an iron-clad bottom. That was why he was not going to make it as a hustler. Gay johns don't want to believe that homeless hustlers might be gay too. Hustlers are supposed to be studs—trade—basically straight, macho guys who will lay back and let their dicks be sucked for a price. Certainly that is what customers would expect of someone as big and muscular as David; no one who would pick him up would be interested in his ass.

At last David gave up on his john. Except for shifting the weight on his shoulders a couple of times, he gave no indication that he was aware of his duffel bag at all and had no trouble keeping up with me and the dog, although we took the most direct—and hilly—route to Adams Park. Fortunately, I had dinner fixings: a can of beans, a can of tuna, and some crackers stashed away with my gear, although I had to lie about their origin to get David to eat. My bedroll was quite large enough for the both of us.

What Nina Hartley Knows

Sallie Tisdale

The parking valet in the tiny parking lot took the keys to our unfortunate car with courteous disdain. We walked through metal detectors into the pink, neon-lit foyer, and passed the tuxedo-clad bouncers with their beefy hands and thick necks and watchful eyes and slipped into the club.

I was in New York for a conference on sexuality; I was speaking after Candida Royalle, who makes hard-core porn films for women. Candida and I had never met, though we both belong to a cheerful little anticensorship organization called Feminists for Free Expression. This trip to Goldfinger's, a venerable strip club deep in Queens, was a last-minute field trip for a few FFE members. Candida's friend and colleague, Nina Hartley, was doing a show at Goldfinger's, a kind of porn star concert, and so we piled into the beater and went.

One of the young women in our group had never been in a strip club before; I recognized her combination of intense curiosity and skittish nerves because I'd felt the same way the first time. Then I was filled with foreboding and wonder, with no idea how to behave. The traditional male world of voyeurism, with its simple cash economy, has its own rituals and its own manners. Women rarely learn these things. To enter means to enter as a foreigner, an alien bound to make mistakes.

That was then. I like strip clubs now. I like the perfume of sex like a fine fog in the air. I like the beautiful dancers and their erotic, animal moves, the no-windows closure from the ordinary world. And I like the fact that it is the men who are a little bit scared, not me.

I believe men (straight men) are much less comfortable with sex than women. A great number of lies have been told about this; I was a grown woman before I realized that all those high school assumptions about how readily men talk about sex among themselves were imaginary. In my experience straight men hardly ever talk bluntly about their own sexual experiences, desires, or concerns. They genuinely worry about what women say about sex, about their belief (based in truth) that women talk easily about sex even when they don't know each other well. I think maybe men are just shy about sex—it means too much, and not enough.

Thus, a massive cultural delusion—that men are unconcerned with female desire, and that male sexuality is obsessional and fierce. In the midst of this, strip clubs are a strange, perhaps inevitable, phenomenon, not at all what they seem or claim to be. Men come to strip clubs to look at women, to fantasize and drink and sometimes masturbate. They also come to share with other men a peculiar intimacy no one ever talks about. In strip clubs, I can watch men in a rare way—they turn away from me after a quick glance, away from the few women customers. They turn to the stage and look instead at the dancers; they look up, with studiously blank expressions, to be confronted by dominant women full of control.

We stood around the stage at Goldfinger's awhile, watching the dancers. The customers sat below the strutting, high-heeled feet, in dimness, gazing up, silent. The music was the usual loud, disco house blend. The lighting was all gauzy-pink and soft. Two women, one wearing only a pair of strap heels and a thong, the other only a pair of close-cropped bikini panties, leapt up silver poles in the center of the oval bar and slid slowly down, pranced along the edge of the stage between fidgeting hands, slid along the waxed wood bar top like snakes. The customers sat still, except for a few tapping fingers; the bartender quietly poured drinks and picked up five- and ten-dollar bills.

Sylvia Plachy

Then a tall brunette appeared, her hair cropped short, clad in tight black leather shorts and a little black top, and climbed up on the stage. After a few minutes walking back and forth, surveying the crowd, she squatted suddenly before two men with the fluidity of a cat. She leered at them and then, without warning, pulled open her blouse for a few seconds, exposing her breasts. In a while she would certainly take the blouse off. Two other women on stage were topless, but suddenly the customers seemed to have forgotten that. They were thinking only that they wanted to see this woman's breasts again, and to encourage her, one slipped a five-dollar bill into the top of her boot. She smiled, stepped back, pulled her shirt open another moment, then closed it with a smile. And reached down to receive another bill.

Later, an enormous guard in a tailored suit guided us past the bar and through a line of patrons waiting to meet Nina and pay twenty dollars to have their picture taken with her. The men in line were big and unpolished, guys in jeans and khaki jackets with broad shoulders and creeping bald spots, joshing with each other in undertones. The guard seated us at a small table, a waitress brought us tiny glasses of white wine, and we waved at Nina and watched her work.

Nina Hartley has been a porn star longer than most people stay in the business. She is a celebrity where many remain anonymous, and inspires unusual loyalty in her fans. Nina has shocks of golden-blonde hair, pink, healthy skin, stiff, enlarged breasts, and hefty oval buttocks. When I asked a friend of mine why he liked her films, he said, "She has the best butt in the business." Her face is a nice, ordinary face, an open face. Her work is marked by intelligence and humor and sly fun, qualities which are magical combined with sex. On the screen she surrenders to her sexual appetites and then, without warning, looks directly at the viewer with a nudge and knowing glance.

That night at Goldfinger's, she wore only a thong, heavy stage makeup, and extraordinarily high stiletto heels. Real sexual confidence is a mysterious, enviable quality. It's a great fantasy—this ability to strut one's stuff without apology. The men stood in line, murmuring, and Nina walked back and forth in front of them, slowly, with a persuasive conviction in her own alluring power. They were like shy boys meeting the superhero they've only read about in comic books—a mythic figure suddenly real, suddenly here.

Nina turned on a huge golden smile, sauntered with long steps over to the first guy in line and took him by the hand. She spoke into his ear, low and private, and planted his palm squarely on the far side of her naked waist, and leaned against him a moment. "What kind of picture do you want?" she asked, almost purring. "What's your fantasy?" And he told her. She set up the scene on chairs under bright lights—him on a chair, herself kneeling at his feet, looking up with adoration. Her brother-in-law shot the picture, Nina signed it with a flourish, and exchanged it for his money. Then she gently sent him on his way, and turned to the next customer.

After a while, she took a break to say hello and drink some mineral water at our table. I thought it would be strange to meet someone I'd seen before many times on screen, a woman I've seen fucking, twenty feet tall in a dark theatre and on my own television in the living room, right beside me. It is not always easy to grasp this—sex work is work. Just as regular sex can be more performance than not. It all comes full circle: sex is performance is work is sex. Nina was glad to see Candida, with whom she is making her next movie. We talked about the plot, and what to expect from the conference the next day, and how the show had gone. And then the break was over and it was time to pay the rent.

Nina repeated the brief encounter again and again, whispering to each man, asking him his name, his fantasy, how he wanted her to stand, to sit, to kneel. One mustachioed fellow laid her across his knee and she smiled playfully while he pretended to spank. Another, like many, only wanted her on his lap. They posed, smiled self-consciously in the crowd's spotlight, while the brother-in-law quickly focused and took the shot. Again and again, she signed her name and parted with a smile. The brother-in-law slid mounds of money into an envelope. Between customers, Nina stood with her back turned, artlessly erect, and her eyes were distant and relaxed before she turned to the next man.

She came to the conference the next day, arriving late and looking tired. She sat beside me in the back row in a sweatshirt, jeans, big shoes, and too much makeup. She whispered in her fast, high voice a while, and then we turned to the lecture. After a while I looked at her beside me—tall, slender, sitting upright, in perfect control, and fast asleep.

Sex and *the (Somewhat)* Celibate Prisoner

Evans D. Hopkins

The mail line is extra long today. There is a new female guard in the control room, and I suspect several of the men know damned well they have no mail, but just want to get a good look at her.

To see through the seven- by fourteen-inch slot in the control booth cage, you have to climb two wooden steps. As I address the guard, all I see is her pelvis—a tantalizing eighteen inches or so from my face. The dowdy uniform does not diminish her hourglass figure. I ask her a question so that she'll bend down a bit and I'll be able to see her face and hear her voice. But neither quite live up to that body.

The guard hands me a single manila envelope. It's not the fan mail from female admirers I had been hoping for in the aftermath of my *New Yorker* article, but it is an intriguing offer nonetheless.

"They want you to write an article about sex in prison," says Shorty, reading over my shoulder. "You can interview me for this one." He lowers his voice conspiratorially. "I can tell you about how I screwed that faggot

Sweet Tee, you know, the one with the titties? Man, I tell you, after ten years being locked up, it was just like screwing a *real woman.*"

I start to tell him that's not what I have in mind, but I can't help but feel sorry for the bro'. He was locked up at such a young age, I'm not sure if he's even had a woman before.

Back in my cell, as I think about the editor's proposal, the old adage "write what you know" comes to mind. Well, sex is a subject I once believed I knew a lot about. Indeed, during the early part of my incarceration, sex was something of an obsession. But after I was transferred to the Nottoway prison several years ago, I worked hard to relegate sexual thoughts to occasional private moments with, shall we say, visual erotica. And for the last few months, I've attempted to completely rout such thinking from my mind. I've served sixteen years of a life sentence for armed robbery (an incident, I'm inclined to add, in which no one was hurt), and as I await word from the parole board, hopeful that I will be released this spring, I've resolved to remain completely celibate. So I don't particularly relish the idea of surveying prison sexuality (which, for the most part, is a solitary affair behind bars). As far as I'm concerned, Portnoy should have kept his complaint to himself.

But there was a time, during my imprisonment, when I was actually, in a sense, sexually active. That period is worth recounting, even if it's still a bit painful.

I. The Visiting Room

"Those definitely were the days," I.B. says to me. "A man could at least try to satisfy his woman with those three visits a week."

I'm talking to a man who was at the Virginia State Penitentiary with me during the '80s. We reminisce about the now-demolished maximum-security prison, which was but a stone's throw from downtown Richmond. "The Wall," as it was called because of its fortress-like appearance, had two visiting rooms: one for visitors with children and the other for adults only, where many couples engaged in nonstop necking and *heavy* petting. These rooms looked rather like lunch rooms found in small factories, with vending machines lining the walls. The more daring would actually have intercourse, often by sneaking into the visitors' bathroom, but sometimes, in more remote parts of the visiting room, under the folds of floor-length skirts. Other couples would slip into gaps between vending machines. The guard on duty more often than not turned his head, either out of sympathy, embarrassment, or fear of confrontation.

I tell I.B. that I'm thinking of trying to "pull" again, to seduce a woman, if only for the pleasure of the correspondence, and I show him a letter I've received from a female "fan."

"I remember when you were like I used to be," says I.B. "Homeboy, you *always* had a woman kicking the doors down to see you, *every* visiting day at The Wall. You say you haven't had a woman in what—eight years? Now if you're really getting ready to go home, and you've done without a woman for *that long,* you damn sho' don't need one now."

I.B. tells me that his wife, whom he met when she worked as a guard, has "stuck with me through thick and thin, even though I can't do anything for her sexually these days, with the way they got the video cameras in the visiting room here. And since the last lockdown, you can't even kiss—much less hug and get close—but at the beginning and end of the visit. Let me tell you, homeboy, after all my wife's been through—humiliating herself, cocking her leg up to let me get a quickie, or workin' my joint under the table—she *deserves* my loyalty once I get out. If you get a woman now, no way she can deserve to have you, over all the women you'll have becking at you when you get out."

II. "Ho-ology"

Locked in for the night at 8:00 P.M., for a half hour or so I pace the nine feet between the cast-iron cot and steel door of my cell, trying to quiet my libido for the night's work of writing. I must take care not to knock over all the books and papers stacked on the makeshift shelves along the wall. After a quick series of contained tennis strokes—the only exercise this forty-two-year-old tennis jock enjoys—I sit and smoke a cigarette, thinking about my conversation with I.B.

Contrary to the way he remembers it, I was never the real ladies' man; in fact I was fairly shy at one time. I never got the chance to do much dating during my teenage years. I joined the Black Panther Party when I turned seventeen, and thereafter my days were filled with political work and writing for the party's newspaper. Of course there was an air of sexual freedom in the party during those days in the early '70s—especially in California, where

I joined the newspaper staff. But most of the comrade-sisters were older than I, and a little out of my league. Consequently, despite my brief period of marriage before my incarceration, my courtship skills were limited before I was locked up.

It was in prison that I developed something of a "smooth rap"—though I was hardly on the level of players like I.B. who served as my mentors in "the game." Men like I.B. came from the streets, and being able to "mack" and "play ho's" was part of a culture in which it was both a badge of honor and an economic expedient to be able to control women through the combination of psychology and sex (better known as "ho-ology" among practitioners).

While I never was as successful with women as I.B., there was a time when I pursued women with all my wiles. To a man in prison, having a regular woman visitor is part and parcel of the code of manhood. It's about exercising one's power despite incarceration, and—more than that—about finding someone to provide emotional comfort, financial help, and those mirages of freedom that hours in the visiting room can bring.

So why have I chosen to do the balance of my time all alone? Partly it has been because dealing with a woman can create more emotional tension and sexual aggravation for a convict than it's worth. But there is a deeper story here, which requires going back eight years or so, back to when I was still at the State Pen...

After the first few years of loneliness, I learned how to attract women by placing classified ads, and wooing those who responded with long romantic letters laced with my poetry and with bits of erotica. No doubt many of these women were attracted to the outlaw/rebel mystique, and the promise of forbidden sex. Frequent short visits create a heightened sexual tension that also seems to be a turn-on for them—at least for a while. I learned the hard way that such relationships were rarely sustainable, usually lasting no more than six months. Therefore, when one began to wane, I'd begin seeking another.

Then, shortly before I was transferred here to Nottoway, a rural prison fifty miles southwest of Richmond, I met Nancy, who began visiting me with such loyalty I believed that she'd be with me "for the duration," as I used to say. However, a month or so after my transfer here, her car broke down as she drove back to Richmond from a visit. The following weekend she decided to travel here, along with her three-year-old son, in one of the transportation vans that a church group sponsored for visitors. The van crashed in a rainstorm, and both Nancy and her son died. I recall watching the tape of the accident's aftermath on the six o'clock news, and recognizing her suede boots, extending from beneath the sheet that covered a lifeless form. With this tragic turn of events, the game of prison romance became too serious for me, and my days as a player came to an end.

III. The Fan Letter

After receiving cards and letters from women in distant states, I finally get a live one from northern Virginia. She writes that she would like to correspond with a prisoner "because I want to give." While her writing is sharp and effervescent, the tone is that of an ingenue: "Is this your first fan letter?" she asks.

Well, years ago I'd have jumped all over her with the full power of my prose. Instead, I send but a short reply, along with a copy of one of my earlier pieces from the *Washington Post,* and hope that her next letter might reveal that 1) there is some intellectual substance there, and 2) she's above the age of consent, now around twenty-five for me (which is relevant should correspondence lead to something more once I'm released).

Her next letter answers the second question, and makes the first one moot. "I can't believe I'm corresponding with a *real writer!"* the letter begins.

I jot a few words on a postcard, telling her politely that I'm busy with a deadline for an article and will try to write more next time.

———

Have I become a prude, in prison, you may ask? I don't think so. Rather, I have chosen celibacy as an exercise, as a means of withdrawing from the immediacy of the visceral world, in order to see things with greater clarity. Standing at some remove is almost a prerequisite for sanity in prison; the immediate world is one of clanking bars, piercing announcements, echoing shouts. The discipline of celibacy is a means of escape, of transcendence, of maintaining self-control.

So no, I am hardly a prude. Sometimes I want a woman so bad I ache—longing not just for sex but for the feminine voice, the gentle touch, or just the image of someone who cares for me to hang on my wall. But I have come to understand that human sexuality is a precious and powerful force that affects us both in its presence and its absence.

IV. Home

I'm the lone inmate in the prison van, on my way home to the sleepy mill town of Danville, one hundred miles south of Nottoway, on the North Carolina border. Sixteen years of numbing captivity is finally ending.

The guard turns the radio to a Top 40 station. Amazingly, "Fantasy," the Mariah Carey hit of a few years back, blares out of the radio. The end of the song has a question-and-answer chant which repeats several times: "Watcha gonna do when you get out of jail?" The reply: "I'm going to have some fun."

I am sitting on the porch of my parents' home in the country, enjoying the night air, the stars, the lawn and trees bathed in the amber glow of a street lamp.

The desire for sex is often a guise of the broader need for human joy, and sex doesn't always satisfy that need. At the risk of sounding square, my period of celibacy has helped me to call upon that emotional quality referred to by early philosophers as *agape*—love of truth, justice, beauty, and humanity and to ground myself for this greater purpose. I no longer feel in danger of losing moral focus, or relying upon a relationship to define myself. I am by myself beneath these trees and great sky, but I am not alone.

I turn to a fresh page from my notebook, and begin to draft an ad for the personals: *Single Black Male, seeking special lady who wants something real this time...*

Hustler's Measure

Aaron James

I work part time as a "male escort," which is a euphemism for a prostitute who gets his clients through an agency. Before joining the agency about four months ago, I occasionally went to a well-known East Side bar in New York, now closed, where negotiations were made on the spot, usually to my disadvantage, though not always. I prefer working for the agency because there is less hassle and less involvement with the marginal elements of hustling—competing with other hustlers, chatting with potential johns, and so on—which, though sometimes interesting, is more often time-consuming and boring. And you never know whom you'll see at a bar; the agency, on the other hand, gives me the name and address before I go out. They also set the price, which is regular and fair. And they "pitch" me to the client beforehand, preparing him to be pleased with me.

Getting the job was easy. I called the number on a printed ad and after responding to a couple simple questions, agreed to come in for an interview. I arrived precisely on time since the agent had asked me not to be early, and waited a few minutes on a red upholstered chair, overhearing the owner speaking to a client on the telephone and his colleague interviewing an aspiring escort in the next room. The owner sat before a small, elaborate desk; I could see on the desk only index cards, pens, and fifty- and hundred-dollar bills. He was wearing tight shorts and a tank top, and nearly everything he said was in a surprising tone—more aggressive or tender or nostalgic or mean than I would have expected.

During the interview, we frankly discussed my versatility and experience, I was told how the business was run, and then I was asked to show the agent my body. I removed my shirt and then let down my pants. I was a little cold and more than a little nervous, so I was worried that the impression I made was, well, scant. But I was confident, I said, that under different circumstances my true endowment would make itself apparent, and I told him I had never had much in the way of complaints from lovers. The agent seemed to believe me and took down a measurement I was happy to accept. He and the owner, who joined us, told me I was hired on the spot, and that I should get a pager with the proceeds from my first call, which would turn out to take place that very night. Their commission would be 40 percent, and I would be expected to bring them cash at the end of each job. I left the bizarre apartment—lots of chandeliers and mirrors in the two small brown rooms, and a dog in the kitchen—and went downtown, in the opposite direction of my residence. It was 8:45 P.M., and I didn't feel like going home. The interview had taken forty-five minutes: three times as long as they had said it would take, which I noted with some satisfaction. I felt they had liked me, and I was glad. I needed the money badly.

The first time I ever hustled, at the bar, I had (aside from a real but customary need for money) a dubious motive. I had just been left by a boyfriend I was in love with, and he had hustled. I wanted, I guess, to experience something intense he had been through, hoping that it would help me to understand him better, or, even more dubiously, that it would draw us back together when he found out about it. Immediately after I went through the first, disturbing episode, I phoned him in tears from the street and told him what I had done. He reproached me brusquely and told me not to do it anymore. This, of course, compelled me to do it again—to plunge myself into what was then, for me, a neurotic, sacrificial activity, to ease the hurt of being left by doing something I hoped would hurt him. I don't think it hurt him much, and in any event we never got back together for any extended period. I am still, unfortunately, in love with him, though I don't believe that's why I continue to prostitute myself.

When I hustled out of bars, I almost always felt sad and lonely as I left the client. In the taxi afterward, the money was a lump in my pocket. I felt that I had reminded a lonely man of his loneliness and left him to it, exploiting his desperation for a small stack of cash. Usually I had the idea that he couldn't really afford it.

On the downtown subway after the interview, I thought to myself that working through the agency would be different. A relationship that develops in a bar and subsequently on the taxi ride to the john's home is often loaded with the suggestion of a developing friendship—thus the ugly feelings, at least in my mind, when the little *amitié* comes to its abrupt, commercial termination. The mediation of an agency gives a more businesslike dynamic to the whole transaction and, as in psychotherapy, both parties benefit from the structured time and the payment of a set fee. And the men who can afford the agency's "high-end" rates are generally wealthier than the men I met at the bar, and therefore less troubled by the experience.

I had something to eat, phoned my answering service (no messages), and went, too early, to my favorite East Village bar. I had a drink and found, to my surprise, that I had no interest in meeting anyone, or even in sex—if it wasn't going to add something to the nonsexual till. I felt arrogant, as if my services were too valuable to give away, which was a wonderfully empowered state of mind. (Since then, I have found that this feeling has contributed to my difficulty in sustaining sexual interest in men I am attracted to but not in love with. It is a psychological nuisance, an unwanted defense.)

I phoned my service again and found the agent had rung. After a brief phone call, I nervously got into a taxi and headed for a fine hotel on the Upper East Side. The agent had told me that the client, a businessman from Texas, wanted to take me to the hotel bar for a drink before going back to his room, which was fine with me, though the agent didn't like the idea. He said it was a waste of time, and as it turned out he was right.

I was surprised by the ease with which I was able to walk through this fancy lobby and into the elevator, with no questions asked, especially so late in the evening (it was about 11 P.M.). I suppose if I had been dressed less well, or arrived later in the night, or was black, I might have been stopped. I went to a high floor and knocked on the room door. A nice looking man in his sixties answered the door and spoke to me in a moderate, soothing Texas

accent. I asked to use the toilet before going down to the bar. While I was relieving myself, the red-faced Texan peeked in and politely asked me if he could watch.

In the bar we sat in a corner and John (I believe that was actually his name) put his hand on my knee, which several people were able to observe. I thought it was strange that he did not mind being seen with me in this cozy, almost romantic public situation. He was married, he told me, and wealthy. He had children and was in New York for business. But I figured that if he wasn't afraid, I had no real right to object, and I tried to enjoy the situation. He asked me what I did besides this, though he didn't appear to be very interested. He told me about his wife and his children, one of whom was older than me. John was cheerful and a nice enough guy, though without a great deal of charm: he neither attracted nor frightened me. He asked if I had condoms with me—the agent had told him I would. I didn't. I explained honestly that this was my first night working for the agency, and I hadn't had the time to stock up. I said I would go out and find some on my own time and come back as quickly as possible. He wanted to come with me, so we got into a taxi and found a deli a block away. I got out and paid for the condoms, and we took the taxi around the block and went back into the hotel. John seemed almost proud to walk through the lobby with me at a few minutes before midnight.

That first night, especially after my forgetfulness, I was very nervous and it showed. I found it impossible to relax and John was wonderfully understanding and forgiving. I could sense that he was disappointed, but I believe he got the pleasure he felt himself entitled to in the long run. It was the hardest work of its kind that I've had to do. A relaxed atmosphere and a hard-on are preferable to tension and its physical repercussions, both for the client and for the escort, but they can't be forced.

I spent just over two hours with John, including drinks and shopping. He handed me slightly more than the fee for one hour and asked if that was alright. I was too unsure of myself, then, to get the full fee. I did manage to say that the agency expected him to pay for the full time I had spent with him, and he turned over a small additional amount of money. What I had made, then, wasn't enough, but it was a lot. It was roughly equivalent to what I make doing other kinds of work in about half a week. And it was untaxable cash.

I had assumed that hustling was dangerous, and no doubt some of it is. But I have never felt afraid of a man the agency has sent me to see, and I have never been hurt in any serious way by any of them. The men have always paid me without complaint. What would have happened if I had insisted on a full two-hour fee from John? Probably he would have turned it over. We were, after all, in a quiet, posh hotel in a room under his name, and I'm sure he would not have wanted trouble.

On a Thursday night about two weeks later, I did two jobs within six hours. The first was with an executive in midtown, at his apartment. He had a fake leather sofa upon or around which, it appeared, he lived his entire domestic life—a life which involved drinking, smoking, reading popular magazines, watching television, and listening to a dismal collection of a dozen or so compact discs. He smoked ultra-light menthol cigarettes and had a mustache. He began to tell me about himself, about his job and his past. He had had one lover, he told me, and they'd just split up a few months before. I could see, by then, the signs of too much friendliness, and I took my shirt off in order to get things moving along in a more sexual, less intimate way. I led him away from the sofa and eventually brought him to orgasm on his bed. I showered in his clean, plain bathroom, and he paid me, with no tip.

I thought my work for the night was done, and went out for a drink. At 12:30 A.M., my pager thrummed in my pocket; it was the agency again. The agent said that he really needed me to do another job if I could, that he would appreciate it very much because this was a regular, wealthy client. And he was known to sometimes tip extremely well. I reluctantly agreed to go. Again I jumped into a taxi and went off to a ritzy hotel, this one on Central Park South. I could hardly believe it when a young, handsome man answered the door. He was wearing a beautiful white terrycloth robe. (I later found out that he was quite well-known, first for his previous job in magazine publishing and now for his position working closely with a successful fashion designer, and for his good looks, wealth, and charm.) I liked him and we had very good sex. After he paid me, with a generous tip, we talked for half an hour before I left.

On a Saturday night I was to work in a mid-priced Times Square hotel. The agent said he'd only agreed to send someone to this inferior address because the client was an out-of-town regular; he was reliable; he was staying in this hotel only because there was no vacancy at his usual, fancier one. I was greeted by a diffident, fat man with glasses—a computer programmer from Washington, D.C. The air conditioner hummed in the chilly room, and we quietly removed our clothes and lay on the bed. He said that he wanted to be touched very, very gently—in fact he wanted to be touched almost not at all—for about half an hour. I slowly stroked various parts of his body with the extreme tips of my fingers, occasionally pausing to rest my arm, which I held in the cold air above the man's body while my fingers did their delicate work below. At what seemed to me an arbitrary moment in our exquisitely calm session, the large, pale man sighed softly and released the subtle sexual tension inside of him. He washed and dressed; I followed suit, and left with the money I had earned so easily. I envy the man his sensitivity, and the refinement of his sexuality, which I suspect gives him uncommon pleasure on the rare occasions he indulges it.

I have been with a number of famous men. One of them I grew up watching on television. He was a normal enough guy in bed—quite sweet in fact. He offered me a plastic bottle of water when I arrived, and led me through several darkened rooms to the back of his large hotel suite (he told me he rented it year-round, though he spends most of his time in California). He answered the phone once during the hour, telling someone that he was just relaxing and was going for a run in Central Park later. He spoke to the person affectionately and softly, almost as if the person were a child, though I don't believe she was. He told me afterward about a book he was writing, which sounded very bad. He underpaid me by ten dollars, which I didn't notice until I had left the hotel—I have since learned to count the money right away. He said goodnight to me in the same careful tone he had used with the person on the phone.

Since that first night with John on the Upper East Side, I've been doing several jobs a week for the agency. I have learned to relax and perform better. With some later clients, I have enjoyed myself, and I have reached orgasm many times, usually by fantasizing about someone other than the client, but occasionally as a natural result of the sex. I have never, though, been tempted not to take my pay, nor has a client ever suggested it.

I like the freedom of the job, since I'm never required to work, only requested; and, its disruption of my life notwithstanding, I like the startling feeling of my pager vibrating against my thigh, telling me that I will probably be in bed with a new man within the hour, making money.

If there is anything that nearly all of these experiences have in common, it is that the time I spend with these men is quiet and unhurried. It is often now, for me, similar to meditation of a kind: we are both focused, breathing, and relatively undistracted. We are together in a rare, structured, mysterious way for about an hour.

And then, a little richer, I go away.

A Conversation
with Richard Kern

O n a sweaty June day, the stoop of Richard Kern's East Village apartment building is crowded with guys shooting the shit and eating takeout. They stop talking and watch me approach. "Kern is 3F," one of them says. "Oh. Thanks," I mumble, blushing. I push the buzzer to the apartment, whose walls could—and do—tell stories. Hundreds of "girls" have shown up here over the past decade—Kern's *New York Girls*. The walls are all bare, save for a Rita Ackermann oil painting of a (premakeover) Courtney Love lookalike sticking a needle into her scabby arm, and a couple of the infamous artist's own prints. There are bolt-holes in almost every doorway, where some of Kern's more daring models have been strung up for the lens. He leads me into his office and proffers a glass of water. "Hope the slice of lemon is okay." The photographer's southerly sliding vowels and gentle indifference somehow render moot the question I came here with: why the women in *New York Girls* seem so blasé about being so nasty. Best known for the brutally sordid films that sent audiences

Richard Kern

running from theaters in the '70s and '80s, and for his noir-inspired photographs of predaceous women who look like they have a taste for pain—perhaps *your* pain—Kern is now more interested in "making sense" than causing a stir. The photographer seats himself in a sunny corner and looks out the window onto a vacant lot for most of the following conversation. In the silences he incrementally raises and lowers the shade, adjusting the light. *—GF*

In your introduction to New York Girls *you say that you were first inspired to photograph sexy women when you were hitchhiking and got into a car filled with "New York City glam girls." Are your photos today about glamour, or something else?*

That was definitely something I remembered. Those girls were not "glamour girls," they were "glam girls," like David Bowie, platform shoes and shag haircuts. But the shots I take aren't about glam, they're about getting someone to show me something I don't normally get to see, about walking down the street and seeing someone you wish you could see naked, and getting to see her naked.

You've described how in the process of making a particular film, My Nightmare, *you got ideas by fantasizing about your model and then asking her to act out your fantasies. Is this an approach you use in photography as well?*

I still do that. But it's hard to go as far as I want to because naturally there's fantasy and then there's reality, and what I might imagine in my fantasies goes a lot farther than reality, that's for sure. I would like the reality to go a lot further. *(laughs)*

Do you let the models call the shots and decide how far the session will go?

After I shoot with them once, I know who will do what. A lot of times they're supernervous at the beginning. I just went to meet with a girl that I shot for the first time because I want to shoot her again, and I went all the way to her place to show her the contacts. I never do that, but I wanted her to see how good they turned out. There's nothing like that to make someone want to do it again. And she said, "Wow, I look really skinny. I thought I was a lot fatter than this." That was a good sign. We're shooting again this weekend.

Why do models do it?

A lot of them would do it for free, but I pay them because it makes everything clear-cut. But there were a lot of girls who worked for free in my first book.

They're the strongest looking women I've seen in this type of photography. They look like they get a charge out of being photographed.

Of course they get a charge out of it. Why else would they do it? It's not just for the money, that's for sure, because if it was just for the money, I'd have a lot more people willing to do it.

What is it about working with you that makes them look and feel so confident?

It's editing. Or maybe the fact that I'm groveling at their feet most of the time.

What do you look for in models besides how open they are?

That they don't have a whole stack of restrictions and that they appeal to me in some way.

What appeals to you?

That's pretty broad. *(laughs)* Recently I've had a desire to get away from all the tattoos and piercings that you saw

Richard Kern

in the first book. It depends a lot on the person, on who calls up—that's the way I meet a lot of them. I've been getting a lot of calls from guys. I'm photographing them on the side. It's a whole different thing. I thought it would be a nice counter, 'cause it's really hard to stay interested in the same thing past a certain point.

Are you getting into slightly safer territory now?

I don't know, I'd just like to find some new gimmicks, variations. It's not easy trying to give a justification to a picture of someone with their clothes off, so that it's more than a pretty picture. I've sure taken a lot of those. I think my art history background is starting to interfere with everything. That's why I'm trying to shift focus, so it can make more sense to me again.

What you said about art history reminds me of what Serrano is doing with his newest portraits—presenting his subjects in almost classical poses.

If I was an artist on the level where I was able to do a body of work, have people pay a fortune for it, then pick something else and have people pay a fortune for that, I'd be doing it. It would allow me to think about stuff more. But I can't just say, I think I'll shoot a bunch of dead people, and then go to the galleries and show them and be guaranteed sales. Serrano's pretty much got that going on right now. He can make a living from gallery sales, and I can make a fraction of a living from them. But then again, he can't go out and shoot porn and sell it to porn magazines, and I can.

Serrano's obviously going for shock factor. Is that what you're doing?

That's what I used to try to do. But that's when you're more of an artists' artist. Serrano is more conceptual. He's using the medium of photography to document this, this, and this. He takes aspects of the sexual underworld and rips them out of that world and pastes them onto this neutral scene. My favorite thing about his *History of Sex* series was the backgrounds, 'cause I'm really into backgrounds.

Why did you make the leap from performance art to photography?

Because I needed to make money.

You're well known for your films, Fingered *being one of the most talked about.*

Let's talk about the conceptual idea of *Fingered.* Lydia Lunch and I had made this movie, *Right Side of My Brain,* and people said, "This is pornography." And we said, "You want to see pornography? We'll make some fucking pornography." All the dialogue was cheesy porn dialogue. I had just seen one really long trailer for a horror movie and it had everything in the entire movie that was good, so I thought, Let's just make it really condensed and make it one long trailer-movie. That was the approach there. Just the good parts, no character development, just make it fast.

Psychologically, what were your films trying to say?

They were all anti-sex.

Would you say your books are pro-sex?

Yeah, things have turned around. I used to be a real nihilist and I felt that sex was just a big distraction and I was so obsessive about it in my twenties.

Everything was done to get to the sex part at the end. Going to a bar, going to a club, that's a big part of being young, always looking. And I used to think, Gosh, if that was gone, I would be free. But then I started doing heroin to get all that out of my mind, and that clouded my whole viewpoint.

Is that where the darkness in the films comes from?

Yeah, but I was probably pretty dark anyway during that time, and drugs were only there for a part of it. Now I've taken that whole search for sex or for people to hang out with and have sex with, and turned it into an occupation. *(laughs)* I'm a little easier to get along with.

That brings me to the question: Are any of your models your lovers as well?

In the past they were, but not so much now. I started shooting the people I was going out with. The person I'm seeing now doesn't want to be photographed. I've never photographed her and that's just fine.

So she gets to retain the mystique of being the woman you can't photograph.

Richard Kern

Not only that, I like not having to look at her with that hard, cold camera lens. I like not putting her in that position.

Do you think you're putting your models in demeaning positions?

I don't think so. Some people would see some of it as demeaning, but I don't feel it's demeaning them. I do try to make the models look ridiculous sometimes, but it's not a personal thing. It's just something funny. The fact that they are almost all women might make it come off that way. I can see that. I mean, bondage, I mean give me a break, how obvious can I be?

Well, bondage works both ways.

Yeah, it works both ways. But I showed my work and spoke to a class at the School of Visual Arts and the first question was, "How many more images of abused, tied up women are we gonna be forced to look at?" I was like, "I dunno. I haven't even gotten to the porno part yet."

Did the idea of putting the models in bondage make you uncomfortable?

I was fine with it, and it's still really fun sometimes. It's like a period in the summer when it's really hot and you say to yourself, I would really like some iced tea. And you get into drinking iced tea all the time for a month. Then, one day, you get tired of it and say, I'd like something different now. Maybe ice water . . . Now, I only do it if I don't know what else to shoot. In my personal life, tying up a partner requires a certain outlook towards them, and I'm not so comfortable with that outlook right now.

Are the women who pose in bondage into it themselves?

Most of them say pretty early on, "When are you going to tie me up?"

The Purr *publication of* New York Girls *contained some gory pictures of men, but the women weren't nearly so messed up.*

I thought it would be funny if all the men were dead, and all the women were doing their thing, whatever it is. The new version of the book took the gore out. I'm not doing the fake dead stuff anymore. I'm tired of fake.

What would you say to those who claim that your photographs incite violence towards women?

"Okay, if you say so." I don't know what makes violent guys do what they do. I would doubt it is my photography. But when my book *New York Boys* comes out, people are going to have a hard time with that complaint. *(laughs)* It just depends on the society. In France, where my stuff is really well received, it's a whole different outlook. People don't have all these political questions about what the images mean, they just say, "This is really pretty."

Your stuff has been edgy for so many years. Do you find it difficult to keep that edge?

Yes, it's hard. It's so hard. I've got maybe five shots in my new book that I feel have a jolt to them. But then again, if I looked at my bondage stuff again, I wouldn't get a jolt.

Trust me, other people do.

Richard Kern

Taryn Simon

I'm standing on a ponyskin rug in my first-ever pair of stiletto heals, trying to keep my balance as other partygoers jostle past. "Isn't skinning a horse, like, taboo?" says the guy I'm having a nonconversation with, virtually hairless himself.

"Fuck taboos—who needs 'em?" snorts a recent arrival, a heavily tattooed woman wearing a skull-and-crossbones nose ring and a T-shirt that says STILLBORN STILLWARM. "Clearly, *you* do," says the bald guy. Stillborn's eyes narrow, she takes a drag of her cigarette and ashes on the pony. It occurs to me that the bald guy has a point: if there were no taboos, this girl would have no shtick, no cause, no one but herself in the mirror to flip off every morning.

Don't get me wrong: I appreciate Stillborn's commitment to existing outside society's OK Corral. After all, if it weren't for the stillborns of the '70s, it might still be taboo for professional women to wear pants and flats to work. Of course, some fashion statements are merely cultural semaphores: tattoos, nose rings, even miniskirts, tell us who we are and who we aren't, where we belong and where we don't. Where I went to college, for example, wearing makeup and shaving one's legs was frowned upon. The ideologies that spawned the hippie movement were alive and well there, but they'd been embraced unquestioningly for so long they were no longer radical at all. Still, I felt like a traitor to my sex when I wore the sexy clothes I'd bought in Paris during my year abroad, so I packed them away until moving to New York, where it's hard to find a good taboo that hasn't been smashed to bits.

Of course, as cofounder of a literary sex magazine I've managed to stumble upon most of the taboos that are still-intact. Friends have asked, "Don't you find the subject matter limiting?" What I suspect they really mean is, "Don't you worry about your *reputation*?" At my last publishing job no one ever asked me if I got tired of editing books about television shows. The truth is: Yes, sometimes sex embarrasses me, but not enough to pack it away like I did my French dresses.

So, here I am, heading for my ten-year high school reunion, having finally figured out why everyone thought I was a goodie two shoes back then: I've always been more curious about rebellion than invested in it, and although I publish "literate smut," I'm still more an observer of the sexual vanguard than a member of it. For me, flirting with taboos—dancing around them and occasionally dipping into their mysterious waters—is preferable to waging an out-and-out war against them. Of course, the Stillborn chick I met the other night—and feel I've met a hundred times—would disagree...

Freud said the guilt we feel when transgressing a taboo is what makes us "civilized," prompting us to set boundaries for ourselves. Some of these boundaries are clearly necessary, like prohibitions against murder and incest. Others no longer make sense, but we continue to observe them out of custom. It's important to examine our guilt, to decide whether it's really ours or if it's been handed down to us like an older sibling's ill-fitting clothes. When Rufus and I first talked about launching *Nerve,* I have to admit I had some reservations, mostly about being perceived as a pornographer, even though what we had in mind, and what I think we have created, is about as similar to *Hustler* magazine as sushi is to tuna-on-white. Would I be exploiting women by publishing nude photos of them? Would I be exploiting men by publishing nude pictures of *them?* Wasn't there supposed to be something horribly wrong with exposing the human body? I thought about this—a lot—and for the life of me couldn't remember why sex (the real stuff, not Madison Avenue's homogenized, sweetened brand) was supposed to be such a big secret. It wasn't my conscience that needed examination, but the taboos that lurked there, crumbling in my fingers when I held them up to the light.

This chapter is about the fragility of taboos, as well as their allure and tenacity. There's the remarkable case study of Mr. M., a tireless masochist who fascinates novelist Rick Moody; there's Ben Neihart's fictive rock star, who pays a young stud to let her pee on him for musical inspiration; and there's Elissa Wald's story of callous lovers, overplaying their roles in each other's fantasies. The most daring of all these explorations may be Cammie Toloui's diary of working as a "live nude girl." Toloui's words and images betray her sympathy for the men who pay to watch her, upsetting the classic notion that it is she who needs the sympathy. Though her story is not pretty, it's real, and far more illuminating than any dogma.   *—GF*

The #1 Song
in the Country

Ben Neihart

I was twenty-eight, tall, bony, a bit stooped when I walked. Maybe it was a little bit late in the season for another sexy rage-filled singer-songwriter chick, and maybe I wasn't that angry or horny, but I got a contract anyway, with Warren Brothers, after a photo of me getting my pussy shaved by Mr. Michael Stripe appeared in *Playboy*. The photo accompanied his interview, in which he said he wanted to fuck me. A bitch profiled me in *Salon*. I fucked ICA agent Benet Little, from the L.A. office, and got a bit part as a witch on *Days of Our Lives*. The suits at Warren Brothers tried to fix me up with Ballart and Warden and Kidface and the Rust Brothers but I was like, We can talk about producers, no problem, when it's time for me to go into the studio, but I'll write my songs, okay? I told them I'm moving home to Lancaster, Pennsylvania, as a matter of fact, until I finish them. There's a music scene, Ed Kowalski from Alive is in town, and he's definitely fuckable, and so on.

I rented the top floor of a rowhouse in the city. I wasn't used to being alone, so I wrote fourteen songs in a month. The suits loved them, called them tight and hook-filled, and they went on about the sampling we could use in the song they thought would be the second single, but for the first single they wanted a song with hard-core lyrics. Couldn't I talk about my pussy or maybe pee in a guy's lap? I got on the phone with my agent, but she was no help, so uncreative. I got Michael Stripe on the line and asked him what I should do. "I need urine for the single, and it can't just be a fucking blow job where he dribbles some piss into my mouth," I said. "I need raunch. I mean, it can't be an accident. I think if I'm going to do this I need to pee on a guy so I know what it's, um, like."

"Let me ask Ed Kowalski," Michael started, "he might know a guy."

"Call me back." An hour later, Michael called. "Ed set it up with a guy who needs the money. If that's okay, meet the guy tonight at this park, I think the address is..."

"I know the place you're talking about," I interrupted, and hung up.

I went near dark. I watched ducks descend into a mucky pond. A few cars were following the park roads, headlights off and tires rolling across the loose gravel. The sound made me smile. I wasn't sleepy, and the air had achieved its cobalt heaviness. The ducks were really a splash I couldn't see.

I wasn't there long before a boy rounded the near shore and came up to me, dropped to his knees. "I could smell you from way fucking far away," he said, "so I followed my nose. I'm glad that I did."

"I'm the singer," I said. "I hate asking you this, I mean, if you don't want some chick pissing in your lap...'

He licked the palm of his hand. "I want you to piss in my lap more than anything." He had shaggy brown hair parted in the middle, thick eyebrows, a fat round nose. He wore a tight tan T-shirt and jeans. Good shoulders, flat belly, strong arms.

"Can I tell you how genuine you sound?" I said. "You're good."

"I'm in a band, too. Ed's gonna maybe produce our record."

"Oh, I'll totally mention you in my publicity for my disk."

"I have a great body. I work out all the time. You wanna, like, touch it?"

I reached out and gave his arm a squeeze: soft soft skin over hard round muscles. He flexed for me, and I was impressed.

"Look, I need to be up front with you," I said. "I'll pay you a hundred an hour, but you have to be creative. I'm looking for sensations I can use in my single, and I've been fucked before and I know what it feels like. There's the pee and all, but I mean, I might have to prod you and lick you, like that. Let me taste your hair? I mean, I'm sort of famous so I'm used to being objectified but for now you're a nobody and so maybe you don't like it."

"I want to fuck you. You don't even have to pay."

"No, I wanna pay. I can expense it. And then I won't feel bad about the pee. Now, I really do wanna taste your hair."

He laughed, but when he understood that I was serious he bent his neck and presented me with the top of his head. I took a lock, a big mouthful, and held it there. My mouth was slippery, pumping out saliva as I moved across the top of his head, wetting him, and then, before I knew what was happening, the boy slid his hand along my inner thigh and pushed a thumb up my panties.

"You, like, shave your pussy?" he asked. "I thought that was a thing just for the magazine."

"I like the way it feels," I said. "By the way, you taste so, um, briny. Let me taste under your arm?"

He held out his arm as if I were going to give him a shot. I rolled the short sleeve of his T-shirt up over the hard round cap of his shoulder and dipped my nose and mouth into the nest of hair. He brought his upper arm down tight against my cheek and along the side of my head, clamping my face in his pit, and I took deep deep breaths, almost laughing, licking and wetting the hair. With my other hand, I played with his nipples. Slowly, he loosened his hold on me, and slowly I pulled my face away from him and told him we should go to my place.

He followed me up the stairs—three flights. My apartment was the only one on top. As we trudged the final couple of stairs, he pushed his face up my skirt and traced his nose down the crack of my ass and licked my crotch. I stood there, feeling the wet of his tongue, and then I started to squat, and I could feel my ass sort of open as I let him support some of my weight. The boy had a bull neck and those shoulders, so I wasn't worried. He wrapped his arms around my lap from behind, with his face still buried in my ass, and tipped me forward so I was on my hands and knees. My door key fell out of the slit pocket of my skirt. As I reached for it, he put his thumb and forefinger in my pussy and took my ass in the rest of that hand, flipped me over, supported my back with the other arm, and picked me up, carried me to the door.

"I have to pee," I said.

He smiled. I liked the way he looked, holding me. Shoulders straining, neck veins and muscles standing out. "Piss on me."

"Yeah," I nodded. "You're good."

As soon as we were inside, with the door still hanging open, I started to pee, through my underwear, down his fingers, down the front of his T-shirt and the lap of his jeans.

"The record company wants me to call the song 'Territory,' but I don't like that. It's too cerebral. I don't want real punk, you know, either. Like not 'Golden Showers' or 'My Yellow Stream.' Am I too heavy? You can put me down, although I have to admit I really like a guy who's clearly physically stronger than me. You wear a T-shirt well."

"How about 'Jasmine Wine?'" he asked.

I gulped. "That's so damn Steelie Nicks. I love it."

He sat on the toilet while I hung my pissy clothes inside the stall shower. I got a fresh wash cloth and rinsed off and stood in the shower and douched with something fruity and put in my sponge.

"I'm going to start fucking myself," I said, two fingers still up my pussy.

"I don't know why you cleaned up," the boy said. He pulled off his T-shirt, unbuckled his jeans and just sat there, legs wide open, and I pulled the denim off, down his hairy thick legs. I was in a sort of kneeling position in front of him, and he lifted his feet, rested them on my knees so the pouch of his white briefs was right there in my face. "You might as well fucking taste this now, I mean if you like stick as much as you like hair."

I peeled the waistband down and cupped his dick out of the fabric and he leaned forward and sort of rested his balls on my chin.

"I have to pee now," he said. "You want it?"

I started to hear a melody. It was simple, strong, it was a great fucking tune but it was just outside of me. I nodded, and he put the head of the dick in my mouth. I spit it out.

"Keep your dick pressed against my neck," I said, "I don't want any on my face. Stream it down the front of my body."

It was warm, and there was a lot of it, some pooling in my belly button, my lap. As soon as he was done, I took his balls in my mouth for a quick kiss and then I told him to start beating off, we could get off together. I heard the melody again. God it was sweet. A song was coming together. The words warm like blood kept going through my head. Warm like blood, saffron, and then, with twin rhythm guitars, the chorus: *I can smell you from far far away far far away ooh I can smell you from far far away far far away . . .*

The boy sat back down on the toilet and I lay at his feet on the bathroom floor, rubbing my swollen labia with my knuckles. The head of his dick looked like a fat extra thumb in his fist—and as he stroked it, spitting down there, wiping his mouth with the back of his other hand, I looked at his nipples beneath the hair of his chest and they were the same color as his lips and I liked that and I told him and he said, "I want to come over and fuck you."

I didn't say anything at first but then the chorus of my song came to me, and the melody, and I sang it to him: "I can smell you from far far away . . . "

He got down on the bathroom floor beside me, supporting himself on one thick elbow, and pulled me onto his lap; I watched his dick go inside me, shaved pussy lips swallowing him, and I started to come right away. We tangled our fingers up together as he bucked against me. I heard my words, I heard my melody, my fucking song, my first single. He was singing it back to me, and it occured to me, in a flush of generosity, that the song would work as a duet.

The rest, of course, is fizzy bitter pop music history: the infamous "Yellow Wine" video, *Nightline,* the fights over the boy with Iona Apple and Murielle Shocked, my bomb second single, the one I sang alone, my triumphant power-ballad comeback with the re-mixed version of "Crestfallen," the flings with Tawnie and Nick Flexum, and the very public debacle of Thick Boy, as he was calling himself now, dissing me at the Grammys and walking out of the Maverick party with that bitch, Jule.

I ran after him, out into the crowded plaza swarming with fans and media. "Hey," I called out to him. "Are you sure you want it to end this way?"

He stopped in his tracks. Jule took him by the elbow, but he shook her off and took a couple of steps in my direction. "The way we started," he said, shaking his head, "I mean that was beautiful and real, but now you're all about glamour and gowns and shit. What do we have left?"

"We've got jasmine wine, baby, jasmine wine. We shared that. You've got to admit we shared that."

"Yeah," he said, touching the crotch of his Versace leathers. "But Jule knows that vintage, too." He winked at me, those cruel cruel eyes. "We're going home now to uncork."

On "Polysexuality"

Rick Moody

Intellectually, I don't really have any taboos. Or at least, there are no limits to what I am willing to admire in the literature of sexuality. I have always found virtually anything provocative and satisfying and, on the other hand, very little upsetting or abject. It's the elimination of boundaries and the practice of liberty in the realm of erotic imagination that affords the keenest revelations. Thus, I'm a practicing heterosexual (well, most of the time), who nonetheless likes gay and bisexual sexually explicit literature as well as bestiality, necrophilia, transgender imagery, intergenerational sex, psychoanalysis, continental philosophy, fetishism, etcetera. None of these interests have had much effect on my more intimate pursuits in the real world (well, most of the time), but as far as literature and the life of the endocrines goes, permanent revolution—as Trotsky described it—seems to be the best approach.

I wasn't always this way. Like most kids from the suburbs my early training in the literature of the sexually explicit was confined to period sex manuals spirited away from various adults—*The Sensuous Woman, The Joy of Sex,* and page 28 of *The Godfather*—manuals whose cabalistic secrets I

Andres Serrano

pored over with the intensity of a hermeneuticist. When you're ten or eleven, words like "vulva" or "orgasm" or even "blow job" seem impossibly mysterious. Anyway, I had no idea of the catholicity of my tastes in these things until I was away at college and studying, among other things, literary criticism. This was during the heyday of deconstruction, when theorists like Jacques Derrida, Michel Foucault, and Roland Barthes were in vogue, and *Semiotext(e),* the Columbia University–based magazine of postmodernity, was at the peak of its sway. In 1981, *Semiotext(e)* published an issue called "Polysexuality," devoted, as the title would suggest, to the idea that sexuality is a continuum, not a structuralist economy of either/or's or do's and don'ts. Among its contributors were William Burroughs, Jacques Lacan, Gilles Deleuze, and Felix Guattari, and such venerable pornographers of the past as Klossowski, Bataille, Verlaine, Rimbaud (these last two in a collaboration entitled "The Sonnet on the Hole in the Ass") and Anonymous, that heavyweight of the field.

"Polysexuality" didn't avoid a single sexual expression that I could think of, then or now: bondage and discipline, incest, necrophilia, coprophagy, etcetera. And many of its essays, befitting the intellectual intensity of its contributors, were excruciatingly exact in their depiction of these practices. For me, it was a tremendous eye-opener. I read it the way other people read techno-thrillers or romance novels. Not only did I interpret "Polysexuality" as an act of political rebellion (that such work would be published is itself political), and as a philosophical investigation (what is sexuality, and what separates it, at its most arcane, from other human endeavors?), but it was also a tremendous turn-on. Especially the pieces relating to theory. I was also, however, quite dizzy with the language of case histories. (I never felt the same about Freud's Dora or Little Hans after "Polysexuality"—they seemed, in that context, patently sexualized. It's no surprise, therefore, that such debased examples of erotic literature as *Penthouse*'s "Forum" now seem to me reminiscent of the style and language of the Freudian case history.) No question about it: The intellectual revelation is closely related to the orgasm. At least the boy model of the orgasm. The life of the mind and the pursuit of sexual expression are often one and the same.

My favorite piece of all in "Polysexuality" was called "M." It concerns a happily married man who subjected himself to the most baroque expressions of masochism. And it follows here. The life of a writer or reader or intellectual, I'm trying to suggest, is always about liberation. Don't allow any social or economic force to abridge or coerce or limit in any way your own expressions of sexuality, as you would not allow any other speech act to be limited. Be free, consider every possible point of view, the ones that horrify, the ones that delight, the ones that you refuse to admit delight you, and thereby know yourself.

M. [Mr. M.'s Story]

Michel de M'Uzan from "Polysexuality," an issue of Semiotext(e)

Mr. M. was sixty-five when he came to me for the first time. A radiologist colleague of mine discovered him after he had consulted her about a hemoptysis which proved to be of a short-lived duration. My colleague examined him and made a careful inventory of all traces indicating perverse practices: she discussed his state with him and advised him to see me. Mr. M. acquiesced at once, remarking that his case might be useful to others with the same perversion as his. He also admitted that by agreeing to consult me, he might also be hoping for an opportunity to be humiliated, and at the same time to better understand his curious status. His curiosity about himself had never been satisfied: he had read all there was on the subject of masochism and had always been disappointed in his findings. Actually, many other factors played a part in his decision to see me as I shall indicate later on.

Mr. M.'s appearance and habits were those of a calm and collected person. He was extremely careful to conceal his perversion from those around him. He had been a highly skilled technician in radioelectricity before his retirement. His employers held him in such high esteem that he was able to obtain special working conditions, and in particular arrangements affecting his hours and his vacations. He loathed the idea of personally exerting any form of authority or of holding a commanding position and considered both giving and receiving orders to be sure ways of losing his freedom! He was very fond of this freedom which involved long, solitary walks during his holidays. He lived in a small suburban cottage with his adopted daughter and her husband. In short, his daily existence was singularly devoid of any moral masochism.

But what a contrast between these outer appearances and his naked body! Provided that certain thresholds be exceeded, quantitative considerations and intensity factors can modify the qualitative aspect of a phenomenon and its sense. Going on the assumption that masochistic practices are no exception, I shall describe them in detail and thus possibly modify certain conceptions of masochism.

To begin with, Mr. M.'s body, except for the face, was almost completely covered with tattoos: "All big cocks welcome," and laterally, with an arrow, "Big pricks enter here" on the buttocks; in front, in addition to the penises tattooed on his thighs, one found the following impressive list: "I'm a slut," "I like it up my ass," "Up with masochism," "I'm not a man, I'm not a woman, I'm a slut, I'm a whore, I'm fuckmeat," "I'm an ambulating shithouse," "I love swallowing shit and piss," "I love to be beaten all over, and the harder, the better," "I'm a slut, give it to me up the ass," "I'm a whore, use me like a female, I'll make you come but good," "I'm the stupidest cunt around, my mouth and my asshole are for big pricks."

Mr. M.'s scars and marks of torture were equally startling. His right breast was literally absent, having been seared with a red-hot iron, pierced by sharp objects, and torn off. His navel was a sort of crater: molten lead had been poured into it which was prevented from spattering out (as it would have done because of rivulets of sweat) by introducing a red-hot metal rod into the lead. Thongs of flesh had been cut along his back, through which hooks were passed so that Mr. M. could be suspended while a man penetrated him. His small toe was missing: it had apparently been sectioned with a hacksaw by Mr. M. himself, acting on the orders of a partner. The bone surface was rough even after the amputation and he had filed it even. Needles had been pushed almost everywhere into his body, even into the thorax. His rectum was enlarged, "so it would look like a vagina." Photographs were taken during this process. It is interesting to note that none of these tortures were followed by the slightest suppuration, even after foreign bodies, such as needles, nails, and pieces of glass had been inflicted on his body. The daily ingestion of urine and excrement over a period of time did not cause any apparent upset. The internist asked Mr. M. to show him various "instruments of torture": boards imbedded with hundreds of needles, a wheel full of phonographic needles with a handle that was used to beat him. Lastly, and most remarkably, Mr. M.'s genitalia had not been spared. All of this could easily be verified. The tortures mentioned above left definite traces which incontestably proved that Mr. M. was not lying.

The death of his first wife, caused in no small amount, one feels, by the tortures she had endured, had a profound effect on M. He was overcome by depression and developed pulmonary tuberculosis in his turn, but was completely cured after two years spent in a sanitarium.

He married a second time but the marriage soon ended in divorce: his second wife was a prostitute whom he had selected in the hope of finding an experienced partner. The fact that she was a prostitute and a procuress put M. in danger of being exposed if she were arrested for her illegal activities and he wanted to avoid that possibility at all costs. He also intimated that his wife's lack of morality shocked him. He legally adopted the young girl who was their maid during their brief marriage. M. was forty-six or forty-seven at the time. It was then that his perverse activities ceased altogether. From then on, he lived completely within the framework of the family life he had created and to which he was very much attached. Nothing of his singular past was known to the persons involved. Correspondence was practically the only contact he maintained with his real daughter from his first marriage. He told me that he did not think she was masochistic, "except for the fact that she had ten children."

M. described his parents as having been very considerate and kind to him. He was an only child and his parents were not young when he was born. His mother was very affectionate, his father was a little more rigid. All of this is very ordinary, one might say. Nevertheless, M. at four years of age had seen a little girl in his neighborhood eating her excrement. He even remembered her name. He said, "I was disgusted. But later on it came back to me." Another time during our talks he made the following statement about a book he had read on fakirs: "At first I thought it was horrible. But later on it came back to me."

The appearance early in life of erogenous masochism—often cited by writers on the subject—was verified in M.'s case: his practices began when he was ten years old. He became aware of his punishment-seeking penchant and his attraction to urine at boarding school. He went through a short period during which a certain repugnance apparently held him back, but when this was over his masochistic practices started in earnest and grew in importance. After being sodomized by a monitor, he became the target of maltreatment by his classmates, the sexual aspect of which is obvious. His classmates, however, often backed off, not daring to actually commit certain deeds: they dared not, for instance, push needles through his arm themselves but would give him orders to do so. In sexual "games" he would always assume the female role. As he said, "I was really the local slut. And it satisfied me."

During his first marriage his masochism developed to its fullest. M. and his wife, although engaging as I have stated in normal sexual activities, were at the same time indulging in shared masochistic relations: "I liked it when she made me suffer, and she liked it when I made her suffer." Then came the idea of incorporating another person into their activities. One person, then two, shared their sexual existence for three years.

M.'s case reveals that the phenomenon of physical pain and its mysterious ability to trigger erotic pleasure and orgasm is not what certain specialists have claimed it to be. Theodore Reik, for instance, claims it is terror and anxiety which are associated with pleasure and then with orgasm: M.'s case disproves this, indicating clearly that pain itself is the trigger. The basic link between the intensity of the pain and the intensity of the orgasm underlies everything M. described and at times mentioned openly: "On the whole, it was pain that triggered my ejaculation." This explains the characteristic attitude of the masochist who constantly demands that his partner increase the pain. M. was quite aware of this outbidding. Fear of pain would be absent from him and it was his sadist partner who would back off because of the extreme nature of his demands: "At the last moment, the sadist always backs off."

It appears moreover that pain has a double function: on the one hand it apparently acts as a catalyst for sexual arousal. On the other hand it would seem to increase sexual excitement and push it to its climax while losing its own specificity. In this sense, pain has no boundary. "Every inch of my body could be aroused through pain." This would indicate an extreme mutation of the body's sensitivity.

Yet pain in itself was not the ultimate leisure. It was but a means. M. made the distinction very clearly: "At first, and on the spot where pain was applied, it hurt, but then I got an erection. More pain, and still more, and the feeling of pleasure gradually became sharper, clearer. Ejaculation occurred when the pain was at its most intense. After ejaculation, there was pain again and it hurt." This aspect of pain as a means was identified by Freud in *The Economic Problem in Masochism*, where he posits that, in the case of masochism, physical pain and unpleasure are neither ends in themselves nor signals, but means to attain a goal which is always pleasure. From M.'s endless search for pain, we can logically infer an equally endless need for pleasure. M. orchestrated the brutal tortures inflicted on him in order to obtain the keenest possible pleasure. He undoubtedly experienced "the feeling of happiness derived from the satisfaction of a wild instinctual impulse untamed by the ego." One would be incorrect in assuming, however, that M. was free to desire or to refuse that joy. The paradox is that it was forced upon him. In a sense he was condemned to pleasure and this is why his case is so difficult to unravel. Suffer the worst torments to obtain pleasure under absolute compulsion: such was M.'s destiny for the greater part of his life.

Holding Fire

Elissa Wald

Late August.

The filmy sun fading between buildings.

Six o'clock in the evening and Alicia is waiting for Jake. She has in fact spent the better part of the last few months waiting for him, something she hates to acknowledge even to herself. Certainly no one else would know it. Her waiting is a near-miracle of camouflage and self-containment. She doesn't sit by the phone, doesn't even stay home. It's something invisible: an inner ear cocked, an ache.

Jake has been her lover since early June. Now he is going back to Caryn, his fiancée, whom he is trying to convince himself to marry. And she will be left with the dregs of summer, swirling like backwash at the bottom of a glass.

She stands at the window and watches the street. He is coming over after work to return her keys. And then it will really be over, whatever "it" may have been. For her own part, it required too much discipline to be called a fling.

Alicia's apartment was just a few blocks from the firehouse. He would walk, as always. It pained him a little to think he wouldn't be over there anymore. She had continued to flirt with all the guys in the firehouse but so far no one else had ever gotten an invitation to her room.

She had admitted him into her private sanctuary and like all women was probably trying to weave him into her web. She had her dance of seduction like all the rest, her wiles and stratagems. It would be nice if he could be drawn in, if one of them ever had the strength and grace to keep him under her heel. Ultimately they always fell for him, always wanted more than he could give, probably because he could give so little and made no effort to pretend otherwise. For some reason never failed to draw them in.

Of course, this was fine too; he was nothing if not conquest-oriented. But as in any hunt, after the kill there was nothing left but the trophy, the ghost.

He was already infamous for his successes. There was one he was supposed to be marrying and another on the side. A would-be wife and an unwitting mistress. And there were others, so many others. For a short, half-ugly guy he'd had more than his fair share and it was like a testimony to something special about him. Something they all recognized. Maybe it was his spirit—wild, kindred to all the creatures he'd ever slain. That was part of why he had to slay them. Sometimes it even felt like self-impalement—and who could resist that?

He loved the way Alicia had been drawn deeper and deeper into him in spite of herself. She knew him for what he was and she imagined herself a sexual stable-mistress, doing what she liked with whomever she pleased. She projected this image onto everything she did, but whenever Jake had a block of free time she took it, and every time he saw her she was wearing something else, another dress, probably a new one just for him.

She was leaning toward loving him but she knew better, and every move she made in his direction was so elaborately casual. She had an airtight pretext for each visit to the firehouse and every strut past it. How she loved to strut past it *Hi boys* doing her best Jessica Rabbit, slinky in Spandex or short tight skirts...

And she did look damn good too, he had to admit it. She looked edible, like something he wanted to sink his teeth into, ravish, dismember. The other guys at the firehouse were jumping out of their skin; they were openly jealous, almost gnawing on their own arms, and sometimes during an unguarded moment they looked at Jake with hatred. This glint of malice—sudden, unmistakable—always caused a perverse thrill to leap within his heart. He was envied. These other men, taller than him, more conventionally handsome, coveted what he had.

Yes, he would miss her. A little. She had entertained him very well.

—————

It was her rape fantasy that made her give him her keys in the first place. A set of keys along with her work schedule of the next several months. He could only use them once, she said. She didn't want to know when.

And in fact it was so many weeks before he did that she had no longer believed he would. She was no longer mounting the stairs with trepidation; her heart wasn't pounding as she unlocked the apartment door. By the time he used them, she would have screamed had his powerful arm not cut off her air, coming around her throat in the dark. She had a moment of unadulterated terror as her hand flew to claw at that arm. In that first second of contact—as soon as her fingertips touched his muscle—she knew exactly who it was and it made sense but even in the wake of relief her heart hammered on with leftover adrenaline, exactly as she had fantasized. And then he was dragging her, one hand over her mouth, the other like a steel band around her waist. Not to the bed but to the table, where he forced her over it face down and pulled her head back by the hair.

What else had they done? They took a bath together once: scented, candlelit, where she took a sea sponge and polished his whole bronze body: shoulders, chest, rock-hard thighs, and callused feet. A magnificent body that the water made newly radiant. As if reading her thoughts back to her, he said, "Look at you, your beautiful body, your pretty face, that *smile*..."

She smiled a lot with him. She had straight, even, very white teeth and he made her feel like smiling. He had roused her from sexual latency and after so many months it was an immense relief. Her job as a stripper had driven her real sexuality underground, but like a man drilling for oil he had found it and it was exploding like a geyser.

There had even been some romance. An old fire coat he had given her. A present of striped bass, caught one afternoon in Montauk, which he blackened on her stove before his night shift. He brought her other treasures of the sea as well: fresh caviar, a jagged shark's tooth, bits of beach glass: azure, mint-green.

She brought him offerings too. Two weeks ago, she brought a dozen Rockefeller oysters to the firehouse, gotten to go from the South Street Seaport. A brazen gift: a veiled invitation to come by after work.

She also liked to cook, would have cooked elaborately had it not cost so much leverage. As it was, she often painstakingly put something together and then took equal pains to mask its virginity—she would cut it into pieces, stash it in the fridge, say it was leftover from something and offer to "re-heat" it. She would set a place for him at the table as if it were an after-thought, and with a half-ironic smile as some kind of disclaimer, she might light a candle.

"I made a pie for Josie's party, there's one piece left, are you hungry?"

And the slice would be taken from the fridge, having been separated from the rest of the pie that afternoon. The rest, wrapped in tin foil, had been hidden at the back of the freezer. One of several elaborate charades; one of many efforts to be kept under wraps.

She had to do it this way. The truth would not be forgiven. Though it seemed that none of it had made a difference, in the end.

They acted out a lot of fantasies but Jake had to admit that the "rape" gave him as much pleasure as just about anything he could remember. It was almost like hunting—his stealthy, unannounced arrival at her apartment at quarter to four in the morning. She always worked the last shift at her strip joint, always from eight at night till four. He could've come earlier, could've read her damn diary or something if he'd had the slightest interest which he really didn't, and besides she was the kind of girl who had probably devised some ingenious way to *know* if anyone ever fucked with it.

No, he arrived close to when he knew she'd be getting off work and didn't even bother to snap on the overhead. He'd memorized the apartment already with a fireman's flair for spatial detail; he knew where everything was and he stayed just inside the entrance, positioned himself behind the open door of the hall closet and waited.

It *was* like hunting, crouching patient and knowing in the dark with the intimate apprension of his prey. He heard her coming up the building stairs, knew it was her beyond a shadow of a doubt, knew her tread as he knew the gait of every animal he'd ever lain in wait for. When her key

Andres Serrano

turned in the lock he felt a stab of predatory joy and no sooner had she bolted the door behind her—reflexively, the light not even on yet—than he was upon her, with full, instinctive, perfect knowledge of exactly how to do it. She never had a chance to make a sound and he felt her panic, her not knowing who it was, and it aroused him almost to the point of creaming right there, that female panic and ineffectual blind struggle.

One hand flew to the arm he had locked across her windpipe and with this he felt her body change. Recognition and understanding trailed her runaway pulse, and then almost immediately excitement—receptivity, *surrender*—set in; without a word exchanged, he felt all that in succession. It was like his exchanges with the animals: the giving over, the abandon, of one wild thing to another, of prey to predator. He dragged her to the table and flung her over it, for the first time now somewhat inefficient, clumsy in his haste. He could not get his pants unbuckled fast enough, couldn't impale her a second too soon. Sinking himself into her like planting a flag on enemy territory, like staking a claim.

Tears were building inside like a storm. Green like a sky before rain; not to break until after he had come and gone.

She had done her best for him. Been nothing but sanctuary, inspiration. Not one demand ever passed her lips. He never even gave her his phone number, and she never asked for it.

When she discussed him with her friends, she didn't say she was in love. Or in pain. Or in despair. She said she was horny. This was allowed. The woman of the '90s was allowed to be horny. She was permitted (as long as she insisted on condoms) to take whatever measures were necessary to satisfy, gratify herself. The only thing she wasn't allowed to do was need. Therefore, in accordance with this rule, Alicia did not need Jake. She was merely amusing herself. Toying with him. He was, perhaps, her favorite toy.

The problem was that, in acting this role, she was no match for Jake, who didn't appear to be acting. He seemed to be getting exactly what he wanted. It was clear he was enjoying her, that he would come over and play whenever the impulse was upon him, and that his intentions did not extend beyond playing. He was appreciative, kind, but never fervent or passionate. No declarations would be forthcoming.

Sometimes this was all right. The picture pleased her: the stripper with her different lovers, one of them a hard-muscled fireman. They came in turn, paying homage, bearing gifts, bringing her pleasure. And she received them each with equanimity, a gracious hostess, a mysterious lady in her tower, a girl who had to have it. Affection and carelessness.

Jake's permanent departure was not in this script, and suddenly Alicia did not see how she could do without him. His callused palms and cracked nails. His air of absolute competence. He might not be a deep or complex thinker, might not spend a moment of his life pondering unanswerable questions, but he would be competent at whatever he put those strong square hands to: steering wheel, pick-axe, rod and reel, bow and arrow, a woman's body.

Only once had he ever lost an ounce of his cool. And this had to do with his own fantasy. He had a secret one he had never told anyone but her, of a woman strapping on a dildo and fucking his ass.

Alicia mentioned this to her friend Liz, a lesbian, who supplied her with a lavender one.

"You know," Liz told her, "this was the first dildo I ever bought and I was scared, I didn't know what I was doing, and I didn't want to hurt anyone. So I got this little one. But really, it's *too* little...it's embarrassing ...I never use it, anyway. But it would be perfect for fucking someone in the ass. You can have it, and borrow my harness too, if you want."

So she took this paraphernalia home and stashed it away in the loft and the next time Jake came over, she showed it to him.

"Look what I've got," she teased. She was unprepared for his response: the sharp intake of breath and sudden gravity.

"Can I see it?" he asked.

She watched while he examined it. He appeared transfixed. He turned it over and around in his hands and finally looked back up at her.

"Would you do me with this?"

"You mean *now?*" Alicia asked, startled. *"Today?"*

"Please," he said. She couldn't recall his ever being so serious before. "Would you? I mean, this is—I don't know how to tell you, this is a very heavy fantasy of mine. It would mean a lot to me."

Alicia was taken aback. "Well," she said finally. "I could *try*...I mean, I've never done it before, I don't really know *how*..."

"That's okay," he said. "Try. Just do it, I mean, what's the worst that could happen?"

"Well..." she said, "...all right, I guess you've got me. I mean, you know I'm not going to be the one to deny anyone their fantasy...and you've helped me fulfill a few of mine..."

She opened her closet. "I know exactly the right thing to wear with this, I've just got to find it."

It took several minutes for her to unearth it—a kind of half catsuit, a bustier attached to pantalets, made of some black material. She took this and the strap-on and a pair of stiletto heels into the bathroom and shut the door. Once inside, she couldn't figure out how to put on the harness and had to ask Jake to help her.

To her surprise, he did so without any derision. And back in the bathroom, the catsuit stretched without too much difficulty to accommodate this new appendage. A snap closed a flap between her legs, which she sprung to pull out her purple cock. Perfect; it was perfect.

When she emerged, Jake was staring at her, a strangely naked expression on his face. Not since the night she danced for him had she felt such a surge of power. She gripped the rubber member lovingly, holding his gaze. *So this is what it feels like to be a man.*

"How do you want me?" he asked. When had he ever asked for direction?

"Go bend over my bed."

Marvelous, the sight of him assuming this position. She smeared some cold cream into the crack of his ass first. She had never dreamed of doing this and could barely imagine how. "They've got a phrase for girls like me," she said, entering him part of the way. "Chicks with dicks," and then she saw that his jaw was clenched in pain.

"Am I hurting you?"

"A little, yeah."

She withdrew to apply more cold cream, then re-entered to the hilt. He moaned. She thrust tentatively, not knowing exactly what to do. It was not, after all, a real extension of her body. She had no idea what it felt like to be inside him—was it touching his prostate gland, was it a tight fit?—and this cluelessness made her cautious.

But it turned out that none of this really mattered. Just the idea of it was taking care of Jake. She reached around to grip his cock but he demurred: "You don't have to touch me, what you're doing is enough," and as if to demonstrate the truth of this confession, he shot almost immediately, all over her Indian quilt.

———

Jake made his way to Alicia's with a pleasant sense of purpose. Bedford Street was dusky and peaceful, dappled with shadows from the trees. Her door keys were heavy in his pocket, a weight he was soon to be rid of. As in a hotel, returning them was the act of checking out.

Out of the frying pan and into the fire, really. Caryn would be waiting for him in Montauk. But he didn't have to think about that yet.

Well, if he was going to get married, he was glad to have had this thing with Alicia first. Girls like her didn't come along every day. Game for anything. And she really was.

How had she gotten his ass-fucking fantasy out of him? Probably it was when he asked her if she'd ever had anal sex.

"No," she said, unexpectedly. "I've always wanted to...but by now I kind of think about it as a second virginity. I really want to give it to the right person."

"How about you take mine and I'll take yours?" he asked.

She smirked at him. The bitch. "I'll take yours," she said, and at this, her first flicker of one-sided greed, his pulse quickened, and his cock got hard. They left it at that. He wasn't going to confess that she could have his cherry on a silver plate if only she'd *take* it as her due.

It didn't come up again for several weeks, until the afternoon she pulled *it* out of some sleeve. A dildo, and more important, or as important, a black harness to strap it on with—a tangle of narrow, ominous strips of leather like bondage gear, like sex itself.

"I borrowed this just for you," she said, smiling with something like good-natured ridicule, and went on with some story about the dyke friend who provided it. Already he was erect, his heart pounding. Watering at the mouth.

"Let me see that," he said, reaching out almost involuntarily. She handed it over. He touched the rubber cock, fingered the harness straps. They put a tremor in his hands and knees.

"It'll be waiting here, for whenever you're ready," she teased, but waiting was out of the question.

It took some time to convince her to do him on the spot, still longer for her to equip herself. He waited on her sofa, hot with anticipation and unable to sit still. At one point she emerged, a sheepish look on her face.

"I can't figure this out," she said. "The harness contraption. How are the straps supposed to go?"

Jake took it from her, figured it out immediately—it wasn't that different from how you improvised a rope harness, creating loopholes for the legs. He unbuckled the straps where they were mismatched and refastened them to girdle her. He did this with deference, a slave equipping his mistress to mount him. She took it and disappeared again. The next time the bathroom door opened, she was ready. Clad in a black one-piece outfit that stretched from shoulder to mid-thigh, with a lavender cock jutting out between her legs. She was heeled, as tall as him now or taller.

Jake was ready to burst. "Where and how do you want me?" he asked, his voice gone husky with submission and a rare humility.

"Go bend over my bed," she said, command edging delightfully into her tone. "Take your pants off but leave your underwear on. Pull it down around your thighs where you'll feel it."

He complied—obeyed—in silence, trembling.

"Stay there," she ordered. "I'm going to get some cold cream."

Bent over, waiting, feeling the breeze from the open window against his ass—this might be the finest moment of his life. And here she came, a five-foot four-inch women turned Amazon. Striding over on authoritative heels. A woman with a cock.

"They've got a phrase for girls like me," she said, dipping four fingers into the cold cream. "Chicks with dicks," and then that hand was on him, in the crevice of his ass, such an intimate, hidden, vulnerable spot—and the cream was cold, a shock of cold—and the hand was sure, it was opening him up, priming him for invasion, readying him for her use.

"All right, then," she said, and he felt the tip of her cock enter him. "How's that?"

"Fine, go ahead," he said through gritted teeth.

She pushed part of the way in and ah, the pain, it was pleasure and pain so perfectly commingled as to be inseparable but yeah it did hurt, it *hurt*.

"Does it hurt?" she was asking.

"A little, yeah," he gasped, and she withdrew as suddenly as she'd entered. Relief, yes, and loss...

"I'll put some more cold cream on you, then," she said. "I don't want to hurt you," and of course she didn't, that was maybe her fatal flaw though he never would have admitted as much. The hand again, the cold spreading over that sensitive membrane, and then she impaled him all the way. It was amazing, much less painful, a sensation of the deepest, most profound penetration and it was happening to *him,* being done to *him.* He was squirming against her like a woman would, like a bitch in heat, and he felt his climax imploding at the very picture of it.

"Ah yeah," he moaned, "yeah..." and she reached around to stroke him but no, she mustn't, that would bring it on in an instant...

"No, no, it's okay, you don't have to do that," he said, but already it was too late. He came in the next moment, spurted helplessly and explosively everywhere.

Her laughter stayed with him for days.

Cammie Toloui

Diary of a Live Nude Girl:
Snapshots from the Lusty Lady

Cammie Toloui

From 1991 to 1992, I was a stripper in a one-on-one "talk to a live nude girl" booth at the Lusty Lady in San Francisco. I charged five dollars for three minutes minimum of my services. The customers usually just wanted to watch me through the window as I stripped and masturbated, and if they paid extra I would use my toys: dildos, zucchinis, vibrators, and whatever else I happened to bring in. They could do any number of things during those precious minutes: many would masturbate, some would tell me their problems, and others had detailed fantasies which I would act out with them, though that cost extra.

Of course, there were some who just came to visit me because they were curious. They would pay their five dollars, watch me go through my routine, then, when the three-minute indicator light would go on, they would thank me politely and fumble out the door, usually to a waiting group of friends. "What did she do? Did she take it all off? Did she use her fingers?"

After one and a half years of working there, I finally brought my camera in with me. I never thought anyone would consent to letting me photograph them during such a private moment. But because of trust and the offer of a free dildo show in exchange, over one hundred customers allowed me to take their pictures.

As a photographer, an observer, I enjoyed most of these men and women. They were fascinating people who I respected for their honesty and openness, and I appreciated them for sharing their humanity with me.

The following accounts are from a journal that I kept about my most interesting customers, some of the weird and wonderful

Cammie Toloui

things that they did or said. I used to tell all the other dancers to refer the strange or unusual ones over to me if they were too much to handle. The stranger the better, as far as I was concerned. For the most part, however, my customers were just average men or women—your neighbor, your boss, your husband or wife—and I appreciated them, too.

The Guy Who Sucks His Own Dick

I see him in the booths when I'm dancing. He usually creates quite a stir because when he shows up, all the dancers run over to the window to watch and encourage him to drink his come. He takes off all his clothes except his socks. He's short with curly brown hair on his head and all over his body.

Sometimes he lies on his back when watching the dancers, then when he gets attention from one of us, he flips his legs up over his head and manages to get his dick into his mouth. Usually he'll turn so he can let his head hang upside down over the side of the bench—we can see the dick-to-mouth penetration better that way. He's a favorite of the newer dancers because his act gets old after a while. The more experienced dancers don't give him the attention he wants so badly.

The Slug

The Slug owns his own business and he's always trying to get me to be his secretary. Supposedly, his old secretary used to play along with his submissive fantasies. She would have sex with her boyfriend in front of him, call him names, and otherwise humiliate him.

He likes to come in and tell me what a bad boy he's been. He'll look all sheepish and say "Do you want me to lick up this mess?" meaning the come that other men before him have left. I make him kneel down in it and tell him to lick it up off the floor—he shows it to me on his tongue, and then swallows it. Sometimes I have to look away so I don't gag, other times so I don't laugh. He puts on the funniest-looking expression—like a dog who's about to be hit. I would never demand that anyone do this, but he wants to, so I don't feel so bad.

Cammie Toloui

Sometimes he comes in when the booth is clean, so he waits out in the hallway. After someone else has been with me, the instructions are that if he has left some come, I am to signal the Slug by flipping him off. Then he comes to clean up. He's married and doesn't allow himself to come for fear of getting his wife suspicious when it's time for him to perform in bed.

The Rulerman

The Rulerman is kind of roly-poly. I don't know if I would recognize him without his hat on. He likes the new dancers because he can only do his trick once before they figure him out. He likes to go into the Private Pleasures booth with a small ruler—like five inches long or so. He pulls down his pants and puts the ruler up to his puny dick and asks her if she thinks it's the smallest dick she's ever seen. Then he asks her to laugh and make fun of it while he jerks off (still holding the ruler in place). He tells elaborate stories about how his wife makes fun of him. In one story, she fucks their friend who has a huge dick—right in front of him. In another story, his wife brings over her friends and they make him pull down his pants and they all laugh and point.

I begin to get very involved with his stories, almost believing his wife's cruelty, feeling sorry for him, yet he keeps asking me to laugh at him and humiliate him. It's difficult for me to actually be convincing. I don't enjoy making people feel bad—unless they deserve it.

Eventually, he comes and the full extent of his penis is realized. In other words, he's been hiding its true length. I'm infuriated—this is humiliating to *me*.

I've seen him in the side booths in the live show. One time I said "Hey! Did you bring your ruler?" and he put his finger to his lips like he wanted me to be quiet about it. So the other girls wouldn't know, or so the other men wouldn't know?

The Sex Addict

He's a middle-aged business man with a small brown mustache and beady eyes. At first I was really annoyed with the way he jerked off. He holds his dick gingerly with his thumb and forefingers. The other fingers stick out as though he were a society lady holding a teacup. He flicks his hand back and forth quickly then stops, pulls his hand away, then does it again, like a violin player with his bow, only not as elegant. I hate this, but I've since learned to ignore it. He always wants me to be on my hands and knees at a certain angle so he can see my butt and part of my face. This is better for me because I don't have to watch him jerk off.

He lives with his mother, which leaves him with extra money to spend on sex. Somewhere in the thousands per month. He usually pays two women to have sex with him a few times a week. They usually meet at a hot tub place or at one of the women's homes.

The first time he came in to see me, he said one of his mistresses left town, so he needed a new one. He said I was just what he was looking for. He was spending a lot of money on me that day so I didn't come right out and decline. I think I just said "Oh, that's nice."

The second time he came to see me, he spent most of the time trying to talk me into becoming his mistress—all the while I was on hands and knees with him jerking off. I finally turned around and told him I wasn't at all interested and that I wished he would stop asking. He did exactly what I thought he would do—he put his dick away and left.

The third time he told me that after his visit he was off to a group therapy meeting for people with sex addictions. His mother had recently found out about his problem and made him go into therapy. She intercepted his phone bill and saw how often he called the phone sex lines. He said she often catches him masturbating, which he does many times a day. He visits the massage parlors in the area and rents porn films every night.

He never again asked me to become his mistress, but he wanted to know if I would pose for pictures.

I often see him downtown in his suit. I think he recognized me once because he walked away very quickly—but that's okay, because if he didn't, I would have.

Habits

Fabrizio Rainone

Our earliest brushes with desire embed in our memories indelibly—the smells, the textures, the places our eyes fell. The redolence of suntan lotion, cracked vinyl car seats, grape Bubblicious, the retinal print of hands gripping stick shifts, dimples pooling, crotches testing bikini tensile strengths. Some would say desire runs deeper still, traceable in Play-Doh, Band-Aids, Mom's hair. Before we had a word for it, sex was a warmth, a flush, a reflex arc of sensation that mingled blindly with anything available, with anything that gave us pleasure.

Those minglings are of great consequence—early associations with sexual arousal can become aphrodisiacs, or if we are scolded, blocks. Sensations repeated become deep body memories: Youthful habits, chosen or developed for reasons long obscured, press into the mind like crooked teeth into an orthodontist's dental mold. I have known women who could only come while lying on their stomachs, holding their breath, with their legs together, as they did the first time it happened under the covers, late at night, in the room they shared with their sisters. Attempting to undo such habits can also be like orthodontia: slow, exasperating, and not sure to hold.

Of course plenty of habits subside over the years, and come to evoke the time periods of their origins. Most men have trapdoor memories of lubricant scents, which can peg years past like top ten songs. Vaseline was my fall of '83, before I discovered that the tacky residue could be avoided. Nivea was my summer of 1984—I smell it occasionally when women open purses in grocery stores. The impact of these scents always startles me, but of course it makes sense: What conditioning could be more powerful than smelling something—or looking at something—in the moments before orgasm?

The Nivea of my sophomore year was personal, but the accompanying *Playboy* was universal. Most American boys look at soft-porn magazines as they feel the first kindlings of desire, and the conditioning effect is considerable. While I don't think those magazines cause men to objectify women more than they would otherwise (sexual desire is inherently objectifying, in my opinion), they do teach boys to desire a very specific body: thin, taut, big-busted, with pubic hair trimmed and edged like rich people's lawns. This may bolster the hair removal industry, but it limits everyone else—it produces fruitless complexes and shores-in the pool of romantic opportunity.

Of course habits, whether or not they are beneficial, make us who we are. They are the mark living leaves on our personalities, like creases in long-worn leather. I hum when I eat, yawn when I'm nervous, scratch my ear when low on patience, and compulsively twist off the pop-tops of beer cans for no reason at all. I take baths a few times a day and have a weakness for aggressive but slightly flighty women in business suits with wool tights and messy hair. The longer I'm around, it seems, the more habits I have, and the more beholden I become to them.

The five essays that comprise this chapter all convey the pleasure of repetition. M. Joycelyn Elders councils us to take a saner, more appreciative view of masturbation; Gloria Mitchell remembers the creak of saddle leather and thrum of horse flank; Quentin Crisp enumerates the charms of lethargy and self love; Fiona Giles dissects the involute relationship between women and penises; and Lisa Carver explains her penchant for gruff, buzz-cut guys who like to do it in truck stops. The common ground is affection for the details of each day and the loyalty—sometimes stubborn, sometimes unwitting—that makes of these details habits.   —*RG*

Some of My Best Friends Are Sensualists

Lisa Carver

There are two main ways of doing it: sexually or sensually. Sexualists are into sex. Sensualists are into eroticism: stuff that isn't sex but involves the suggestion of sex. Sensualists are romantic—they set the mood. They notice details like texture and scent. They light candles. They have plenty of time and they are ready to *explore the options*. Baths have a purpose beyond getting clean if you are a sensualist. You take retreats and sabbaticals. You lie in mud. You kiss for a wicked long time. And I suspect you of liking jazz.

Sexualists, on the other hand, are more enthusiastic, garish, brutal. We're on a mission. Food is something we eat when we are hungry. We don't see the whole picture. While the sensualists toil over preparations for the perfect evening, sexualists make do. We screw in our work clothes at a truck stop in five minutes flat. We're just that way. I'm not waiting around while someone lights some damned candles. If you know what you want, why do other stuff first? We sexualists are propelled forward in life, not

117

sideways. While sensualists luxuriate among the world's endless possibilities, sexualists live with definite goals, which we pounce on and pummel into submission.

I had sex with a sensualist once. He hung his long hair (ugh!) around my face like a tent, cutting off all my light, and said, "How does that look and feel?" Then he paused. I realized he was waiting for me to compliment him on his eroticism—and until I did, he was withholding. Withholding thrusts! So I lied and said, "That's so cool."

Kim Weston

Sensualists have sex without orgasms on purpose. They call it tantric sex. I'd call it a bad date. Let's tell it like it is: sensualists are sick. They sniff feet and get a hard-on. I'm fixated on a single star—I jump on a rocket ship and explode in orgasm, and that's it. So much is *going on* with those other people. They have a richer world. Secretly, I wish I too could get all excited about colon hydro-therapy and the rest of those wacky fetishes. I just don't understand it at all.

Sensualists do stuff with their fluids. Why? When giving a blow job, the obvious thing to do is swallow the semen—it's neat, polite, and efficient. I don't smear it or drip it into the guy's mouth, or any of those other things that I know sensual people are going around doing. The guy already came; he doesn't want to be doing anything messy anymore. Getting come sprayed in your hair or on your breasts or wherever is fine, because it adds to the excitement of the ejaculation. The woman gets to be defiled (which is always a good time) and the man gets to actually see his claim being staked on the woman's person. It makes sense. Of course, being a little anemic myself, I always prefer to swallow (for the protein).

Sexualists hate nothing more than someone who takes too long. Oh god it's so awful—they peer into your eyes and they stroke you and say,

"Mmm." I read recently that 51% of Canadians surveyed said that they valued their partner's satisfaction above their own. Above their own! Quit looking at me, Canadian lover! It's a lot of pressure having someone hovering up there, worrying about my orgasms. Just leave me alone—I know how to get there. I mean, don't leave me alone, but...

Sensualists write long letters. Erotic letters should be two lines: "You are the most attractive person I have ever met in my entire life. I'm dying with desire—dying!" This should get your message across with a minimum of fuss. I wonder about people who send four-page single-spaced letters about what they'd like to do. Just come over to my house and do it already! Once you've figured out your feelings, wouldn't acting be the next logical step? The Scorpions said it best: "There are no words to describe all my longings for love."

Sixty-nine is strictly for the sensualists. They want to have their mouth on an organ, scent in their nostrils, and flesh in their fists while you-know-what is going on down there. Not me! I need to concentrate. I can't even think, much less perform, while that's going on. Why do two half-good jobs concurrently instead of two marvelous deeds separately, one after the other? One must prioritize.

One activity I'm not sure about is anal sex. It works and it hurts, two things we sexualists like. But it's considered gross and deviant, so their kind goes for it as well.

I recently learned there are two ways to fuck a tub. In a conversation with a sensualist, it came out that we both masturbate by lying under the bathtub faucet. But she likes to let it just barely dribble onto her you-know-what and let the pressure slowly build, while I turn it up all the way and swivel right up to the opening where the water rushes hardest. That's when I understood: the sensualists are in for the long haul—they want to be enfolded in sensation, they want to expand their consciousness to the breadth of the universe, encompassing everything. Whereas I want to lose everything. I want to be smashed to pieces.

You can tell right away which category people fall under. Well of course if the man has long hair he's sensual. Oh lord, protect me and my kind from the long-haired man and his slithery ways! Dangling hair in their faces,

Kim Weston

dangling pauses in their speech (to show how meaningful they are), dangling promises (threats) of future love, strange hands and arms dangling all over me. They're big danglers, those sensualists. They wear soft, spongy foot-wear and sculpt designs in their beards and bestow multitudinous casual compliments to all. They're messy human beings, with all that dangling and complimenting and beard-growing. They're billowing with layers. Layers of issues, layers of scents, layers of spirituality, layers of meanings to their song lyrics, layers of vests and scarves and belts and brooches and other ungodly items I can't imagine having the time to collect, store, coordinate, and put away at night.

Whereas there's something startlingly accurate about the sexualists. They're unfettered by facial hair or accessories or issues. They have no is-sues. None! They have one or two beliefs, to which their lives are de-voted. You see them so sharply focused, so unswerving, and it's such a challenge...you're dying to swerve 'em just a little. The externals might be slightly in disarray (shirt half tucked in, half out), but inside they are robots on fire. They can appear cruel and emotionless...and, well, on a bad day, they are. But at least they're not hypocrites, issuing protestations of caring for others in order to show off their soul and paw your body. Plus, sexualists have better shoes.

I can spot a sexualist on the street blocks away. They pass by me, and I am briefly but utterly possessed by their voracious yet uncaring eyes. Oh my god I do like them. I want to be had in a doorway by each and every one of them. Sexualists burn everything out—habits, towns, lovers—because they are so ravenous. Burn me out, please!

Henry Miller and Marilyn Monroe stand out as sensualists. Jack Nicholson is a big sexualist, though I hate to admit he's in our camp because he's such a letch. That's okay—we have Joan Collins and Xena the Warrior Princess too.

Some of my best friends are sensualists. Though I don't understand their ways, and would rather they didn't have their way with me, sensualists do make interesting and loyal friends. Like Rachel. Rachel will dance for hours naked in front of the mirror. If I found myself all alone in the house, naked and dancing, I'd say, "What am I doing?!" and put some clothes on and go back to work. I always read you're supposed to do little things just for yourself to bring out your sensual side, but what kind of game is that? Can you really flirt with yourself? You already know what the outcome is going to be. I can make myself come in two minutes. Why spend two hours? I suppose I admire sensualists for their patience, just as I admire babies for having such a good time with round plastic things all day. I envy aspects of their experience, but finally both babies and sensualists are aliens to me—I can't imagine trading places with either one.

Sensualists have us seriously outnumbered, and they're closing in. I see an army of massage-oiled zombies looming and leering, promising pleasure, as we cower, shaking, in the middle of our small wagon-circle defense. It's not enough that they have each other—they want us too! They want to play our bodies like fine-tuned cellos, employing all their acquired love-making skills. But we'll fight for our right to cram our pleasure into a few minutes—a powerful concentration of destructive joy—rather than letting it linger on, seeping all over our precious afternoon. We'll fight for the right to ram and be rammed! Um, do you want my phone number?

Horse Lust *and the*
Would-be Equestrienne

Gloria Mitchell

I was a girl who liked horses. Most girls do; an early passion for those sleek and shining muscled bodies, those dark liquid eyes and tender, velvety lips and noses is not an unusual thing. I wonder now (as I wondered then) what richness of experience and satiety of delights must be accorded to the daughters of the wealthy who, neatly turned out in boots and jodhpurs, are welcomed into the rich, dank, musky air of stables for frequent riding lessons, where they are mounted on steeds of their very own. It is an intimacy I can scarcely imagine; I worshipped horses mostly from afar, and the exceptional, divine interludes when I was actually able to sit astride one as it walked and trotted were just slightly burdened by my need to note every nuance of the experience, so that I would have something left of it when it ended. I can remember descending, dizzy, from the solemn heights of an Appaloosa, and watching with longing as it was led away, twitching its white-and-gray dappled hide, by a careless nasal-voiced girl a few years older than myself.

The psychologist Bruno Bettelheim had an explanation for this form of worship: girls, he said, like horses because horses, being large and strong, represent the masculine, and to ride a horse is to exert some kind of control over the masculine. Girls derive a sense of mastery from the experience. But a fortunate effect of postmodern thinking (if there is one) may be that it has slowed down our rush to categorize and dichotomize, to think that all things are either male or female, light or dark, rational or emotional, aggressive or submissive, destructive or generative. I think we're learning that the fact that the human race is divided into two sexes does not explain everything.

For me, the interplay of power in riding was something more subtle, less obviously Freudian. I had stacks of books about horses—their history, their physiology, their psychology (to whatever extent they might be said to have one). The books illustrated the myriad styles of bits, saddles, and bridles with which one could outfit a horse. They also discussed the range of signals a rider might give to a horse: fingers massaging the reins, calves squeezing, heels tapping gently to "collect" the animal; weight forward, reins high on the neck to signal *faster.* The rider's posture and balance had to be perfect, her touch light. All this suggested a tandem being, horse and rider, subtle signals transmitted from flesh to flesh. And it all had to be practiced, so I piled pillows in a heap on the edge of my bed to represent the rounded back and flanks of my steed. I mounted the pile holding a length of clothesline, which served as reins (English style or Western, single reins or double; I had to be versed in every kind of riding, to be ready if and when I was called on to put these skills to use). I sat perfectly straight, pressed my knees into the pillows, strained dangling feet to keep my heels down and my toes in. As I balanced I thought about how unpredictable horses could be, how a sudden noise or movement could spook them into rearing or running. The thing was to be prepared (I told myself), to have thighs strong and ready enough to hold you to your mount. You could then ride it through whirlwind moments of arching movement and unanticipated direction and speed; you would come out on top, breathless but unblemished.

This was control. But what was being controlled? It's hard to say, because the fascination with horses was not just with riding them, not just with watching and touching them, but with pretending to be them. A friend of mine and I had a game in which we spent hours on hands and knees on her living room rug, lifting our limbs delicately, shaking our hair, and whinnying. As horses we were treated cruelly. We strained to pull heavy carriage loads while snaffle bits pinched our tongues and whips descended on our helpless backs. At last, in the game, we would find rescuers, kind masters or mistresses who fed us well and groomed us till our hides glistened all over, and whose weight we were glad to bear. Horses are connected in my mind with other girlhood fantasies of capture and release: being bound to railroad tracks by a lecherous, mustached ne'er-do-well or chained to a rock in sacrifice or sold into a harem.

Could I say, then, that the horse, existing to be exploited or admired (or both), represents something feminine? In many of the pictures I drew of horses, I gave them billowing manes and thick eyelashes, as though I were trying to depict an equine Miss America. Then again, an indispensable attraction of the horse, that bestial engine of churning muscle mass, is that it is huge and strong and fast, an organic Harley-Davidson. I used to dream sometimes that I had a stable of racehorses, all about two feet high, impossible to ride. Like the drummer's dream of being onstage with his drums and holding a pair of tiny, ballpoint pen–sized sticks, this dream was one of helplessness and ineffectuality—castration anxiety, it might be averred.

So whether the horse represents a masculine force domesticated, controlled, and literally reined in or a feminine one empowered and enlarged, stronger ultimately than its captors, is difficult for me to say. I tend to think that the attraction of horses was not that they suggested one sex or the other, but that they suggested sex itself. At least, as I remember it, the experience of riding was an undeniably sensual one. It involved motion and rhythm and heat; it involved spread thighs and pressure against the crotch. And one of its challenges was that you had to control not only the movements of the horse, but the movements of your own body. You gripped with your legs and rose from the saddle, then fell again (but not too hard—control, again). You moved in rhythm with the horse as it trotted—"posting," this was called, a term that even then must have had just a faintly obscene ring to it. Your breathing, too, was timed with movement, and every breath brought in the scent of the other creature whose body interlocked with yours, who made your hips rock and sometimes jolted you with a heart-stopping, unexpected stumble or sidestep. Horses are sexy, as I am not the only person to have discovered.

Pornography sometimes makes use of the equestrian motif: the slave is strapped into position, perhaps gagged; the master or mistress wears boots and carries a riding crop. Sometimes the reference is quite literal: a dark-haired dominatrix sits astride a muscular fellow and pulls reins attached to his headgear. All this ought to be appealing to someone with a childhood fetish for the smell and creak of leather, the metallic jingle of riding accouterments, and the mystique of controlling or being controlled. And it is, sort of. But ultimately, "You are my slave, you belong to me, you must do as I tell you," seems to lack drama. People who really engage in such activities have told me that the dynamics are not so clear—the sweet, submissive young thing relates how she persuaded her master to let *her* tie *him* up. Still, despite such self-conscious crossings of self-imposed boundaries, the participants seem to like defining the relationship in terms of symbiotic need, rather than murky, changeable desire. It strikes me that there is an unwillingness, on both sides, to take risks.

Compare this to riding a horse. Riding a horse may be a kind of mastery, but the reason it is exciting is that the rider is not in complete control. Perched atop this great, strong animal, you know that you could be thrown off and trampled. You have expectations of the horse—you trust it and think you can govern it—but the horse has not signed any agreement with you. (Instead, you have signed an agreement with the stable owners releasing them from liability for your injury or death.) The bigger, faster, and more active the horse is, and the wider the ground over which you can ride, the more exhilarating the experience. (That was another flaw in my real riding sessions, as I recall now. They were too restricted, and didn't measure up to the fantasy of a graceful canter or a wild gallop over endless fields.) What you want from the experience is suspense, uncertainty, possibility. In contemplating those scenes of dominance and submission, I have to wonder: if riding a horse can be so complicated, why should sex be any less so? Why would I want a lover whose relationship to me was predicated on his entirely controlling me, or else entirely submitting to my will? I don't, mind, mean to suggest that B/D and S/M relationships are sick; I just wonder if they don't get a little boring.

In my postpubescent life, I seldom think of horses—I suppose that erotic contact with other human beings has diminished the need to climb on top of animals. Sometimes I dream of them, though. The horses in my dreams are not two feet high anymore; they are real ordinary horses, but they are still out of reach, unattainable objects of desire. These dream horses are housed in fields or stables nearby, and in the dream I make plans to go out riding, but can't find the right clothes or can't seem to wrap up a frustrating conversation with some earnest but confused stranger. And sometimes, when my waking, masturbatory fantasies involve fetters and blinders or other, subtler forms of control, I feel a connection to that early fascination with the kind of heavy, curving horseflesh that gets groomed and saddled and strapped and mounted.

But do I want to be the rider or the horse? I'm not sure; I only know I want one to be a match for the other. I like the acute awareness that comes with mutual uncertainty—the strenuous, shifting connection of two bodies, muscles taut, breath meting a jagged rhythm. I like to wake up saddle-sore.

The Art of Celibacy

Quentin Crisp

Celibacy is a word most often used in connection with the priesthood. Mr. Webster, in his famous dictionary, gives its meaning as the state of being unmarried, but we have all become much more outspoken and nastier than we were in Mr. Webster's day. We know that the state of being unmarried does not necessarily involve chastity—a more exalted state.

In the film entitled *Priest*, one prelate was having a shameless affair with his housekeeper and the other, newly arrived, made himself comfortable in the vicarage, took off his turned-around collar, and made straight for the nearest notorious gay bar. The film was, of course, absurd. If one arrived in a small town to work for McDonald's, one would not be as indiscreet as that—let alone if one had arrived to work for you-know-who.

Why is God so against all forms of self-gratification? There seems to be no reasonable answer, but we all accept that he is. I would think that if a man were physically satisfied, he could concentrate his attention on "higher" things, whereas if he were not, he would think about nothing but his continual battle with the flesh.

When Mr. Clinton appointed Dr. Joycelyn Elders to the post of surgeon general, she recognized that preoccupation with sex is a particularly onerous problem in the schools. The goodly doctor also said that it wouldn't hurt for adolescents to be taught about masturbation in the classroom. Mr. Clinton was shocked. His surgeon general was sacked.

Upper school was certainly where it all started for me. I spent most of those four miserable years slaving over knowledge that would prove useless, and (like the other boys) indulging in the solitary pastime of masturbation. It was such a dark subject, so surrounded by shame and mystery. We were all terrified of the consequences. How much was too much? Would one go mad? Could other people tell if one indulged? And so on.

No one was there to allay these fears, to say that it was the least complicated, the cheapest form of self-gratification, and that, as has already been noted, one doesn't have to look one's best. What more is there to say?

And if you do not enjoy having sex with *yourself*, why fly to the opposite extreme? Why get married? For human beings, marriage is such an unnatural state. If you want monogamy, it has been said, you should marry a swan.

When Miss Streisand stated that the people who need people are the luckiest people in the world, she was correct to use the plural and thereby avoid the common misconception that people who need only a *single person* are the luckiest people. If you allow anyone into your life who can claim the dreary role of "best friend"—almost as threatening as "wife"—he will weigh you down with guilt. When you meet him in the street he will say with feigned surprise, "Oh, you are still here. Naturally, I thought you were dead since you didn't telephone me all last week."

In view of these snags, it is well to dispose our interest horizontally, to cover the whole human race, rather than in-depth so as to burden some single unfortunate person. For this it is necessary to live in a large city so that any number of strangers are available.

People are always asking me how I deal with bores but, when we say of someone that he is boring, it is often ourselves that we criticize. It means that we have presented ourselves to the public as a shallow, wide-open vessel into which strangers can pour anything. I used to say that no one is boring who will talk about himself, but I was laughed to scorn by the press, so now I have revised my statement. I say no one is boring who will tell you the truth about himself. I mention all this to answer the question often asked of the celibate: "Aren't you lonely?"

Those people are lonely who don't know what to do with time when they are alone. I do nothing. I am a dab hand at doing nothing. I do not subscribe to the Protestant ethic of needless activity. Before I do anything—before I can even lift a finger—I always ask myself one question, "Can I possibly get out of this?" and if I can, I do.

And what does one think about when there is no one else to consume his thoughts? He thinks about himself, which is the only thing that he can change by merely thinking about it. And he must be alone to

Vivienne Maricevic

do this. How can anyone decide to work on his public image if, the moment he opens his eyes, an all-too-familiar voice beside him says, "And another thing..."

The last words on celibacy—or the advantages of onanism—must belong to that wonderful but neglected writer, Miss Katherine Mansfield. In her diary, there is an entry that says: "On living alone. If, by some awful chance, I find a hair in the butter, at least it is my own."

The Dreaded *"M"* Word

M. Joycelyn Elders, M.D., with Rev. Dr. Barbara Kilgore

Masturbation: it's not a four-letter word, but the president fired me for saying it. In this so-called "communications age," it remains a sexual taboo of monumental proportions to discuss the safe and universal sexual practice of self-pleasure. No doubt, future generations will be amused at our peculiar taboo, laughing in sociology classes at our backwardness, yet also puzzled by it given our high rates of disease and premature pregnancy. We will look foolish in the light of history.

Over the months since I left Washington and settled into my home in Little Rock, I have pondered the rage, embarrassment, and shock with which the word "masturbation" is met in our culture. What other word, merely voiced, can provide justification to fire a surgeon general—or anyone? What horrible betrayal of our proud race does masturbation conjure in our minds? As a physician, and as the nation's physician, it was important to answer every question posed to me with clear information. Informed decisions require knowledge. To insure the health and well-being of a patient, age-appropriate information must be made available. Some call it candor—

I call it common sense and good medicine. On the other hand, coquetries can be more than deceptive: both the refraining from self-gratification and the concealment of it can result in sexual dysfunction.

Yet to study masturbation would be to admit its role in our lives—one that many of us are not comfortable with. Instead, we discourage the practice in our children, dispensing cautionary tales that read like Steven King novellas. These myths were more understandable before Pasteur enlightened the world to the presence of germs in the 1870s; prior to his discovery, no one really knew where diseases came from. Masturbation was blamed for dreaded conditions like syphilis and gonorrhea, as well as for their ramifications: dementia, blindness, and infertility, to name a few. It's remarkable that some of these rumors still circulate despite clear evidence that they are unfounded.

The wall of myth surrounding self-sex is just beginning to crack—thanks, in part, to President Clinton who put it in the news. For the first time the topic is being broached on popular television shows, and comedians are able to joke about it without alienating their audiences. You can even find a variety of how-to books in the "sex and health" section of most bookstores. The overwhelming majority of psychologists and medical professionals seem to believe that sex-for-one is a natural part of living; we all touch our hair, necks, knees, and many other spots on our bodies in public to calm ourselves or to scratch itches, and it is no less acceptable, they assure us, to touch other body parts in private.

A friend, a senior citizen, stopped me after church one Sunday and said, "Please tell the children that masturbation won't hurt them. I spent my entire youth in agony waiting to go blind, because my parents told me that's what would happen if I masturbated. I guess I could have stopped, but going blind seemed the better option." We all want to tell our children the truth about their bodies and sex, but many of us are afraid of the consequences. Parents need to let go of the idea that ignorance maintains innocence and begin teaching age-appropriate facts to children. Informed children know what sexual abuse and harassment are, what normal physical closeness with others is, what should be reported, and to whom. Rather than tell children that touching themselves is forbidden, parents may gently explain that this is best done in private.

One enlightened friend shared with me the story of how she taught her preschool-aged daughter about her anatomy: the mother told the girl about her vagina as they examined theirs together with mirrors. There was some discussion and admiration. Later that day, friends came to dinner at their home, and at the dinner table the father asked his daughter what she had done during the day. Of course, she told him the most interesting thing that had happened: she and Mommy looked at their vaginas. But hers was prettier than her mommy's—"Want to see?" The stunned dinner guests were silent as the mother quickly retreated with her daughter to explain privacy. It is never okay to shame children for natural inquisitiveness or behavior: that shame lasts forever.

Masturbation, practiced consciously or unconsciously, cultivates in us a humble elegance—an awareness that we are part of a larger natural system, the passions and rhythms of which live on in us. Sexuality is part of creation, part of our common inheritance, and it reminds us that we are neither inherently better nor worse than our sisters and brothers. Far from evil, masturbation just may render heavenly contentment in those who dare.

Dick Love

When asked, as I frequently am, if the book I recently edited, *Dick for a Day: What Would You Do If You Had One?* proves that Freud's theory of penis envy is true, I can only reply that I have worshipped many dicks in my life—not to mention in my bed, on the grass, in the sea, on the hoods of cars, in a hammock, in several nightclubs, even in the back of a suburban daytime bus.

As the faces of ex-lovers fade and blur, their dicks stand firm in my memory, an avenue of saluting guards to rakish highlights in my sexual archives. Smoldering resentments might reignite years after an argument is lost, yet I can still feel affection for the owner's penis, neither as conquering sword nor symbol of unjust outcomes but—quite the opposite—his single most innocent and endearing part.

There was the one that bent to the right, adding width to its already impressive length, and which dipped and softened slightly before it came. There was the one that throbbed with veins so prominent that once, on a bad trip, I ran out of the room in fright. There was the one I met only briefly,

133

advancing through the papers on my desktop where I sat with my dress hiked up, a hot red birthmark glowing on its head like a fevered fog lamp. Then the several that refused to harden despite my earnest devotions. The tiny one, small as my little finger. The one that pounded on and on but never came.

Do I have a favorite dick? An ideal dick? A Platonic dick of all dicks? Not really. Knowing they're everywhere thrills me more.

Yet I don't envy dicks or their owners, with the anxieties and responsibilities attendant on power and privilege, not to mention the baldness and enlarged prostate that hormones bring later on. I get the impression from men that they are riddled with anxiety about coming too soon, about not getting it up, about unbidden hard-ons in public places, and even about the existential point of it all when they're not in bed. Who needs to live with the endless fear that even if I secured the girl safely in my arms, my own penis might betray me and refuse to fulfill my lust?

But I have loved certain penises, as well as the idea of them, cherishing the moment I can slip my fingers inside boxers or briefs and discover the heated weight of a hardening cock in the palm of my hand—a memory I will dwell on long after the affair has begun.

What would it be like, I wonder, to have a woman on her knees unbuttoning my pants, pulling my cock straight from its huddled confines with her warm mouth as I regard her tilted profile, my fingers resting gently in her hair? What would it be like to go weak at the sight of a naked breast, its delicate rising curve too enticing for me to resist grazing with a palm. How would it feel to enter her body, knocking against the subtle resistance of her muscles, luxuriating in the welcoming clutch of her textured vagina? How would it be to relinquish my all-too-hard and well-defined edges—not so much to invade and conquer but to let loose my fences and dissolve into somebody else?

Whenever I have been without a man for a number of months, and without sex, I have gradually felt my physical edges blur, and my sense of where I begin and end becomes less clear. I have commented on these things to my absent boyfriend, or to a girlfriend if I'm single, and I have noted their strangely disordering effects in my journal, like a poorly colored-in figure in a children's picture book. Not a matter of losing my personal identity, it is a more physical vagueness, even a slight invisibility, that comes from not being held and touched. I remember walking down the street thinking I should

Peter J. Gorman

ask someone for a hug. I also miss the weight of a male body lying on mine after sex, fearing that I might float off into the stratosphere or vaporize.

Even if Freud was wrong about penis envy, perhaps he was right in another respect when generalizing differences between men and women. I know I don't want a penis nestling all day long between my legs, nor do I feel that my genitals are a deficient or a miniature version of a man's. But my own case of penis curiosity points to a certain narcissism, a wanting to know what I'm like from the point of view of the viewer, to sneak into his warm soma on the sofa and check myself out. ("First, I would like to fuck myself," to paraphrase a number of women in *Dick for a Day*.)

When asked what I would do if I had a penis for a day, my answer is that I would like to be a young man at the height of my sexual appetite, but also a virgin. I would then like to meet someone like myself, in her thirties, at the age when women are also at their sexual peak. The story would trace the pattern of European novels in which a young man is inducted into the ways of women's bodies by an older, experienced woman, sometimes a prostitute, and sometimes presented to the young man by his father acting as the pimp. As this young man on the threshold of his first sexual encounter, I would be unknowing, eager, uncritical. In a word, I would be innocent. I wouldn't see her various softnesses and shadows as something less than perfectly molded flesh, but rather as reassuring cushioning for my clumsy landing. In the exhilarating rush of my desire to try out the delusions of possession, her myriad faults would escape my notice. And I would know what it is to be in the grip of a woman's much-vaunted sexual power, something it is difficult for me to imagine from within.

When Freud suggested that women are more narcissistic than men, his theory held a kernel of social truth. Just as penis envy can be acknowledged to exist where penis ownership ensures greater freedoms and cultural dominance, so can female narcissism result from the very real awareness of being looked at. It is a truism that women are forever being watched. And when they look at themselves there is no such thing as an innocent glance—they are always a little worried or picky or anxious, conducting their small appraisals and spot checks or, on a bad day, casting a blanket of self-disgust over the whole sorry mess. Either way, the constant need for review can be tiresome.

It is only by becoming a man that I could really know how gorgeous I am. I could be sure of my power, and relax.

Those dicks I remember are *seeing* me. Still.

Debauchery

Richard Kern

My debaucherous impulse—id, if you prefer—is greedy and sloppy, sexy and ravenous. Sometimes she gets the best of me, and I have to stop what I'm doing and let her out of her cage for a while. The last time I let her out, *she wandered into a crowded bar, where all the heads turned to watch her because she was alone and licking her purple lips and dressed in just enough rough black silk to cover her garters. She sat down next to a man whose girlfriend had just trotted off to the bathroom, purse in tow. She ordered a Jack Daniels, neat, turned to the man on the stool and saw that he was the one she'd fuck before her next drink.*

It would have to be soon, because the JD was just a dusty red flag in her throat, and she was already thirsty again. She told the man, whose hair was long, but not too long, whose clothes were shabby but expensive first, she told him in no uncertain terms that he was to find an excuse to ditch the girl and meet her outside in five minutes.

To make a short story shorter, she stayed out all night and did things that *I* would never do, because I'm much too sensible and monogamous and forward-thinking to have sex with strangers—that is, unless I'm in the insular world of my fiction. Aside from occasional stress-relieving bouts of drink followed by the raunchiest sex my boyfriend and I can be bothered with, I pretty much restrict my debauchery to the playground of my imagination and, of course, to *Nerve.*

Like most adults, I have retired a portion of my debaucherous self in the name of self-preservation. We all learn, sooner or later, that mortality is not a bluff. In youth, debauchery is unwittingly suicidal; later, it becomes wittingly so—a transition few of us are willing to make. At twenty-eight, the impulses still surface—to drive like a madwoman, drink till I'm sick, have sex in stairwells—but I'm more likely to satisfy them vicariously through characters in a film or book. The heroes of *Rebel Without a Cause, Thelma and Louise,* and *One Flew Over the Cuckoo's Nest* enthrall us because we respect, on some level, their refusal to make the concessions the rest of us do. At the same time, it's not lost on us that sooner than most, they all end up dead.

Having sex may be the closest we ever come to fearlessness, to boundless enthrallment with the moment, to forgetting everything but our pleasure. The stories that follow capture that abandon, but not without perspective. Courtney Eldridge renders the pleasure quest of a sexual compulsive with a lithe humor that betays the addict's deeper self-awareness. Barry Yourgrau's tale exaggerates the shock of witnessing a lover transform into a debaucher. David Teague's thick-skinned art collector has all his wits about him when he spends a sordid night with an inspired but physically repugnant artist in pursuit of the art he really desires. Contributions from Norman Mailer and Poppy Z. Brite, two very different icons of sexual openness and bad behavior, bear out a line from *Kissed,* a film about a winsome necrophiliac: "Crossing the line depends on where you draw it."

Debauchery changes with the times. It's almost impossible, today, to completely let loose without some fear of the consequences. William Vollmann and Dale Peck confront these fears for all of us in the most sobering way possible: their protagonists knowingly risk AIDS in exchange for the briefest human encounters.

Vollmann and Peck's stories illustrate an interesting cultural shift: In the age of AIDS, when we indulge our debaucherous impulses, we sacrifice our health, rather than our morals. Perhaps this is why I feel free to write about sexual excess but not to live it. Having grown up in the shadow of deadly sex the way my grandparents grew up in the fist of the Depression, I'm part of a generation whose coming of age was chastened by fear first, guilt second. Good old-fashioned right-and-wrong makes less sense to us than it might have if we'd never held our breath for two weeks at a time, waiting to know if we'd already paid the ultimate price for our indulgence. When this looming physical danger is finally conquered by science, and sluttiness is no longer an oblique form of suicide, will we simply revert to the old way of thinking—that chastity and virtue are one and the same? Or will we learn the lesson of this generation—that our most reckless sexual impulses are like teenage kids: If we don't give them a safe place to play, they'll play elsewhere. —*GF*

Ethics and Pornography: An
Interview with Norman Mailer

———————

We had heard that Norman Mailer was not a fan of the Internet, but knowing him to be a provocateur and sex enthusiast, we made him an offer nonetheless. A response came, through his assistant, in the form of a ten-page fax. It was an out-of-print interview, conducted almost seventeen years ago by Jeffrey Michelson and Sarah Stone for the sex magazine *Puritan*.

The story behind how Mailer came to do this interview is of some interest: Michelson was hired as Norman Mailer's houseboy at the age of twenty in 1966. When Michelson wasn't helping around the house or running errands, Mailer, an avid boxer, trained him to spar.

After a year in Mailer's employ, Michelson went on to a career in the music industry and then cofounded *Puritan* in 1977, which he describes affectionately as "art you could jerk off to." Michelson and Mailer continued their friendship, vigilantly boxing with various friends on Saturdays in the late '70s and early '80s.

On December 28, 1980, Mailer sat down with his one-time student to discuss sex, love, and the nature of desire. Mailer later counted this among his favorite interviews. Michelson is now an infomercial director, and *Puritan* has shelved its literary interests in favor of straight hard-core.

—GF, RG

Jeffrey Michelson: *What do you think makes for great sex?*

Norman Mailer: Great sex is apocalyptic. There is no such thing as great sex unless you have an apocalyptic moment. William Burroughs once changed the course of American literature with one sentence. He said, "I see God in my asshole in the flashbulb of orgasm." Now that was one incredible sentence because it came at the end of the Eisenhower period, printed around 1959 in *Big Table* in Chicago. I remember reading it and thinking, I can't believe I just read those words. I can't tell you the number of taboos it violated. First of all, you weren't supposed to connect God with sex. Second of all, you never spoke of the asshole, certainly not in relation to sex. If you did, you were the lowest form of pervert. Third of all, there was obvious homosexuality in the remark. In those days nobody was accustomed to seeing that in print. And fourth, there was an ugly technological edge— why'd he have to bring in flashbulbs? Was that the nature of his orgasm? It was the first time anybody had ever spoken about the inner nature of the orgasm.

Okay. Looking at it now, that marvelously innovative sentence, with all it did, one of the most explosive sentences ever written in the English language, we can take off from it and say that unless sex is apocalyptic, we can't speak of it as great. We can speak of it as resonant. We can speak of it as heart-warming. We can speak of it as lovely. But we can't speak of it as great. Great is a word that should never be thrown around in relation to sex. My simple belief is that sex that makes you more religious is great sex. I'm going to live to pay for, to rue, this remark if it gets around.

Michelson: *I'll never tell anyone.* (laughter)

Mailer: Remember that awful priest who said, "There are no atheists in foxholes"? It was a remark to turn people into atheists for twenty-five years. I remember every time I got into a foxhole, I said to myself, "This is one man who's an atheist in a foxhole!" *(laughter)* Well, what I do believe is that you can't have a great fuck and remain an atheist. Now it seems that the atheists of America are going to excoriate me. This is striking at them; this is a true blow at their sexual happiness.

Michelson: *I would like to get on to your feelings about sexuality. Not to intrude on your own life, but just to discuss certain things. What do you think you know about sex that most other people do not?*

Mailer: Jeffrey, I can't possibly answer that. I'd have to believe it's true... Really, all I believe is that I'm more aware of my limitations than most men. I have less vanity about sex than most men.

Michelson: *You've grown to have less vanity?*

Mailer: Yeah. I used to have an immense amount when I was younger. I needed it. I had an immense amount to learn. Sexual vanity probably has an inverse proportion to sexual sophistication. When we're young, we have to believe we're the greatest gift given to women because if we didn't, we would know how truly bad we are. When I was a kid, I remember I had an older cousin who was immensely successful with women. And I was always obsessed with performance. He used to say to me, "You're wrong on that; performance has nothing to do with it." I never knew what he meant. It took years—he was considerably older than me—to come to understand what he was talking about. Performance is empty sex. Performance is push-ups. I mean, we've all had the experience of making love for hours, and getting that airless, tight, exhausted feeling, you know, my God, will she ever come? For God's sakes, please, God, please, let her come! *(laughter)* I have a bad back today and one of the reasons is that I worked so hard when I was younger.

Michelson: *At sex?*

Mailer: I didn't work at lifting furniture, I promise you. If I'd been a furniture mover, at least I'd have some honor. *(laughter)* No, I have a bad back because I was stupid. Because I tried to...you see, the minute you try to dominate sex through will, sex escapes you. The connection of female sexuality with cats is not for too little. You cannot dominate a cat with your will. If you do, the cat goes right around you. Sexuality is the same way:

can't dominate it. So over the years as you come to recognize this, you begin to approach it from the side, so to speak.

Michelson: *Tell me about your first experience with pornography. Do you remember the first magazines you had as a kid?*

Mailer: I think it was *Spicy Detective*.

Michelson: Spicy Detective?

Mailer: There used to be magazines called *Spicy Detective* and *Spicy*—I can't remember the others, maybe *Spicy Romance*. The girls always had marvelous large breasts, with tremendously pointed nipples. I don't know how to describe these breasts, it almost fails me. You couldn't call them pear-shaped, nor melon-shaped, somewhere in between. They were projectile-shaped. Literally, they looked like the head of a 105 Howitzer shell, about four

Barbara Vaughn

inches in diameter, and went out about five and a half inches, with those tremendously pointed nipples. The girl always used to be tied to some sort of hitching post with an evil man approaching. They always had one arm under their breasts. I remember that it made the breasts project out even more. They'd have a wisp of clothing. A torn panty would cover their loins. I've never seen anything I enjoyed as much. Now, I didn't learn much from it.

Michelson: *Do you feel that there are any social benefits that result from a sexually free press, or do you feel that sexually explicit material must be tolerated simply to protect the wider benefits of the First Amendment?*

Mailer: Well, the first benefit is sexual sophistication. Talk about pornography always revolves around: Does it excite more violent impulses, or doesn't it? The women's movement is absolutely up in arms about pornography. An encouragement to rape, et cetera. I just can't agree. I think they don't know quite what they're talking about. Of course, some kinds of pornography are on the cusp. I wouldn't have anything to say for pornography that uses children as models. I'm against anything that sets people's lives on certain tracks too early. Using a child to make money from sex is obviously offensive. If you were a magazine that had pictures of children performing sexual acts, I wouldn't be in it. That's where I draw the line.

But you asked what the social value might be. Pictures of men and women making love is not going to hurt people as much as it's going to help them. It gives them—and I would include pornographic movies—an education in that part of sex which is universal, as opposed to the part that's particular. Those tragedies of high school kids who get married too young, only to discover three, five, eight years later, with a couple of children between them, that they weren't meant for one another at all, and so split, come about because sex is so compelling when they're young and they know so little about it. That's a profound error we've all made one way or another. We mistake the beauties of sex for all the beauties of the particular person that we're with, that is, think the particular person beautiful because of the sexual feelings they arouse in us. We don't understand those feelings are more or less universal, and could be felt with someone else. The faculty of choice is not present. Now when I was a kid, and I've never known a kid who wasn't riveted by pornography, I wanted more and more of it. I never saw enough of it to satisfy myself. That's because there's tremendous knowledge there, tremendous knowledge about human behavior.

You also get a sense of the sexual behavior of a panorama of people that you couldn't possibly have in your own life unless you devoted your life to sex. One of the ironies of pornography is that it enables people to free themselves from chasing after sex. A lot of that knowledge can now be obtained in a secondary fashion, through pornography.

Michelson: *Knowledge as opposed to pleasure?*

Mailer: Yes. If we all had to go out and acquire every bit of understanding through our own experience, it would take us forever to learn anything. That's why, in fact, civilization moved so slowly for so many thousands of years. From Gutenberg on, there's been an incredible rate of acceleration. Now, people are able to acquire most of their knowledge by reading. They don't have to go through the experience themselves. The worst thing you can say against pornography, I mean, the only argument I would use if I were determined to stamp pornography out is that it tends to accelerate the same things that are being speeded up by all other communications. Pornography, right at this present point, is a peculiar frontier of communications.

Sarah Stone: *What exactly is accelerated?*

Mailer: The consciousness of people. In the simplest literal sense, a kid of eighteen will now know what he wouldn't have known till he was twenty-eight.

Michelson: *Do you feel comfortable about appearing in* Puritan?

Mailer: Not altogether. I've thought about it, and finally decided I probably ought to. I'm not opposed to pornography—in fact, I think it probably has a social benefit. On the other hand, in *Playboy* I've had the experience of seeing my work printed between shots. Now, *Playboy* happens to treat its writers exceptionally well. No magazine is nicer in terms of courtesy, and you get fine pay for your stuff. They're a godawful magazine, however, in terms of layout, at least from the point of view of the writer, because the last thing you want for your prose, is to have a photo of a gorgeous model with her legs going from Valparaiso to Baltimore right in the middle of your prose! I'd rather you took an axe and drove it into the middle of the reader's head. Because the reader's not going to follow my stuff. His eye is on the bird. So there have been times when, despite the attractions of *Playboy,* I don't really want that piece there. It's not going to be read properly. In that sense, pornography is a tremendous distraction for a writer.

Michelson: *I'll try to make sure the layout keeps all your words together.*

Mailer: At least let me pick the pictures.

Michelson: *When does a graphic representation of a sexual act become art, and when smut? Can you suggest any criteria on which to base a judgment?*

Mailer: Let me ask you: What would be *your* idea of smut?

Michelson: *Things that are particularly degrading to either sex.*

Mailer: Get specific.

Michelson: *I guess it's stuff that turns me on in a way I think I shouldn't be turned on.*

Mailer: Excellent.

Stone: *I feel the difference is if it's commercially and sloppily done just to get another page in the book, then the insult is to the art. Where it's a true and honest representation of feeling, then no matter what it represents, it's got to be respected.*

Mailer: Mmm, that's very well put too. You would be saying in effect then, Sarah, that smut is the equivalent of a sexual act that's casual, what we call sordid, no love, no real pleasure in it, a cohabitation with a rancid smell to it. So a lack of respect for the seriousness of the occasion when a photographer takes a picture of a woman in a pornographic position makes for smut.

Jeffrey is saying, as I gather, that there are certain acts that tend toward the bestial, the fecal (I assume these are the sort of things you're thinking of) that may be arousing, but you find that your moral nature disapproves.

Michelson: *I'm wondering: Is smut to pornography, to good pornography, as trashy romance novels are to good literature? Is it just the lower end of the genre?*

Mailer: It's certainly complicated. Take Sarah's criteria, pictures that are transparently cynical. The model's worn out, the photographer's worn out, disgusting. Yet that can be arousing in a funny way. For instance, in *Hustler*, often I find that the most interesting section is those cheap Polaroid pictures that untalented photographers send of women who are not models.

Michelson: *The reality turns you on?*

Mailer: The sordid reality. My sexuality, I expect, is aroused by knowledge. The moment I know more than I knew before, I'm excited. Those gritty Polaroid shots in *Hustler* are often more interesting. They communicate. You know, the picture of some waitress who lives in Sioux Falls. I know more at that moment about Sioux Falls, about waitresses—even if they're lying, even if she isn't a waitress, there's something about the very manifest of the lie that's fascinating. It arouses your curiosity. Whereas superb pictures of models can get boring. There tends to be a sameness in them. Aren't enough flaws present. The very question of the sordid is…tricky.

Stone: *In Woody Allen's movie* Annie Hall, *he's on the street and he walks up to this little old lady and says to her something like, "Why are relationships so difficult?" And she says, "Love fades..." As a man who's had six marriages, what is your reaction to this dialogue? Do you think that love fades and do you feel that sex fades?*

Mailer: I don't think that sex fades in marriage necessarily. Without talking about my personal life, I'd say that compatibility is nearer to the problem than sex. What I mean is people can have marvelous sex and not be terribly compatible. That sets up a great edginess in marriage. Some people, in fact, can only have good sex with people who are essentially incompatible with them. I might have been in that category for years, I don't know. If you're terribly combative, then you're drawn toward mates who are not too compatible. Anyone who has a violent or ugly or combative edge is not going to be comfortable with someone who is really sweet and submissive. They want something more abrasive in their daily life. Otherwise they are likely to lose their good opinion of themselves. There's nothing worse than being brutal to somebody who's good to you. Whereas if you're living with someone whose ideas irritate the living shit out of you, and you fight with them every day and feel justified about it, that can be healthier than living with a soul whose ideas are compatible to yours. All the same, if you do choose this fundamental incompatibility, there will come a point where it ceases to be fun and turns into its opposite. Faults in the mate that were half-charming suddenly become unendurable. Every one of us who has been in love knows how fragile—what's a good word for skin?—how fragile is the *membrane* of love. It has to be mended every day and nurtured. We have to anticipate all the places where it's getting a little weak and go there and breathe on it, shape it again. In a combative relationship, obviously, that's difficult. You have to have a great animal vigor between combative people or they just can't make it for long.

Michelson: *What about love fading?*

Mailer: Well, I don't think love fades; I don't think there's anything automatic about it. I think most of us aren't good enough for love. I think self-pity is probably the most rewarding single emotion in the world for masturbators, which is one of the reasons, I suppose, I'm opposed to masturbation, because it encourages other vices to collect around you. Self-pity is one of the first. You lie in bed, pull off, and say to yourself, I have such wonderful, beautiful, tender, sweet, deep, romantic, exciting, and sensual emotions, why is it that no woman can appreciate how absolutely fabulous I am? Why can't I offer these emotions to someone else? Self-pity comes rolling in, and cuts us off from recognizing that love is a reward. Love is not something that is going to come up and solve your problems. Love is something you get after you've solved enough of your problems so that something in Providence itself takes pity on you. I always believed that whoever or whatever it is, some angel, some sour sort of angel, finally says, "Look at these poor motherfuckers. He and she have been working so hard for so many years. Let's throw him or her a bone." So they meet and find love. Then they have to know what to do with it.

Michelson: *Love is a function of having paid your dues?*

Mailer: Truman Capote has got this book he's writing, *Answered Prayers*. I gather from something he said once that its theme is that the worst thing that befalls people is that their prayers are answered. Which is not a cheap idea. Love is the perfect example. Everybody prays for love, but once they get love, they have to be worthy of it. Love is the most imperishable of human emotions. It never fades. That's my answer to the question. There is absolutely no reason why people can't love each other more every day of their lives for eighty years. I absolutely believe that. Without that, I have no faith in love whatsoever. I think it would be a diabolical universe if you're introduced to all these wonderful sentiments that illumine your existence but something is put into the very nature of it that will make it fade. That's the sentiment of a person who is full of self-pity: Love fades. That old woman was full of self-pity.

Michelson: *Do you feel that there is a spiritual obligation to sexual relationships, and if so, what price do we pay if we don't live up to it?*

Mailer: Well, it's always a spiritual obligation. But the trouble with the word spiritual is that we think of churches and priests and clergymen. I do think there's a spiritual demand in love, however, more a demand than an obligation. Love asks that we be a little braver than is comfortable for us, a little more generous, a little more flexible. It means living on the edge more than we care to. Love is always in danger of being the most painful single emotion we can ever feel, other than perhaps a sudden knowledge of our own death. La Rochefoucauld has that wonderful remark that half the people in the world would never have fallen in love if they had not heard of the word. I think that most people I know, maybe three-quarters of the people I know, have never been deeply in love.

Michelson: *Talking about not being deeply in love, have you ever paid for sex, and what is your opinion about hookers and johns and the outright exchange of sex for money?*

Mailer: Well, take it at its best. Because at its worst, there is nothing worse than paying for sex, and being thrown a bad, cynical, dull fuck by a whore who either has no talent, or no interest in you, or feels you don't deserve anything better than you are getting. That's one of the worst single experiences there is. On balance, counting the number of times I've had good sex in whorehouses and bad, I could almost do without it. But, you know, living fifty-eight years, you end up with a lot of experiences. I've had a few extraordinary times in whorehouses, which I'll have to write about someday, too. So I wouldn't put it down altogether. It's just that it's immensely more difficult, I think, to have good sex with a whore unless you're oriented that way.

There are a lot of guys who are not homosexual, but grow up in a male environment. They have four brothers, or they're jocks, or just live in a male environment as so many small town kids do. They're less comfortable with women, and so if all their buddies have been plowing the same broad—and I use the two words, "plowing" and "broad," because that's the way they're looking at it: they're actually looking upon it as a field—the fact that they're going to be mixing their semen with the effluvia of their buddies is tremendously aphrodisiacal to them. So sex can be intense for men in whorehouses. It doesn't mean that they're homosexual; that's too quick a jump to make. What it does mean is that they have to cut that close to the edges of homosexual experience in order to get a real send-off.

Michelson: *You said to Buzz Farbar in a* Viva *interview that you couldn't afford to begin—this is a quote—you "couldn't afford to begin to get homosexual because God kows where it'd stop." Do you feel that homosexual impulses should be repressed, and quite candidly, have you ever experienced such impulses?*

Mailer: I've never experienced them dramatically. I've never ever said, "Oh, I got to have that boy," or "I've got to go to bed with that man." I feel it's been a buried theme in my life but a powerful one. It creates its presence by its absence. I don't think you can be an artist without having a...well, let's try to define the elements a little.

There are homosexuals who have essentially male experience and others who have female. In a funny way, the difference between male and female in homosexuality is more marked, probably, than it is between men and women. When a man and a woman make love, they can take turns: one more aggressive, then the other—there are many ways in which a woman can almost literally fuck a man. The woman can be active, the man passive, then they reverse it. Many good sexual relationships consist of that back and forth. Nothing like the dialectic when you get down to it. But, in male sexuality, there is a tendency to either be top or bottom, back or front. They have an expression: Did you do it or were you done to? There is much more identification with whether you're going to be the male or the female in the relationship.

Now, I think all humans are born with a man and a woman in us. I think that's self-evident: we have a mother and a father, and to the degree that the mother is female and male both, we have a female-male component in ourselves. In turn, through our fathers we have a male-female side to ourselves. At the least, two sexual systems within us, physically, at any rate. I also suspect male artists have more of a female component to their nature than the average male. I think that's why I've always stayed away from homosexuality. I suppose I felt the female side of my nature would have been taken over by homosexuality to a degree that would have been repulsive to me. What you get down to is that it's a man who's doing it to you. And the man in me does not wish to be dominated by another man, not that way.

Michelson: *I know you're now to the right of the Pope on masturbation. Why have you become so puritanical about masturbation?*

Mailer: I'm not puritanical about it. Puritans put people in jail for their activities, or bring social censure against them. I don't go out with a flag and walk it up and down outside certain people's houses.

Michelson: *Ban masturbation!*

Mailer: But, God, I happen to believe, just like the nineteenth-century preachers, that the ultimate tendency of masturbation is insanity.

Michelson: *You think it does lead to insanity?*

Mailer: Well, it doesn't lead to it instantly. People can jerk off all their lives and they're not going to go insane. I said the ultimate tendency of masturbation is insanity. Now the ultimate tendency of driving a car at 80 miles an hour in a 55-mile-an-hour zone is collision. But there are people who drive at 80 miles an hour until the cops stop them or indeed, never get caught, but neither do they collide. The ultimate tendency remains just that. My point, however, is that left to itself masturbation doesn't bring you back into the world, it drives you further out of the world. You don't have the objective correlative.

You see, one of the arguments I would bring against pornography, especially the pornography of my adolescence, is that it encourages fantasy and romance. If I had a fault to find with the pornography magazines in general, it would be that they tend to satisfy elements of fantasy and romance. In other words, they don't—let me see if I can find some analogy. If a kid dreams about football as a wonderful game where he is running for touchdowns, and that's all he ever visualizes, he'd have a rude shock, to say the least, the first time he got into an actual game, was dumped hard and had a headache afterward. There's nothing like the first tackle or block you throw to wake you up to one fact: if you're going to love football, you have to love it with its punishment. And at that point, loving it that way, you have a profound relation to football. To love with the full awareness of punishment is the nature of profundity. So, to the degree that pornography encourages people to believe that sex is easy, it's harmful. But I can't see this as a social harm, since everything in the scheme of things encourages us to believe that life is easier than it is.

Michelson: *Are you against fantasy?*

Mailer: Against sentimental fantasy. That, I think, is our introduction to cancer. A ticket to the gulch.

Stone: *What sexual fantasies get you hot?*

Mailer: I won't get into it for a variety of reasons. Years ago a friend of mine agreed to fill out a sexual questionnaire. He had to go through every girl he'd laid, describe her in detail, what they did, their fantasies, their water sports. After he was finished, for the first time in his life (and this kid was a stud) he was impotent for three months. So one holds on to one's little fantasies. Actually, I have very few left at this point. As you get older, you need fantasy less and less. Let me put it this way: fantasy gives resonance to sex so long as it's on the threshold of reality. If two people are making love and play a little game, and pretend they're other people, well, that's perfectly all right. Finally they have to do the acting job. It's not just simple fantasy. But if a man and woman are making love, and the man secretly thinks that he's fucking the Countess Eloise of Bulgaria, and the woman is visualizing a stud from Harlem for herself, then they're in trouble whether they know it or not. Essentially they are masturbating. The ultimate tendency of such love-making is insanity.

Stone: *Then what sexual realities get you hot?*

Mailer: Nothing remarkable about it. The innermost parts of the female body exposed, that gets me hot. A fine pair of breasts, a beautiful ass. Hands can get me, not hot, but started. I mean, some women have beautiful hands. It's really not important. To find a woman attractive there has to be some one feature that truly keeps pulling you back. It could be her face, her hands, it could be her toes—you don't have to be a shrimper to love a woman's feet, because it isn't literally the hands or the feet that turn you on. A certain statement about the private nature of that woman's sexuality is in the part of the body that excites you. A breast could be adventurous. That would excite certain men. Others might like a breast that's very domesticated, I mean, men that want to dominate a household are not going to be turned on by a breast that's adventurous. It may turn them on, but it's not going to bring them back again and again 'cause such a breast means trouble to them. Brings out their violent impulses. On the contrary, if they find a woman who's got a gentle, domesticated breast, that'll turn them on because it means they can dominate that woman. And so forth. You can go through the various parts of the body. Every body, in effect, presents a possible lock to our key.

Stone: *How can a breast look adventurous?*

Mailer: It can suggest that it would be unfaithful to you unless you're very good indeed. *(laughter)*

Stone: *Why do you think physical beauty plays such an important part in men's attraction to women, and why does it play such a lesser role in women's attraction toward men?*

Mailer: Well, because beauty, finally, is a scalp, no getting around it. When a man goes out with a beautiful woman, he's more respected in the world. I can remember a few ugly women who were attractive to me. Ugliness can be sexually exciting....But I will say that I wasn't very happy to be seen in the world with those women. You could say that was demonstrably unfair to them.

Stone: *There is a certain anger I've encountered with friends of mine when I've said that I know you. You approached this anger in* Prisoner of Sex. *I was wondering if you've discovered whether some of their feelings are based on something real?*

Mailer: More and more I think the reason they feel this antipathy toward me is not because I am a conventional sexist. Anyone who reads this interview can see this. I don't have a simple notion of machismo or anything of that sort—I think the reason is that my ideas about sexuality are more complicated than theirs, and they hate that. They have a very simple idea of sexuality and they want to ram it through. As far as I'm concerned, when they get like that, they're worse than the Communists I used to know in the '40s and '50s. I mean they are totalitarian in this aspect. They do not want deviation from their view of life. Now the only way you can ever learn anything is by deviation from your own point of view of life. You encounter it, you argue with it, you grapple with it, you're convinced by it or you conceive it, and you move on.

Michelson: *You feel like you're dealing with people with blind prejudice?*

Mailer: Well, worse. I'm dealing with people with militant prejudice.

Michelson: *Norman, I'd like to discuss the nature of inhibition, something that interests me. To put it bluntly, why is it that some women like to get fucked in the ass and some women find it distasteful? Some women like to suck cocks, some women don't. It surely is not purely physical.*

Mailer: You can't talk about it generally, you just can't. Everything we do sexually is as characteristic of us as our features. The question you ask is truly bottomless. You could say to me, why do some people have noses with an overhang, and why do some tilt up? Why do we respond to these noses in different ways? I could give an answer; I mean, a nose that tilts up often suggests optimism, confidence about the future, fearlessness, but a nose that turns over suggests a certain pessimism about the very shape of things, an attachment to sentiment of doom. You have to ask next: What is the nature of form? Why do curves do these things to us? But in sexuality, you also have to ask which period of one's life are

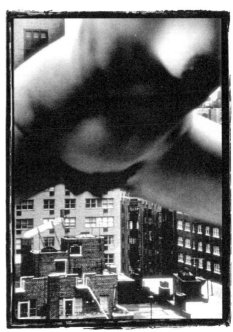

Dianora Niccolini

we talking about? Anyone who's lived with a woman for a few years learns that a woman's tastes can change as much as a man's. There are women who detest being fucked in the ass, as you put it—you see, I refuse to use those words myself.... The woman who wants nothing to do with a phallus in her crack one year is turned on immensely by it another year. I will make one general observation: it's very dangerous to stick it up a woman's ass. It tends to make them more promiscuous. I'll leave that with your readers. They can think about it from their own experience. They can test it out. Those who are scientifically inclined can immediately approach their mate and tool her, if they're able. Then they can observe what happens, watch her at parties, get a private detective, check up on her. So I guess I answered your question: a woman doesn't want it up the ass because she's doing her best to be faithful to that dull pup she's got for a man, and she knows if it blasts into the center of her stubbornness, that's the end of it. She won't be able to hold on to fidelity any longer. That's one explanation. It doesn't have to be true. But you might ponder it.

Michelson: *Have you ever been surprised by a woman because she seemed very proper outside and then was very wild in bed? Or a wild woman on the outside and still wild in bed? Is there a relationship between inhibition and personality?*

Mailer: No royal road to success. *(laughter)* I'm not sure that women have a sexual nature as such. I mean, think of the variation in sexual performance—to go back to that word—you've had over your life. I'm sure you haven't been the same with all women, better with some than others, obviously. With women, I think such changes are even greater. When I was a kid in Brooklyn, we'd walk around muttering, "Ah, she's a lousy lay." You know, sure she was a lousy lay for A, B, C, and D, then E came along. And she was so good, he couldn't even talk about it.

Michelson: *Let me ask you your thoughts about Plato's Retreat and other on-premise swing clubs. I don't know whether you've been or not, but you certainly know what it's about. This type of anonymous sexual expression was once exclusively the province of the gay community. Does it mean anything that it's filtered into the heterosexual community? That you can go, on any given night, with your wife and these places are full of friendly people from Queens, Long Island—you know, regular, human people are going there and having their...*

Mailer: Regular human people as opposed to what?

Michelson: *People with unconventional lifestyles.*

Mailer: People with conventional lives very often are tremendously drawn to orgiastic sex. That's their artistic expression. That's the way in which they are fighting society.

See, I think if there's any guarantee to America, and I believe there is (I hate to say it because it's used so cheaply by all those people who keep shouting, "Our great America, our great democracy") but I think there may be a greatness to democracy. It rests in the profound wisdom that a society can't expand unless, implicit in it, is the acceptance that people are busy working overtime to destroy the society. By that logic, democracy is more dialectical than Soviet Communism. What we recognize is that if you have a society, then you need people who are working to destroy that society. Out of the war comes a metamorphosis, which ideally will be more adaptive to the nature of a changing historical reality than more totalitarian, monolithic states. So—as I say, one natural, normal, healthy function of people is to fight society. The way in which conventional people often do it is through orgiastic behavior. I mean, Saturday night they have a ball with their friends, who either live next door in the next ranch house, or they drive 300 miles to see some other swinging couple. On Sunday they all go to church together. And they're giggling a little. They're living two lives at once. They were having that ball last night, the four of them, now they're in church together. And nobody's ever going to know. Some people can only feel a sense of balance and satisfaction, happiness, I might say, if they're living two lives at once. Orgiastic life provides that. Orgiastic life provides a lot of solutions for people. But it is sheer hell for people who are deeply in love. It's almost impossible, I think, to have much orgiastic life if you're profoundly in love with a woman. You can do it, but it takes the edginess in love and absolutely exacerbates it.

Stone: *Have you been sexually pursued by literary groupies? What's it like being fucked as an image rather than a person?*

Mailer: Well, I've usually been drawn to people who aren't necessarily that interested in my work. My present wife had read one book of mine before we met. She hardly knew anything about me. It's probably analogous to the rich girl, who wants to be loved for herself and not her money, remember all those movies?

Michelson: *Sure.*

Mailer: You definitely don't want to be loved for your literary fame because you know more about it than anyone else and you know that literary fame has very little to do with your daily habits. I mean, finally you're an animal who lives in a den and goes around, and finally, you know, has to be liked or disliked as an animal first.

Stone: *Is jealousy a necessary part of an intense sexual relationship or do you feel that it's a disease?*

Mailer: It's a very good question until you realize that you can't answer it. Because you end up with platitudes. It's my general experience that if you don't feel any jealousy at all, a woman will have profound doubt of your love. A little jealousy is marvelously aphrodisiacal, you know that, but real jealousy, when it takes over, is delusional, and has all the dirty pleasures of delusion. Delusion is one of the most profound forms of mental activity. If we have a delusion, we are, in effect, a detective on the scent of a case, picking up clues all over the place. We're trying to bring in the male factor. So it enables us to go through life with an hypothesis. For some, it is unendurable to live without some hypothesis. So jealousy becomes one of the most satisfactory delusional schemes.

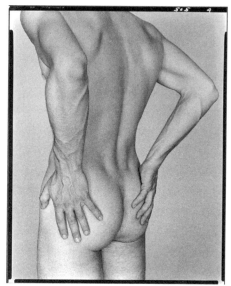

George Platt Lynes

You have an hypothesis. She or he is not faithful to you. Then you study it. You listen to the voice. You check out alibis. It sharpens one's senses. Jealousy gives us a wild ride we would not have without it. People often come into love with their senses drugged by all their bad habits—I mean, one of my fundamental theses is that virtually everything in American life works to deaden our senses. The proliferation of plastics first. So, given the fact that we find ourselves in a state of love with senses dulled, we have to sharpen them up. Very often jealousy hones that point. Taking off on a delusional trip keens our instincts. We can feel more alive than we were before if we don't destroy too much en route. Of course, being on the receiving end of jealousy can be abominable. It mickey-mouses you. You're always saying, "No, honey, honest, honey, no I didn't turn around, no, I didn't look!"

Then there's a lighter form of jealousy that is fascinating. It's jealousy as a way of keeping in touch. Once in a while I'll come home and Norris will say, "What were you doing at three o'clock today?" Not that she does this often, but once in a while, I'll say, "Nothing. I don't know what you're talking about." But then I'll remember somewhere around three o'clock, probably it was three o'clock, I was crossing the street, and I noticed a truly attractive woman. Maybe I turned around and looked at her. It's as if this little act flew through the firmament and lodged in my beloved's head. And at three o'clock she turned around at home and said to herself, "What's that son of a bitch up to?" In that way, that kind of jealousy can be agreeable, can even give you a little glow, Oh, God, that dear woman is sure tuned in to me. You see, so that was okay.

Michelson: *Do you think being in love sharpens psychic connections?*

Mailer: Sharpens certain connections at the expense of others. It isn't that love is blind. Love has intense, laser-like tunnel vision, you know, which probably would be a closer way of describing the nature of how love sees.

Michelson: *One final question. What have you told your daughters and sons about sex?*

Mailer: One of my daughters was talking about losing her virginity, and I said, "Oh God, don't lose it because you come to that decision. Lose it because you can't help yourself. Because you are so attracted to the guy that it happens." That's the sum of my sexual wisdom. Ah, I don't think she took my advice. *(laughter)*

Would You?

Poppy Z. Brite

Whenever I'm asked to write about sex and gender, a number of possible topics come immediately to mind. I could write about my own experiences with sex work, gender-bending, polygamy, torture for fun; my joys and angsts as a nonoperative transsexual; my drag queen ex-husband who used to get mad if I hit him and even madder if I didn't.

I could write about any of those things. But instead, I've decided to share one of my most secret, personal, and enduring fantasies.

It's about how much better the world would be if John and Paul had been queer for each other.

John Lennon died outside the Dakota when I was thirteen. Before 1980 I'd been peripherally aware of the Beatles, as if it were possible not to be, but I probably couldn't have named all four of them. For some reason, though, the media coverage of John's murder fired my imagination, and I went out and bought a bunch of Beatles records, and turned into a hippie for five years, and wrote an underground newspaper, and wore little round sunglasses. (I tell you all this only to explain the germ of my fantasy. Before

I go further, I'd like to make clear that although this fantasy does have some distinctly Manson-like elements, no actual murders have been or will be performed in its service.)

Here's how it goes in my wonderful universe. The Beatles got together and behaved as badly as history would have it up until about 1967. That was the year that Brian Epstein died of a sleeping-pill overdose and John met Y***, She Whose Evil Name Will Not Be Typed. Albert Goldman claims in his compellingly nasty biography, *The Lives of John Lennon,* that John and Brian had an ongoing sexual affair from 1963 until Brian's death. If you believe Goldman's version of events, it's obvious that Brian, despite being male, was one of the erotic/mother figures John sought throughout his life.

How much better if, instead of the art-grubbing clutches of Y***, John had turned to the *one person who was always ready to take care of him,* who kept trying to woo him back until the day he died, and who (significantly) tolerated less of his bullshit than anyone else he'd ever known? "We Can Work It Out" is a love song to a hot-tempered friend, but it's also a warning to cut the crap if the relationship is to continue. We can get it straight or say goodnight. I love you dearly, but quit fucking with me. Beneath his benign nature and his pretty face, Paul has a core of steel. John needed that.

So they realized that they'd always been in love really, and neither of them ever looked at anyone else again. Paul had never been with another guy, of course, unless you count boyhood circle jerks, but John was the perfect person to initiate him into the sweet passageways and rough edges of manlove. They spent days just talking and kissing. Their collaboration became even richer as a result.

They knew there was no use trying to hide their love from public scrutiny. Since the early days of their career, they'd strenuously refused to give a damn about public opinion, and they weren't about to start now. Thus, John and Paul's historic Bed-In changed the world. Media mavens, celebrities of psychedelia, and other rock stars flocked to the Amsterdam Hilton to offer their support. The "All You Need Is Love" video was filmed, with several of the guest stars (particularly Mick Jagger) looking as if they wanted to jump in bed too.

As well they might, for the Fab Two appeared to be having a very good time. Even in swinging, summer-of-love 1967, most heterosexuals had little or no idea what two men actually did in bed together...until the Bed-In.

That mystery came toppling down with a crash that made John's "We're more popular than Jesus now" remark seem demure. They weren't fucking for the cameras, but they obviously didn't care that the cameras were there. They were used to cameras, and no one else was there for them, really, not in those heady, early days, in that heady pearly daze. You can't (I can't) look at Paul's sweet face without thinking how good he'd look sucking cock, John's in particular: those cupid lips wrapped in a pink O around the spit-slick shaft, those round puppydog eyes turned upward in supplication, and John's long skinny hands on Paul's head, pushing and impaling, and probably bruising Paul's perfectly pitched vocal cords (I do not see John as a subtle lover).

The Bed-In footage of these two heroes was broadcast around the world, changing attitudes toward homosexuality everywhere more than anything ever had or would. (I don't mean to downplay the importance of Stonewall two years later...except that in my universe, maybe Stonewall wouldn't have had to happen.)

"Who was the top and who was the bottom?" my husband asked when he read the first draft of this piece. (He actually said, "Who was the pitcher and who was the catcher?" but he is from Texas and must be forgiven.) My p.c. knee jerked and I said that, as in most long-term relationships, it wasn't that simple. But I can't help thinking that John—with his macho-obnoxious public facade and his private hunger for not just closeness, but immersion— was a secret bottom.

Certainly Brian Epstein had John's cock up his ass any number of times, but I'd bet money that they tried it the other way more than once. I mean, they were doing it for four years, and John later said publicly that he was "curious" and had the affair "for the sake of experience." You can't tell me he wasn't curious about what it felt like to be penetrated. I submit that even if Brian wasn't able to manage this, John certainly would have found out with Paul.

(Oh, and remember the bit at the end of "Strawberry Fields" where John's distorted voice is supposed to be saying "I buried Paul," which fueled the Paul-is-dead hysteria? He was actually saying "I married Paul.")

The Beatles eventually broke up because George was too homophobic to deal with all this (see "While My Guitar Gently Weeps"), but John and Paul continued living and writing together. It wasn't all wedded bliss—once in a while, Paul would have to say "Get a fookin' haircut" or something— but it beat the hell out of creative limbo with Y***.

Just think: in my universe there is no Wings, yet some of those Wings songs that are almost sorta kinda good in *this* universe now have the dirty Lennon touch and are fucking *great*. With no Linda McCartney vocals. (Linda's okay. In my universe she married some other nice rich man—maybe Ringo—and did her photography and never sang a note, or even thought she could.)

I think Paul is a nice man now, yes, but back when I was a teenage hippie I hated him. I thought he was a capitalist pig and a sellout and somewhere in my twisted little commie mind I even blamed him for John's death. Paul's a take-charge kind of guy, and John (despite his caustic image and his undeniable mean streak) was always rather passive: if they'd been together, John probably would've been off on some farm in Scotland smoking pot, eating vegetarian cutlets, and raising a brood of adopted kids from around the world, not waiting to die in that creepy old Dakota.

And this line of thought would lead teenaged-me to even worse ones, like that in reality, perhaps Mark Chapman did a mercy killing. That's the kind of thing that people say I am a bad person for even thinking. I don't know. I couldn't do anything about it but write stories, same as today.

The stories I wrote from 1981 to '83 or so were mostly twisted revenge fantasies. Revenge against whom, I'm not sure. I hated a lot of people and a lot of people hated me. Usually my Paul-like characters suffered; occasionally they were redeemed. I hated him, maybe, but I *wanted* to love him. Paul's a Gemini, like me, and Geminis always have volatile reactions to each other...(Oh, God, the Mansonism is creeping in again. Get thee behind me, Charlie.)

Sometimes my characters were cavemen à la the human types in *Clan of the Cave Bear,* just as noble and just as horny, but with a remarkable resemblance to a certain bunch of lovable mop-tops from Liverpool. Sometimes they were direct knockoffs, as in the six surviving pages of my great unpublished rock opera, "London 1968." In at least one memorable instance they were Musicians of the Future. "Jack" had been killed, and his former partner, "Marlie," desecrated his memory by recording a song with the formerly African American, literally synthetic pop star "Jackie Michaelson." The mixing of this number involved, I believe, "guitarbot" and "nuclear percussion"...but that path is to painful to pursue.

At any rate, the story ended with Jack's ghost appearing in Marlie's bedroom and killing him by sucking his beautiful eyes out of their sockets (which even then struck me as ever so erotic). The two of them were together forever.

I'd been trying to sell my stories since I was twelve, but I never sent out any of these. More than the fact that I kinda knew they weren't very good, they were *private*. The stories I sent to editors were about the kinds of things I thought stories should be about. These were just for me. Though I'm loath to admit it, I must call my own bluff: in their way, they were fan fiction, as surely as all those stories you can find on the Internet about Captain Kirk and Mr. Spock doing the nasty. I hadn't yet learned to turn my real fantasies, the constructs of my universe, into publishable fiction.

Now I have, and I've also forgiven Paul for not boning John when he should've…I guess. But my universe is still so much better than the current reality that, in my opinion, it poses a moral dilemma similar to the famous one of "If you could go back in time and kill Hitler, would you?" If you could go back in time and put John and Paul in the right room on the right night with a few bottles of wine, thereby saving John's life, increasing the output of the greatest rock duo ever, and injecting a giant dose of tolerance into the world…would you?

MacArthur

William T. Vollmann

It was nighttime inside the clinic and within his heart, which was hot, black, and wet with a terrible fungoid softness unlike the cool white tiles of the clinic between which the dark cracks reverberated—Again and again you come here! laughed the nurses. Soon you must get the bad disease and die! Why always come here?—The ache was in his bladder and scrotum this time. The medicine would make him vomit for two weeks. It would be six months before he knew whether he had the disease. His wife, whom he'd now infected, went in with the lady doctor and closed the door. A small child wai'ed* him with politely clasped hands, and the mother laughed. He had always been able to joke and laugh defiantly, but this time, shamed and beaten, he sat sweating and blushing, his head wilting on his weary neck. His wife came back and put her sandals back on.—I'm so sorry, he said.— Never mind, she whispered.—He paid the sneering nurses, stood up straight, and said to them as grandly as MacArthur: See you next year.

---

*A wai in Southeast Asia is a bow and/or clasp of the hands before another person as a sign of respect.

Anonymous

Courtney Eldridge

He fucked his girlfriend, and he fucked his wife. He fucked his neighbor, the chesty brunette who routinely powdered, lotioned, dressed, and undressed in front of her bay windows in broad daylight and who requested he hog-tie her with men's ties—so he bound her with whales and sailboats and anchors and then fucked her on the stained hardwood floor until she squealed. He fucked his best friend's wife in his best friend's mahogany four-post bed, and fucked his best friend's wife's best friend, then he came onto a discarded *Times,* and casually kicked the paper under the driver-side seat. He gladly paid the fare, then he fucked his best friend's wife's best friend's chubby seventeen-year-old daughter in her brownstone garden during her lunch break, and she called him *Daddy,* while digging her chipped blue-polished nails into the dirt. And *Daddy,* he fucked a pre-op man from Houston, then a post-op woman from Dallas, about an hour before his own lunch, at which time he returned to his tidy desk and fucked Dallas and Houston both in a transsexual ménage, with a Texas two-step, until his wrists tired.

Robert Stivers

He fucked a Japanese salesgirl, while purchasing hand-sewn lingerie for his mistress; wrapping the salesgirl's coarse, foot-long braid tightly around her neck, he fucked her in the three-way mirror, which she then cleaned with vinegar, water, and newsprint, before she gift wrapped his three-hundred-dollar purchases. He walked home, whistling forgotten show tunes, whistling songs from *Carousel* and *Oklahoma,* and fucked himself with his wife's black vibrator, watching hard-core gay porn in his bedroom, and he chuckled, spilling low-fat-mayo egg salad on his starched, light blue Oxford broadcloth shirt. He grabbed a handful of rippled potato chips, changed his shirt, chose a gray lightweight wool jacket, and hailed that crosstown taxi, at which time he fucked his best friend's wife's best friend, who slumped against the right-side door, crossing her legs, while he gouged a deep hole in the crotch of her pantyhose with his favorite Cross pen, a silver felt-tip, which bled upon her cotton shield, before fucking a long-legged, siliconed stockbroker, after fucking the immaculate Japanese salesgirl and before the seventeen-year-old with dirty nails. He fucked the stockbroker in a stairwell smelling of Lysol and rolls of beige carpeting—they were extremely agitated as they awaited the elevator, before opting for the stairs—and this broker, the blonde, she also wore a lovely satin and lace garter with three latches per leg in which he entwined his knuckles, especially pleased with her splotchy purplish birthmark, about the size of a melted half dollar, partially concealed by the front latch; and he whistled, listening to the echo, while he dipped her over the rail, appreciating the view from the seventh floor.

He fucked a scrawny baby dyke ticket-taker uptown, fucked her up the ass, for novelty's sake; stuck his fingers in her mouth, cupping her chin, and, reaching around her tiny waist with his available hand, balanced her trigone upon his three middle fingers; and then he washed. He fucked an angel-faced bouncer, wearing chaps, off-duty, downtown, after downing a double shot of whiskey, straight. He fucked his statuesque dominatrix, who was also off-duty, in her cavernous black dungeon, after she untied his balls, spat in his face, and repeatedly called him filthy names, deriding him for the hassles of latex care—but not quite up to her usual today, not today—so he fucked her tits instead. He fucked his sister-in-law's ruby lips, his pixie-cut sister-in-law, whose red lips peeled horribly due to her matte lipstick, and kindly accepted her Kleenex, after coffee. He fucked his sister-in-law's scruffy, collegiate boyfriend, then he came in her boyfriend's unshaven face and wiped him clean with the same Kleenex, after tea. He ate a peanut butter chocolate chip cookie, brushing the crumbs off his wrinkled, untucked Oxford, and fucked his extraordinarily beautiful wife the second she walked through the front door that evening—surprised his wife, hiding behind the door, hooded with a French seam, evenly dividing his face—hearing her keys jingle. He fucked his wife upon their kitchen table, twisting her left arm, then right arm, then both arms behind her back; he pinned her fine wrists and pulled her hair, watching her graceful neck and porcelain chin jutting forward, before she changed her panties and primped for a business dinner, her social business. He then drank a glass of milk, rubbing his fingers in her cum on their imported green marble kitchen table, as his wife kissed his cheek and kissed the fingers he pressed against her dark lips, rushing to catch her own taxi, which was honking on the street below.

He showered, then called his girlfriend, whose tits he'd soaped and kneaded that morning, his rosy handprints lashing her breasts, and who was indisposed, by the sound of her hoarse voice; then he called his mother, who was also indisposed, busy with her senility, and who no longer remembered his first name, often confusing him with a man she confessed loving long before his own father, asking when he would make passionate love to her as he once did, breathless as she recounted the first time, at the lake, after he threw her into the water, and gently laid her against the warm, jagged rock or against the juniper trees, wearing her white eyelet sundress, or that once, while she sat on the tire swing kicking her tanned legs through the air, and he gripped the rope, cutting his strong hands—when would he love her as he once did for hours upon hours; then he called me, and spoke to my machine: I know you're home; and so I was. Then: But you know how I feel about you; and so I do, though I still did not answer. I simply listened, before I wept, immediately erasing the message.

Lyle Ashton Harris

Wood

Barry Yourgrau

I'm on holiday with the new woman in my life. She's behaving very strangely.

We're off at an old, picturesque resort, by a lake deep in the forests.

One night before turning in, as I'm brushing my teeth in the bathroom, I hear noise from the bedroom. I stick my head in. I blink. My new love squirms about slowly on the pillows, her hips rolling and luring under the bark brown covers. She hisses at the sight of me, like an animal. "Sweetheart?" I pipe, over my foamy toothbrush. I shuffle toward her in my slippers, in drowsy approval. The covers slide away as I come up. "My God," I murmur, at the sight of her nightgown up around her waist.

I sink down beside her, next to her heat, my toothbrush still lewdly in place. There's a tiny molten pause. Suddenly we grapple, as if possessed. We roll right, then left. I thrust and plunge and grab, in delirious, disbelieving fever. She wheels on top of me. "Oh, yes!" I yelp, writhing minty-mouthed and ecstatic. She bares her teeth, gaping. Her eyes seem to glow with odd,

171

yellowish light. "Sweetheart?" I sputter. She lunges over, and seizes one of my out-flung hands. She sinks her teeth into my thumb.

I screech and thrash loose and wrench against the wall, jamming the toothbrush so hard I almost crack something. "What the hell!" I squawk, spraying paste. I struggle erect. "Are you nuts?" I cry. "Why'd you bite me—look at the blood!" She huddles down into the pillows, hissing softly, grinning. I stare at her. I follow her eyes to my monstrous pajama pants. I swallow in consternation and edge away, back into the bathroom.

In the morning she's full of apologies, meek cuddles. I cuddle in return, my thumb heavily Band-Aided. We put it all down to new surroundings, food, what have you. She's again her sweet demure self, if a bit wan-looking. She doesn't feel up to our planned excursion to a glassblower's. So instead we just go for a walk along the wooded lakeshore.

"Atmospheric" is how the brochure describes this forest. "Dark and forbidding" is how it strikes me. As we huff along under the towering gloom, my companion seems to grow agitated. "Yes, probably just something you *ate*," I murmur again, uneasily, about last night. I watch her pale head twitch from left to right at the noise of the resort workmen off in the foliage, thumping and trimming, at the darting rustle and wriggling in the undergrowth all around.

The "eating" theme comes up again at lunch, in the dim knotted wood of the hotel dining room.

"Sweetheart," I exclaim softly, "easy does it there!" She hunches over her second plate of frog legs, snorting and sucking. "I just can't get enough," she grunts. "Yes, but people are *watching*," I whisper, finding my own eyes weirdly riveted. My mouth goes inexplicably dry. I stare at her lurid throat. I force a prim, congenial laugh, glancing at a table of oldsters nearby. They exchange haughty, in-the-know looks and sip their goblets of water.

In the middle of the night I'm awakened by sounds of lunch. I struggle around blearily, and then I jolt. My beloved squats in her plaid nightgown by the wall. A window is open to the leafy night. Parts of live frog lie scattered around her, torn and twitching and flopping. She swings her head around to me. I garble a scream into my hand. Her mouth is red, messy. She giggles hungrily in her throat. She flips a webbed hunk aside. She wrenches at her nightgown buttons and puckers up gory lips. "Kissy kissy!" she growls, coming for me with glossy fingers and arms, eyes flashing yellow. I squawk. My blood seethes in revulsion. We have an awkward, gruesome tussle in the darkness. She gets a hand into my pajamas, which I pry away, but still it takes me several long moments. "Sweetheart—I'm not—in the mood!" I hear myself gasping ludicrously, fending her off.

I spend the rest of the night in the bathroom on a blanket, with the door locked. The stark phrase, "not in the mood," blares through the turmoil of my conscience.

Because it's a big fat lie. Three times my horrified, bestial heart urges me back toward the bedroom, where my pajamas are pointing. Somehow I manage to resist.

I decide things are clearly now a matter for a doctor's care. I go see the concierge for a discreet recommendation. The concierge is a stooped little man, in a cold, shadowy office. He coughs bronchially into a handkerchief. I flinch in my chair, thinking the flu would be all I'd need, on top of everything else.

"Someone sick?" he asks, seemingly unaware of the irony. "Not—not in the usual sense," I begin uncertainly. "A lady behaving strange?" he demands. I'm taken aback. "Well—yes, as a matter of fact," I stammer. Flushing, I recount to him, unexpectedly, much of what's been going on. I exhibit my bandaged thumb and bare my still-sore tooth. I describe the frogs and the craze for kisses. I touch on my own darkly troubling angle, as much as I dare from shame and modesty. He nods, grim.

"A doctor won't help," he mutters.

"What do you mean?" I protest. He coughs. He squints at me over the cupped handkerchief. "Do you know a thing or two about life?" he says. I feel myself blush at the question. I blink. "Well, actually, I've been on my own many years," I mumble. "If that's what—" "Some women get affected, out here," he goes right on. "Maybe it's being near so many big trees. Maybe from all that clammy water, out in the lake...

The faint din of labor in the branches drifts from the window. "Well then we'll just pack up and leave, right this minute!" I exclaim, mentally despairing of the lost room deposit.

The concierge flaps his hand.

"It's too late for that now," he declares. "Once she's this way. Once you're both..." His voice trails off. He narrows his eyes, and scans me up and down. "I'll tell you what you have to do," he says. "But you won't like it."

He tells me. I clamber to my feet. "You must be criminally mad!" I sputter. "A wooden stake? What d'you think she is—some kind of *ghoul*?"

He shrugs. "Alright, try taking her to a church," he says. "Go ahead, see what happens."

"Sweetheart, why don't we go visit one of these quaint old chapels the brochure talks about around here?" I suggest, with strained nonchalance, after some chaste cuddling back in the room. The notion provokes such a storm of howling and writhing that I have to ring for the bellhop to help restore order, which finally comes as an exhausted, weepy dozing-off.

I wander out all afternoon long, in anguish at what things have come to, for everyone involved. Having no alternative, my footsteps take me into the infernal forest. This has not been my idea of a vacation in any way, I brood, glaring accusatorially at the grandiose uprights crowding and preening all around. My thoughts and worries so distract me, dusk is falling by the time I start back. I pant along, more and more uneasy in the mottled dimness. Something wriggles past and I jump. Then I whirl about, at furious commotion up from the path. I scream.

My companion is there in the undergrowth, in her nightgown, up against a thick-barked trunk. Her hair streams over her shoulders, a rat whips its tail, squealing in her grip, high over her thrown-back jaws. She sees me. She screeches in joy, churns the squirming thing against her and heaves it aside. She comes crashing toward me, wolf-eyed, nightgown flapping wide open. "Sweetheart . . ." I burble. I scream again, but without sound, thrilled by bare predatory flesh. At the last moment I lurch about and flounder off down the darkened path. She chases me all the way back to the resort. On the lamplit terrace, an old geezer sits with a blanket over his knees. He snickers as I come clattering past.

Another stark night in the bathroom, with the door locked and re-locked, gnawing at my thumb, in despair for both our mortal souls.

At dawn I go around in the mist to the workmen's sheds, to find myself a wooden stake. I poke through a stack of them, long and nasty-looking. I grimace sleepily, to think of the work ahead.

"What d'ya want?" a gruff voice demands.

An ill-shaved foreman in overalls scowls at me. I swallow. "I'm a guest here," I inform him. "I'd—I'd just like to borrow one of these stakes, if I may." "For medicinal purposes," I'm about to add, but the words sound too bizarre.

"So go find your own!" the foreman retorts. "We need all we got, for extra work we gotta do ourselves." A couple of his workmen step out into view, mallets up, to make sure I get the point.

The concierge supplies me with a wooden spoon from the kitchen. "It can be just as effective, believe me," he says. "Forget about size considerations and such." I regard the flimsy utensil in my fingers with dismay. Suddenly he leans across and murmurs that for a small extra charge, he'll come along and lend a hand. I look at him. I have half a mind to say yes to this quirky proposal, but right away implications start to suggest themselves. Then he coughs into his handkerchief, and that does it for the notion.

I spend the morning on the terrace with my listless beloved, so meek in the daylight. "Forgive me, it's been such a *demanding* holiday for you," she sighs, shadow-eyed. I smile and pat her limp wrist. I turn my head and stare off at the dark shimmer of the lake, at the colossal, creaking insidious trees. I grit my teeth.

"Not hungry?" she growls at lunch, over her clumps of smoked eel and asparagus. "No thanks, just feel like a drink," I answer, struggling breezily for a grin as my own loathsome blood heats. My glass rattles against the silverware. "I think I'll have another," I add faintly.

I tuck her in for her nap, trembling. "You're so sweet," she murmurs, as I draw the curtains. Hazy dimness descends. I settle in the armchair, ostensibly to read. A stupendous booming fills the room. I realize it's my heart. I strain through it to catch the slowed breathing of slumber. I rise up stealthily, to peer.

Her eyes are closed fast.

I reach over into the bureau drawer and ease out the lethal spoon from under my socks. I pick up a sturdy walking shoe from the carpet. I creep over to the bed. My hands are shaking so hard, I look like the fool in a vaudeville act. I set the wavering spoon in position over her nightgown and raise the appalling shoe. Her wan, snoozing head on the pillow seems so innocent, that I falter. I close my eyes in despair. A hiss jerks them open.

Yellow-glowing eyes blaze at me.

She snarls, open-fanged, and writhes. I gasp. I force myself to ram down the spoon. I strike it with the shoe. She screeches. She claws at me furiously, twisting side to side. I sprawl on top of her. I batter and slog at the utensil, woozy like a drunk from her putrid breath, hot in my ear. "No—no—no," she screeches. Her nightgown rips full open. "Oh god—oh god—oh god,"

I cry, hammering on, hearing the gruesome, delirious squelching of flesh. She bites me and flails with her bare knees. I pound with every last inch of my might, as if fighting through syrupy tides. All at once she screams horrendously, and sways up, rigid—and then swoons back, splayed and lifeless.

I lie there on her grimy breast, bleating, spent. After a while, I roll off. I look at what I've done, and I groan in awe and horror, trembly with relief. I lurch from the bed and totter into the bathroom and turn on the shower.

As I'm drying off with a leaf green towel, I hear a low laugh behind me. I turn slowly around.

She leans against the doorway, naked as an infant, an arm over the crimson wound in her breast. She smiles at me, intimately, radiant and dewy pink. The slimy spoon dangles from her hand. I smile slowly, intimately, back. I step over to her, and sweep her in my arms. "Oh my true love," I whisper. "Brutally butchered, to save us sweetly here in life!" We kiss, tongue onto tongue.

At dinner the concierge sends over a bottle of ersatz champagne to go with our trout, and a table of old geezers show me thumbs-up and a wink. I nod, pursing my lips coolly. I dab at the trophy scratches on my cheek.

Afterward my reborn beloved and I join the dancing in the nippy moonlight on the terrace. She whispers something about forests and trees and I laugh and give her a private squeeze, so she yelps and squeezes in reply. At this point someone coughs beside us and tries to cut in, but we decline.

The next day, in fact, a jarring note arrives, offering to buy the spoon back—or at least get a long look at it. I grunt and tear the paper into pieces, with a shake of my head and a shudder. Of course I keep this nasty business from my companion. But I add it to my newfound wisdoms about life, and to what can go wrong when you're on holiday.

*The Hunger/*Artist

David Teague

Until he came upon her art, he'd trudged through endless galleries of un-desire, stood in the powder white rooms, crabwalked across the hard-wood, sucked on cheese cubes amid the babbling. Fuck Manhattan. What did Mick Jagger ever see in this town?

Her work bloomed on the walls of the redeemed slaughterhouse, trans-lucent boys and girls, gaunt, naked, and sweet, perched on the gunwales of their white boat, tumbling into the greeny water, luminosity of skin, muscles, bones, blood coursing, purple orgasms spasming. He could be certain of her desire, because it was the same as his: to invade what was beautiful and con-sume its heart.

Soon after he came upon the art, he came upon the artist, pulling on a bottle of Chablis at the cold-cut table. She was the artist, he supposed, be-cause nobody that ugly could have gotten in without being the artist. Up close, he could see that her fine mustache became, in the upper registers, nose bristles. She was ragged enough that, even though she was the artist, people stood twenty feet off from her, which was how she seemed to prefer it.

So his intimate approach gave her pause.

In exchange for his name, he learned that:

She didn't have a car. She didn't have cab fare. She didn't have bus fare. She didn't have a way home. Or any inclination to look for one, until the security guard finally locked them both out of the building with their empty green bottle at 2 A.M. Sunday morning.

He gave her a ride.

The pieces continued falling together in New Jersey, beginning with the decrepitude of her Paramus home, the mildewed siding, the moldering studio, the crud, grime, scale, and litter on the walls, floors, work surfaces. Old old old cornflakes in a bowl.

The artist put him on a stepladder above it all, and the artist directed the desire at him, the desire like his own. By touch, the artist studied the groove in his forearm running from elbow to wrist, learned it in a quarter of a second using the dirty forefinger with the crusted nails and the ancient blackening paint, laid down in the whorls of her skin.

The artist suspended his arm in the air, where it remained, and she sketched it and gave it color.

The artist showed him his own arm.

Neck.

Shoulder.

He was thrilled at being taken down, possessed, consumed by such an appetite.

The artist, the stooping artist, with the stink on her of ancient inspiration endured alone, blithely repugnant, came at him again. Unbuttoned his shirt. The fabric sprang back from his twitching muscles. The artist took him again, and showed him the result, there on her sketchpad.

The artist became greedy, which was the same as inspired, and undid his belt and his fly. His pants fell and the artist yanked down his shorts, which he kicked into the corner full of caked and crumpled paint tubes and rancid banana peels. He stood in the midst of desire, which illuminated the place, while the artist took more of him and put it on paper, and showed him. But it still remained for the artist to approach with the stained peeling fingers, grasping, clawing at his skin—his skin now appearing to her, he would tell himself, translucent, white, too, like the paintings, and with the purple heart beneath. It remained for him to feel the artist's stiff greasy hair on his neck, his chest, his gut, to feel her lips on his nipples, to feel the woman's shark-tongue, to smell her foul breath, which made him, the object of desire, by contrast, that much sweeter. It remained for him to struggle to pull the artist off, to fall back with his ass in the damp old underwear and moldy paper towels on the floor, to wind his hands in the artist's hair and yank as hard as he could to learn if the woman's hunger was strong, and to find that it was, to understand that it was stronger than he was, so that when the ravenous sour desperate mouth found his cock and stretched and moaned and sucked and got it all the way down, the mouth would need for him to come worse than he needed to come. It remained for him to forget what awaited him at the end of all this and to think only of feeding her hunger. It remained for him to writhe on the floor nourishing her desire, stronger than his own.

It remained for him to let go white hot long broad and sweet, after which it would be as hard as a motherfucker to look at the place or the unlovely virtuoso standing over him at her easel—no longer aware of him— painting, content. But after he'd unclenched his eyes and dressed, he would not neglect to take what he'd come for: the newly made art.

Dianora Niccolini

S/M or Sunday *Night,* Monday Morning

Dale Peck

One year from tonight it will pull you out of bed. Some urge, call it unconscious rather than instinctual, will guide you to find your leather jeans and put them on, your white Fred Perry, your tan suede work boots, battered now and filled with dust, and then, wearing what you wore on the night we met, you leave the house and begin walking east. Your clothing hangs on you like a sail on a mast; the night, like the night we met, is warm but cooled by the occasional breeze. When it blows you feel it in your bones, in your joints especially, an icy ache that makes walking difficult. Still, you persist. Neuropathy causes your ankles to tingle and buzz, and each time a foot strikes the sidewalk the tingle becomes a shock. Your head hangs. Your hair which has become thin and almost without texture in the past few months, riffles in the wind. When, finally, Mile End Park appears, a wedge of trees lodged between a lawn and a road, you almost don't believe your eyes, for at some point in your walk it has occurred to you that you might not make it. But you have. You cross the canal, you turn off the main road, and with an effort that seems to you almost superhuman, you lift first one leg and then the other over the low rail that borders the lawn. The ground is baked hard as concrete, the grass covering it brown and straw dry. You lower yourself to it carefully and then, for just a few minutes, you sleep. You are twenty-six, the age my mother was when she died.

_____

You walked past me where I stood in a little nook of shrubbery, but some movement of mine caused you to jerk your head around and you saw me, and stared at me, and then stamped into the forest. I followed, you waited, we met, etcetera; by the time we parted perhaps two dozen men were stalking the few twisted paths of the copse. I remember little of you because I paid more attention to the environment: before you, I'd never had sex outside, and I was distracted by leaves rustling when we moved, people walking by on a sidewalk fifty feet away, the breeze on my saliva-covered cock. You smoked a cigarette with me on the lawn, then said, "Well, back to the garden party," and disappeared into the trees. I went home, but ten minutes later I was back, and by chance I came across you. You were busy with a group of men, but you turned and saw me and detached yourself from them. This time you presented your ass to me, and I rubbed my cock against it. You were a pushy bottom, and you brought my hands down roughly on your skin, and I began slapping you. You were thin even then, your flesh wasn't tight, and I wondered if perhaps you had just lost a lot of weight. I hit you with your belt. I threw you against a tree. As you came a second time, I said, "Meet me here one week from tonight." I said, "I'll strip you and tie you to a tree and fuck you. Strangers will stare at you. When I'm finished I will leave you hanging there, and the lights of passing cars will flicker over your body; night drivers will go home and sleep and dream of your uplifted face." After that, you followed me to the lawn again. Another cigarette: your name was Keith; you were supposed to be completing a Ph.D. in Ugandan family history, but in April you had had pneumonia, P.C.P., and you didn't know what you were doing now; you had had shingles since then but anyone can have shingles; you got tired every afternoon at three or four but that was all; you didn't really think of yourself as having AIDS. As you told me these things I wondered what you had been thinking ten minutes before as you begged me to fuck you even though I said I didn't have a condom. Did you want to infect me too, or did you just want to disappear? Or had you already disappeared by then? "Can I say something morbid?" you asked me on the lawn. You were lying with your head on my chest, your right hand resting on my crotch. "I want to die just like this," you said, "lying next to someone I love, outside, while I'm still young and pretty. Before I get old and fat." I said nothing. After a while you started to shiver but pretended you weren't, and I invited you to my house, where we went almost immediately to sleep. You asked me to hold your ass, and I did. You clung to me even in your sleep. You were hot all night, and slept without any covers; I slept fitfully, covered by you. In the morning, as you dressed, you looked thin and sad and disoriented, maybe a little scared. At some point in the night you had said, "You don't even know me, I can tell you anything, it doesn't matter"; but in the morning you could see these words in my eyes. Though they pretended only at prophecy, they are really your epitaph, and against them, all you could do was dress quickly and leave, almost without a word.

————

When you wake you feel warm, almost weightless, not refreshed, but full of jittery energy. You rise, brush the grass from your clothes; your fingers don't notice your protruding ribs and hip bones. In the woods you move without noise. Again and again you appear in front of them, behind them, beside them, and they look up startled every time. In the darkness their eyes meet yours momentarily, but beyond this brief contact none of them engages you. By now you have learned not to try too hard, and so, after a few fruitless minutes, you return to the lawn. You lay down but don't sleep. Every few minutes a shadow or a pair of shadows creeps from the stand behind you and walks across the park, but none of them stops to ask you your secret. The trees are virtually silent now. Leaves rustle, branches whine against each other, the lights and sounds of cars slip through them simultaneously, like ghosts. When you close your eyes you remember what you said to me. You remember my chest beneath your head and wish it were there, instead of hard cold ground. You pull your arms into your chest, roll over, face the ground, use your thin torso for warmth. The forming dew mixes with the sweat leaving your body. You remember our argument. I said, "I think the soul doesn't like being trapped within the body and it aches always to free itself, to move to something better," and you said, "I think you lay down in a box and fall asleep and that's it." At the thought of that box your legs curl up. You shiver. You notice then that the air moving into your body isn't stopping at your lungs: it travels through them, into your abdomen, down into your legs, out into your arms, even your head

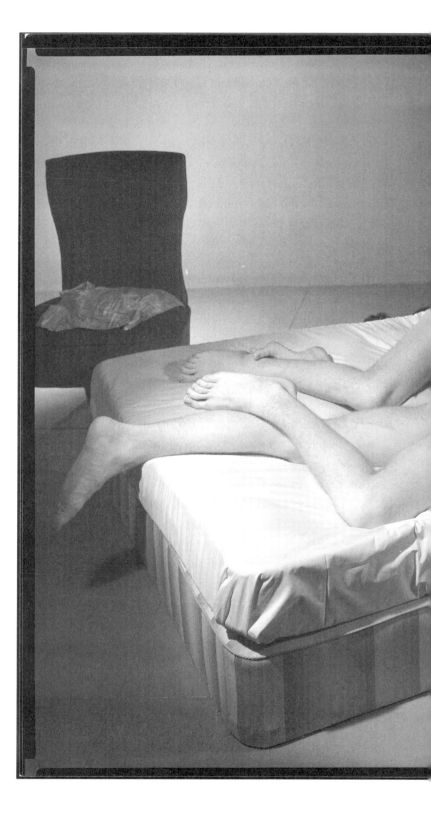

George Platt Lynes

seems to be filling with the cold damp air moving into your body and inflating it, filling it with the substanceless sky. Slowly you uncurl. You roll over onto your back, you stretch out. You are as full as a balloon now, a tire. You are as round as a whale, a beach ball. At last you open your eyes and see the fires of four or five stars in the lightening sky and feel the soft breathing ground under your head and then, for just a moment, you know which one of us was right. In the morning, some granny's dog sniffs at your body, but it doesn't piss on you as you predicted. Instead, it lifts its mouth to the sky and as I am doing now, it howls out its dirge.

Charles Gatewood

As consumed as we *Nerve* editors are by the challenge of trying to get into other people's heads and understand the many personal experiences of sexuality, we are also pretty stunned by the concrete *fact* of sex, by its biological and cultural permutations.

The earliest life forms that appeared on this planet some 2.5 billion years ago had the misfortune of predating sex—they reproduced all by themselves. These single-celled organisms, the primordial equivalent of pond scum, simply split in two—a relatively boring affair. It took another 2 billion years for an amphibious fish to evolve that required a mate to reproduce. While this early copulation wouldn't arouse even the most imaginative of biology students, it enabled the blending of two gene pools and thus rapidly accelerated evolutionary change.

In time, this evolutionary dynamism has produced not only us humans but an extraordinary breadth of species and sexual behaviors. There are countless curious examples: the males of some rodent species ejaculate a gluey semen that seals the vaginas of females to prevent other interested males from having sex with them. These same male rodents, however, have evolved special spines on their penises to remove the secretions, rendering them useless. The males of a species of mites inseminate their sisters while still in the womb and die before they are born. Then their sisters, already pregnant, eat the mothers alive, from the inside out. The kamikaze honey bee's penis literally explodes when he reaches sexual climax, attaching itself with horns and bristles to the pelvis of the queen, forming a natural chastity belt. The male bee, meanwhile, falls to the ground and dies. Male ostriches have penises so large they use them alternately as walking sticks—something boasted in many a locker room but rarely pulled off by males of our species.

Strange as these examples may sound, human sex is no less interesting, particularly when you consider the complexity of various cultural customs. The war between our biological urges and societal prohibitions has been waged furiously for millennia with grave consequences. Medieval monks castrated themselves; Victorians manufactured small domes with inverted spikes that were placed on the penises of teenaged boys at night to discourage arousal; even today, some third world countries continue to perform clitoridectomies. In the West, while prohibitions against sex may have lessened, the pressures to modify the body's appearance through manic exercise, surgery, and voluntary starvation are considerable. Indeed, there are few better examples of the strength of society's sway over us.

All of this is not going unnoticed—the study of sex has metastasized into just about every field imaginable, from biology and psychology to literature, film, advertising, and politics. Sex is now crucial not only to the survival of the species, but also to the survival of Levi's and Colt 45, not to mention Oprah and MTV.

Living as we do in a blizzard of advertising, it's easy to lose sight of our libidinal origins. Yet the act of sex is particularly good at jogging our bodily memories, at reminding us that we are animals—feral, ravenous, playing out an instinctual script. In fact, from an evolutionary perspective, we are mere hosts of our genes, which shed our bodies, one generation at a time, like snakeskin. For the most part we do as they tell us: we search out mates with desirable characteristics, have intercourse with them, and eventually produce offspring with the same proclivities. Rarely do we think of spontaneous sex in an airplane lavatory as a form of genetic obedience; we're more inclined to think of such acts in social terms, as outrageous and rebellious. Indeed, we are torn between genetic and societal obedience, or if you prefer, between societal and genetic rebellion.

These contradictory directives produce some humorous and peculiar cultural products, a few of which serve as fodder for essays in this chapter.

Usually when we commission articles for *Nerve,* we start with authors we admire and brainstorm about what we might like them to write. In the case of these articles, the process was reversed: we started with subjects that intrigued us and approached the most qualified writers.

The full-page ads for "Better Sex Videos" in the *New York Times Book Review* for instance, always seemed curious: millions of highbrow readers appeared to be buying "instructional" videos of people having sex. We were delighted when journalist Ruth Shalit agreed to investigate whether these sales were in the service of self-improvement or self-abuse. We found equally lucid reporters in photographer Matt Harnett and writer Amanda Griscom, who with steady lens and pen took inventory of the accoutrements of desire in a Manhattan fetish club.

As it turns out, the jungles in Zaire contain as much sexual intrigue as those of New York. When we learned of the apparent sexual utopia of the Bonobo apes, we hunted down Cornell anthropologist Meredith Small,

Charles Gatewood

who put their behavior—and ours—in evolutionary context. Japanese animation, meanwhile, seemed to present a curious sexual dystopia. If cultures dream through the films they produce, then never have those dreams appeared more overdetermined—to borrow the Freudian term—than in Japanese anime, or so argues *Newsweek* writer Adam Rogers.

The logic behind each of these selections is that we gain perspective on sexuality by *observing:* sometimes ourselves, sometimes the apes from whom we evolved, sometimes our common fantasies of who we may or may not want to evolve into.   *—RG*

Porno for Yuppies:
The Better Sex Video Charade

Ruth Shalit

Here they are in the *Atlantic Monthly.* Here they are, too, in the *New York Review of Books.* She is arrestingly beautiful, with a wild-rose complexion and lustrous brown hair that falls in perfect waves around her shoulders. He is blond and movie-star handsome, complete with gleaming torso and flat, muscular flanks.

He parts the silken folds of her nightshirt, a fun-loving dimple lurking in his cheek. She gazes at him, her eyes full of astonishment and satisfaction.

The couple in this advertisement is about to have Better Sex. For a mere $49.85, a caption explains, you can join them as they scale the heights of unspeakable ecstasy and journey toward a richer, more fulfilling sexual relationship. All, of course, in the privacy of your own home.

Such are the blandishments of the Better Sex Video Series, a three-volume pathway to erotic expertise that has sold more than a million copies since its 1992 debut. Produced and marketed by the "Sinclair Institute," in Chapel Hill, North Carolina, the series aims its pitch not at the sexually dysfunctional, but at a heretofore ignored silent majority—the decorous masses of "normal adults" who crave new vistas of intimacy. The professional packagers of Better Sex describe their target market simply: "Upper income," says Anne Weston, marketing assistant for the Sinclair Institute. "We advertise in *GQ, Men's Health,* the *New York Times Book Review.* Our demographic is their demographic."

There is a fan club and a Web site; there are ambitious plans for various literary tie-ins. A licensing arrangement with the Townsend Corporation, manufacturer of high-end depilatories and emollients, is said to be in the works. And in the last few months alone, Better Sex has added several new titles to its burgeoning mail-order archives. There's the "Guide to Better Sex Over Forty," for couples seeking to overcome the lassitude of maturity. There's "The Lovers' Guide to Sex Toys," for those who crave a jolt out of life's routine. Lovebirds seeking to elevate their spirit will covet "The Tantric Guide to Better Sex," due out in September. Asked to describe this latest offering, Kathy Brummitt, Better Sex's garrulous marketing director, turns uncharacteristically tight-lipped. "I can't give you a sound bite," she says. What about a one-sentence description? "It would take many, many sentences," she says.

Though the karma may be complex, the sex is grimly uneventful. I popped in "Advanced Sexual Techniques," volume two of the series, expecting an ambient, tasteful frolic, the kind of discreet romp that quickens the pulse while assuring the viewer of his or her demographic pedigree. Alas, the airbrushed wonder couple who gambol through the pages of *Men's Health* are nowhere to be found in the actual videos. They have been replaced by "ordinary couples," a slim, vacant-eyed sexual proletariat. The men have mustaches and bikini underwear. The women are forlorn in their tinkling costume jewelry and pastel clouds of trailing chiffon. They perform their genital aerobics with an air of stoical endurance, accompanied by the restful strains of light disco music. I found myself imagining them clothed.

A voice-over repeatedly declares that these amateur thespians are "real-life couples," authentic, modest married folk like you and me. "Each of our couples have had their own sexual problems," says the narrator as the camera zooms in on a frowning stay-at-home mom. "The kind of problems that come from a discomfort with sex and a lack of information about sex." The couples surmount this discomfort with impressive swiftness: moments later, the shy hausfrau is spread-eagled naked on a bed, chortling with pleasure as her "husband"'s tongue roots around in her nether regions. Now, that's progress. There's Mary, a demure biology teacher who complains that sex with her husband, Rick, is "awkward ...I don't like it." Rick, a musician, readily admits that his lovemaking leaves something to be desired: "It's wham, bam, thank you ma'am." Then there's Virginia, a Lycra-clad, bottled blond who says she is "an executive in a publishing firm." Bill, her husband, says he's "a copilot with one of the major airlines....If they found out I was doing this, I might be loading baggage next week."

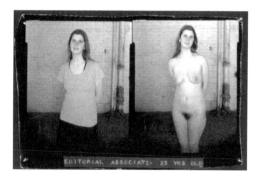

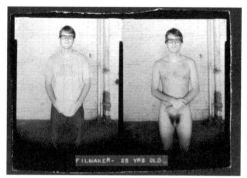

Greg Friedler

Bill's got some baggage, all right. Triple-X buffs will immediately recognize him as Rick Savage, porn star emeritus. Smelling a ruse, I phone up Sinclair's Kathy Brummitt, who readily admits that all is not what it seems. "Obviously we would prefer to use real couples," she says. "When two people are in love, you can see it and feel it." The problem, Brummitt says, is that few mainstream marrieds are willing to truss themselves up for cash. "It's been difficult for us to find real couples who are willing to share their personal behavior," she says. The solution has been hack porn actors "without bionic body parts—no oversized breasts or extremely large penises," she says. "We don't want to have too many people in our videos who model a look that viewers can't achieve."

Brummitt readily admits that Bill, the airline pilot, is a virtuoso of porn films. Rick and Mary, meanwhile, are actually "John and Deirdre, from adult films," she concedes. "They are an X-rated couple. But here's the thing: they were actually married at one time."

There is, then, a central irony at the heart of the Better Sex project. Butterfingered yuppies watch Better Sex in hopes of transforming themselves into kinky, lubed-up sexual dynamos. Meanwhile, the wanton stars of the videos, who really *are* all those things, must pretend to be maladroit sub-

Greg Friedler

urbanites. All of this to flatter the yuppies' fantasy that they are not watching porn movies. Why all of the fuss?

One reason, of course, is the volatile class politics of pornography—a genre long dismissed among the bourgeois as formulaic and debased. It's easy to understand how the Sinclair Institute's upper-income clientele would labor to establish their own distance from the genre's suspect pleasures. And logical that the Sinclair Institute happily confirms them in this self-deception. In the videos, sex becomes a kind of upscale lifestyle accessory, honed through technocratic expertise. "There are golf and tennis pros, literature teachers and nutritionists," explains the narrator. Now, those seeking "formal instruction" in carnality can acquire a new competence, under the sway of authoritative experts.

In forsaking porn for pedagogy, devotees of Better Sex preserve their own sense of moral superiority. They may also prevent themselves from thinking seriously about the sexual problems they wanted to address in the first place. Squeamish suburbanites brought low by sexual ennui are unlikely to be helped by Better Sex's remedial pointers: "Whatever you do, don't bite down"; "Calluses can cause her discomfort"; "Unless you have a remarkable capacity to hold your breath, you'll find underwater oral sex difficult"; "Some women may not want to have a razor close to a sensitive part of their body."

Much more satisfying are the sexual vignettes, replete with counterfeit yuppies in fetishistic garb. Here is "Bill," just returned from a flight from Hong Kong, muttering incomprehensibly about "some turbulence east of the Island." His pilot's uniform, white and clean as starched linen, is a truly thrilling thing to behold. And here is wife "Virginia," resplendent in pinstripes, exuding stern corporate rectitude as she barks into a cell phone. There is a sadistic frisson in the knowledge that within minutes, Virginia's boardroom eyes will become bedroom eyes; that this Judith Regan manqué will be reduced to what she is—a down-at-the-heels porn actress, splayed across her pretend desk, her naughty parts pitilessly exposed. "Since you can't see his face," says the voice-over, praising the merits of a particular position, "you can pretend it's anybody you like." Even an airline pilot.

Prime Mates: *The Useful Promiscuity of Bonobo Apes*

Meredith F. Small

Maiko and Lana are having sex. Maiko is on top, and Lana's arms and legs are wrapped tightly around his waist. Lina, a friend of Lana's, approaches from the right and taps Maiko on the back, nudging him to finish. As he moves away, the two females embrace, press their genitals together and move their pelvic areas rapidly left and right. Both females grin and call out in pleasure.

Although this scene was recorded on video, you won't find it in the back of your local video store. Lana, Maiko, and Lina are bonobos, a lesser known species of chimpanzee first studied in the 1970s in the remote tropical forests of the Republic of Congo, Central Africa. Their heightened sexuality has received public attention since the publication of primatologist Frans de Waal's book *Bonobos: The Forgotten Ape* (University of California Press, 1997), which has been featured on dozens of television and magazine segments, culminating in de Waal's appearance on *Good Morning America*. Bonobos, as de Waal describes them, lead peaceful, egalitarian, and sex-filled lives quite unlike their cousins, common chimpanzees, who are known for violence, male domination, and sexual efficiency. While much has been made lately of the promise peaceable bonobos hold for human passivism, less has been said about what the sexually promiscuous bonobos might teach us about the human inclinations toward sexual experimentation and infidelity.

Why should we *Homo sapiens* take so personally the behavior of these apes? Because we share about 98 percent of our genetic makeup with both varieties of chimp. Chimpanzees, in fact, are more closely related to humans than they are to gorillas. Eight million years ago humans, gorillas, and chimps shared a common ancestor. In the next million years, the gorilla line split from the common human-chimp ancestor; 2 million years after that, humans and chimpanzees split into distinct species. Much later, about 1.5 million years ago, bonobos and common chimpanzees separated into two species.

Bonobos (originally called pygmy chimpanzees) are latecomers to the ape registry because they live in the most remote rain forests of Africa, penned in by rivers they cannot cross (the Zaire River in the north and east and numerous smaller rivers in the south and west). They were first identified, on the basis of skeletal material, in the late 1920s, but it took another fifty years for a scientist—Japanese primatologist Takayoshi Kano—to observe them in the wild.

At first glance, bonobos look much like common chimps: they have the characteristic long arms, short legs, and muscular, compact bodies covered with black fur. But on second glance, subtle differences mark bonobos as distinct. Bonobos weigh about the same as the other chimps but they are built lighter, with smaller heads and more slender arms and legs. Bonobos have dark, pigmented, flat faces with bright red lips and a distinct hairdo, as if each morning they pulled out a comb and parted the hair on their heads down the middle, nattily dressed for a day in the forest.

Bonobos behave in many ways like common chimpanzees. They live in what primatologists call "fission-fusion" groups: large communities that stick together for hours or days, disperse for a time, and then regroup later. Also, females in both species leave their home area when they reach sexual maturity, and males remain. As a result of this dispersal pattern, adult male chimpanzees in a group tend to be genetically related, even brothers, while adult females are virtual strangers until they form social bonds and become friends. Infants are highly dependent and stay with their mothers for years, and to accommodate this dependency, mothers give birth only every four years or so and nurse their infants for at least that long.

But beyond these similarities, common chimpanzees and bonobos are as different as the most dissimilar human cultures. While chimp society is noted for aggression among males and toward females—aggression that sometimes culminates in sexual assault and infanticide—bonobos are comparatively peaceful and egalitarian. In fact, in many bonobo communities, females appear to play a dominant role.

Even more striking is bonobo sexual behavior. As Frans de Waal describes them, bonobos, not humans, are surely the most sexual primates on earth. Like humans, they have sex outside the proscribed period of fertility for females, but unlike most humans, they are constantly having sex of every variety with partners of all ages. In addition to the usual heterosexual matings, bonobos also have same-sex fun. Males grab each other's penises and mouth each other's genitals. Females regularly have sex with each other, and sometimes appear to prefer their female companions. Juvenile male bonobos suck on each other's penises and allow adult males to fondle them, and these youngsters also participate whenever adults have sex by poking fingers and toes into moving parts or jumping on board. Bonobos engage in all of this sex-play with unabashed enjoyment, grinning widely in their copulatory sways.

The behavior of females is so unusual that behaviorists have given it a special name: the "genital-genital rub" or "G-G rub." Two females place their pelvises together, either face-to-face or rear-to-rear, and rub each other rapidly with yelps of delight. Sometimes, this movement is so coordinated that the female on top lifts the other female off the ground as they rhythmically slap their genitals together. Females seem to like the full frontal position best, probably because the clitoris is swollen along with their labia into a pink balloon-like protrusion; a face-to-face position enables maximal clitoral rubbing.

In many ways, bonobo sex bears a remarkable resemblance to human sex. When males and females copulate, they sometimes do so in the typical mammalian back-to-front position with the male entering the female from behind, but they also enjoy the face-to-face position. In fact, females frequently invite males to copulate by lying on their backs. This position, in which the animals can easily gaze into each other's eyes, denotes to some an emotional intimacy seen hitherto only in humans. Although each copulatory bout is rather brief compared to human sexual play, bonobos make up in frequency what they lose in duration.

Bonobos also manually stimulate themselves and each other, both for pleasure and as a preamble to social interaction. A female might fondle the genitals of an infant, or touch the genitals of the mother if she wants a closer look at an infant. Males frequently take the erect penis of a younger male and make "caressing" up and down movements. (So far no one has observed this kind of genital manipulation leading to ejaculation.)

This is what makes bonobo sexuality so intriguing for animal behaviorists: they use sex not just for reproduction, as we expect nonhuman animals to do, but for a variety of nonsexual purposes. They bestow "sexual favors" (as we humans say) for appeasement, to gain food, to show affection and connection, or to reduce stress. In captivity, when food is delivered by the keepers, the excitement usually triggers a round of sexual behavior that calms the group down. Sex functions as a social balm.

This contrasts sharply with how other primates connect socially. Monkeys use grooming and sitting close to reinforce their social connections, and common chimpanzees have a variety of interpersonal gestures and behaviors that establish and repair relationships. For example, after a fight a monkey might smack its lips in submission and groom the victor, a common chimpanzee might hold out a placating hand for reassurance, but a bonobo would probably roll over and spread its legs.

For females, sex is also the passport which allows transfer into new groups. In the wild, a female bonobo will enter a new group rather tentatively, then seek out the highest-ranking females and approach them one by one to initiate a genital-genital rub; with this physical interaction, she signals her friendliness, and the residents' responses signal her acceptance into the group.

In addition to providing hope that our species may have more peaceable roots than previously supposed, bonobos call into question assumptions about the evolution of human sexual behavior. Researchers have previously thought early bipeds lived in male-dominated groups where aggression and violence were the rule, and where female sexuality was useful primarily as a tool to manipulate males. In the traditional scenario, the genital swellings that signaled fertility in prehuman females were lost over evolutionary time because it enabled them to look less sexual and make peace among the males. At the same time, this theory presumed, ancestral females became continuously sexually receptive, willing to mate during nonfertile periods, in an effort to keep one male close to home.

But bonobos suggest another possibility. Bonobo males and females live peaceful, egalitarian lives, and they use sex as an integral part of their calmer social order. Perhaps our common ancestor was more like bonobos in this regard than common chimps. Perhaps ancestral human females "lost" their swellings and became continuously willing to have sex not to manipulate males into monogamy, but to facilitate a more promiscuous lifestyle. Bonobos suggest that our idealization of private, monogamous sexual behavior might be a relatively recent deviation from our evolutionary heritage. Indeed, our ancient ancestors, like bonobos, may have used heterosexual and homosexual sex on a daily basis to make alliances, trade goods and favors, establish friendships, and keep the peace. If so, the breadth of human sexual behavior today needs no special explanation.

Warped Women *in*
Japanese Animation

Adam Rogers

Imagine if the centaurs in *Fantasia* abandoned their chaste little picnic and erupted into a wild orgy. The younger, more girlish colts might not be as into it, so they'd get tied up. Then a 1,000-foot high robot in samurai armor locked in battle with an equally huge demon that squirts fire out of tentacles shaped like penises might crash into the scene, killing all the centaurs.

Or maybe the male centaurs would all die horribly but quickly, while the female centaurs would live long enough to be raped by the penis-tentacles. Eventually a particular virginal centaur, who inherited the mantle of demon slayer from her mother, would finally overcome the duo.

The denouement described above could very easily play out before the opening credits of a typical Japanese cartoon, or anime—pronounced ah-nee-may, a corruption of "animation." While Americans are accustomed to most possible iterations of sex and violence, the often insidious power of women to transform in anime is distinctly Japanese. And though the ragged cityscapes and slinky jumpsuits are new, the gender fantasies are an enduring cultural theme that dates back to medieval folklore.

Heavy Metal notwithstanding, Americans have never gotten the hang of cartoons with realistic sex and violence. Meanwhile, since the 1960s, Japan's output of anime as television series, movies, and made-for-video flicks has been prodigious. They're as much a staple of Japanese pop culture as the ubiquitous comic books—called *manga*—on which they're often based, estimated to comprise 40 percent of the Japanese publishing industry.

Anime's subject matter is so broad, it's really a medium more than a genre. It encompasses historical drama, like a couple versions of *The Diary of Anne Frank* and a treatment of the bombing of Hiroshima, as well as comedy, romance, and just about anything else you can think of. Most of what makes it to the U.S. is more familiar comic-book fare: action-adventure, science fiction, and fantasy. You've probably seen at least half an hour of anime: *Speed Racer*, perhaps, or *Star Blazers*. Maybe it was *Robotech*, or, if you're old enough, *Astro Boy*. More recently a broader range of anime is creeping out of the college clubs and comic-book conventions into the cultish periphery of the mainstream.

The roles that women play in manga and anime run the gamut. "Asking what the images of women in Japanese manga are like is a little bit like asking what the main ways are of portraying women in U.S. television," says Sharon Kinsella, a professor of Japanese studies at Cambridge University. "What you're really asking about is the state of gender relations in Japan, which is a really fascinating and slightly complicated subject."

A recurring theme in anime, though, is the ability of women to transform. Female protagonists tend to fall along a continuum from maternal (though still sexual) through robotic to outright monstrous. "One of the things that intrigued me about the conception of women in manga is there's usually the stereotypical thing about women being horribly treated, and of course they are," says Susan Napier, a professor of Japanese literature and culture at the University of Texas, Austin. "But often the women are if anything more powerful than the men, infinitely more frightening, infinitely more imaginatively rendered."

Napier's main critical target is a film called *Wicked City*, directed by Yoshiaki Kawajiri. It's famous primarily for its opening sequence, in which Taki, the James Bond–like hero, picks up a beautiful woman in a bar. They go back to her place and have sex a few times, in a few different positions. After their last climax, as Taki drowses, the woman's hands elongate into pincers; her legs stretch out and bend back impossibly until she enfolds Taki like a spider. He breaks free in the nick of time, and as he flies across the room we see that the woman's vagina has turned into a fang-lined, gnashing maw. (It's hard to know even where to begin with such scenes. As Napier puts it, "Freud would have a field day with this stuff.")

As the story progresses we meet Makie, an extraordinarily beautiful woman who is actually a denizen of the Black World, a demon realm, and Taki's opposite number on the police force that regulates both dimensions. Her blood-red nails extend into a two-foot-long blade. The bad guy, also from the Black World, has a spectacularly beautiful henchwoman, who, un-clothed, turns out to be one giant vagina. At one point she pulls Taki inside herself, sending him into paroxysms of ecstasy as a method of extracting in-formation. Taki shoots her.

In the end, after Taki rescues Makie from a brutal demonic gang rape, they admit they've fallen in love. In a glowing, empty church they have sex, which turns out to have been the objective of their bosses all along—to unify Earth and the Black World. Impregnated by a human male, Makie's powers are magnified enough so she can defeat the villain.

So the transformation that makes Makie the most powerful is the change from sexpot to mom. Motherhood shows up a lot in anime because, as Antonia Levi, author of *Samurai from Outer Space: Understanding Japanese Animation* puts it, "The Japanese mother is a force to be reckoned with." Even in *Urotsukidoji: Legend of the Overfiend*, a series of films fa-mous for their violent misogyny (they're a prime example of the "naughty tentacles" subgenre), the real power figure is the mother-to-be of the demon messiah. In a manga series called *The Legend of Mother Sarah*, Katsuhiro Otomo, creator of the crossover near-hit *Akira,* tells the story of a mother searching postapocalyptic Earth for her children. In addition to being quite an ass-kicker, Sarah has a bulletproof prosthetic breast; she mutilated her-self in anguish and pain when, after her children were taken from her, she continued to lactate.

For women in anime, transformation—whether from slut to mother, human to monster, or even human to cyborg—is a mixed bag. Though the changes usually increase a woman's power, they tend to evoke concerns about not being fully human anymore, and, for monsters and cyborgs, about not being able to have children. It's an ambiguity that dates back over a thousand years to early Japanese folklore.

From the Manga series, *The Legend of Mother Sarah*   **Katsuhiro Otomo**

The first recorded folktale of a woman's transformation into a fox comes from the Fudoki, an eighteenth-century Buddhist scripture. But more interesting still is a story from the same era in the Kojiki, a primary text from the Japanese folk religion Shintoism, that explains the creation of Japan. Two *kami* (roughly "gods" or "spirits") named Izanagi and Izanami notice their genitals for the first time—Izanami says she is insufficiently formed, and Izanagi says he is formed to excess. She suggests that they, you know, get together, and their first child is a leech. Izanagi says the deformation was a result of Izanami having initiated the sexual contact, which was not considered appropriate for women. So he comes on to her, and their children are the islands of Japan and the sun goddess Amaterasu, the foremost among the Shinto kami.

Everything's honeymoon bliss for Izanagi and Izanami until she gives birth to fire, which fatally burns her vagina. Izanagi follows her to the Dark Realm, the unclean Dark Land of the dead, and tells her he wants her back. Izanami agrees, on one condition: that he not look at her. Izanagi disobeys, and sees that she is decomposing. Izanami is so distressed that he's seen her in this state that she promises to kill thousands of his children, to which he responds that he'll just create more. He goes to a river to ritually purify himself, and in the process of purification creates a whole new set of deities who are the ancestors of Japan's aristocracy. "So there are two types of reproduction," says Allan Grapard, a professor of Shinto studies at the University of California, Santa Barbara. "Sexual procreation and production of deities by a male through the act of purification of his body. Purification has always been connected with the production of culture, and mainly a male practice."

Women, however, have also enjoyed some power in Japanese religious history. Temple maidens, in medieval Shinto shrines, called *miko*, often became possessed by spirits and served as oracles. "The source of speech is located as a presence that only women can communicate with," says Grapard. The miko's power grew out of her sexuality—some scholars suggest that miko exorcised demons by merging with them, or having sex with them. The miko's preeminence, however, was soon challenged. "Once Buddhism came into Japan and located itself in the countryside, male monks began to be the recipients of oracles." The miko were eventually prohibited from practicing. The grappling for power between monks and miko is well depicted in a medieval painting of a Buddhist monk in a temple corridor entranced by the bare breasts of a miko standing across from him.

In much of anime, it seems this battle is still being waged. Both the women of ancient Shinto and modern anime are imbued with the power to transform, and it is linked to their sex and sexuality. While neither Buddhism nor Shinto has any proscriptions against sex the way Judeo-Christian traditions do, both Eastern religions do have real problems with the impure and unclean. Menstruation generally qualifies. Men, through ritual purification, create culture and society, all the good stuff about being human. Women, with their frighteningly chaotic, decomposing bodies, are best at overpowering other kinds of chaos, at least since the Buddhists took over the oracle business. Ultimately, the more powerful women become—monster, cyborg, whatever—the less human and civilized they are.

The most recent fantasy of veiled feminine power may be the current obsession with cuteness, or *kawai*, which is now prevalent in manga, anime, and Japanese pop culture at large. The fascination with cute is so pervasive that the national uniforms of schoolgirls—sailor shirt and skirt—are widely fetishized as erotic objects. The international hit anime series *Sailor Moon*, for instance, is about a schoolgirl in uniform who goes through puberty and gains superpowers with the wave of her wand. The underpants of young girls have been sold out of vending machines on street corners. The broader phenomena is called *lolikon* or *rorikon,* short for "Lolita Complex." But there's disagreement as to whether the fetish is genuinely sexual. "Young women have become the focal point of contemporary Japanese culture, the people who do things, are more lively, insubordinate, and interesting," says Cambridge University's Kinsella. "This state of affairs causes a lot of resentment and complications in a society...that quite firmly places women in an inferior economic and social position." To some, adolescent girls are the ultimate consumer, free of responsibility but with money to burn, interested only in amusement. That's a harsh contrast with the lot of the men in Japanese society, who work fanatically. "Maybe they're not only desiring her as an object of lust," says Anne Allison, author of *Permitted and Prohibited Desires: Mothers, Comics, and Censorship in Japan,* "but actually wanting to be a young girl."

Sexual transformation is, indeed, not limited to animation. Kabuki theater, performed only by males, is famous for its *onnagata,* character actors who perform only female roles, who are considered to be the pinnacle of feminine perfection. The Takarazuka Review is a famous all-female performing troupe, and the actresses there who perform male parts are often the recipients of crushes from young Japanese girls—indeed, *bishonen,* or beautiful males, are androgynous (or outright homosexual) characters popular mostly in girls' manga, but with some crossover appeal. Suffice it to say that the boundaries between genders in Japanese culture are more porous than in the West.

Edo-period Tokyo (during the seventeenth century) was famous for its Yoshiwara pleasure quarter, and equally famous for the Ukiyo-e woodcut prints that represented what went on there in great detail. Why should anime and manga, with their stylistic debt to Ukiyo-e, by any different? "We're reluctant to talk about this," says Napier, "because we don't want to give the impression that the Japanese are any weirder or more sadistic than the rest of the world." Odds are, they're not. The centaurs in *Fantasia* were pretty weird all on their lonesome.

Matt Harnett

Mother of *Bodily Invention:*
Scenes from a Fetish Club

Amanda Griscom

Beneath an unusually thick, black coat of eye shadow, I entered Mother, a top-dog fetish club in New York's meatpacking district. There, on the other side of the flimsy curtain and the stooped, gloomy doorman, was an underground sex carnival. Like a good rookie, I took down some cocktails, and some more, and reconnoitered: there was a stunning congregation of slick red mouths, aggressive nipples, billy clubs, ice-pick stilettos, fishnet legs, thick chains, handcuffs, and vampire capes.

The players were vehement in their presentation, but with everyone caught up in watching and being watched, there was a strained sense of ease. I couldn't figure out, through the smoke and noise and flourish, if I was among perpetrators or victims. It wasn't clear if they wanted domination or servitude. One thing seemed certain: everybody was using costume to act out some heavy-duty conflict. In truth, I never really felt the presence of desire, in me or anyone else, but I saw quite a bit of its exaggerated image.

It's more than I can say for most parties, where the players skulk around, dodging gazes, disguising what makes them vulnerable. A fetish party, by contrast, is forthright: here's my nipple, an electric heap of nerve endings, and I've sliced a hole through it, ornamented it, so come and get me. It isn't a charade, but a ceremony for all things denied.

Matt Harnett

The scene also seemed desperate, because to me desire and arousal are strongest when latent, on the verge rather than full-blown and obvious. The Saran Wrap, zippers, cross-hatched laces seemed more to violate the flesh than enclose it. Maybe, I reasoned, subtlety is not an option for hard-core fetishists—you can't hear sighs and whispers if you're letting out mad, tormented outcries. Or maybe they just find subtlety boring. Some people like sardines, some like golf, some like the clarinet. But why, when it comes to sex, would we fixate on particular, isolated accoutrements of desire? Why fetishize the nipple or the shackle or the bow tie? Do these parts make the mystery of love more compact and obvious, less threatening? You are likely a fetishist of some sort. Most of us endear ourselves to certain body parts and objects that embody and detonate our arousal.

Though I'm not a heavyweight fetishist—I'm endeared, not consigned, to my talismans—I have a particular affinity for broad hands with promi-

Matt Harnett

nent tendons, stretching out like rake tongs. Shoulders really send me, faintly ridged with muscle and bone. It's best if they're smooth, not yet marked by a master's hand.

Love Stories

Lyle Ashton Harris

Genevieve: On a windy morning three years ago, I met Rufus outside the offices of the small book publishing company where it was his first day of work, my 360th. We introduced ourselves and shook hands; he was tall and lanky (how I like 'em), but my thoughts were elsewhere. I had a deadline *and* it was moving day. Soon, my boss had informed me, Golden Boy here would be installed in a corner office, while I'd earned a cube in the back near the watercooler.

I didn't give him another thought (except obliquely, during periodic fits of rage over my office real estate) until the next morning when I stumbled into work after three hours of sleep. He was sitting on some boxes outside my door, pouring coffee from a deeply dented, stainless steel thermos. "Want some," he asked, one dimple flashing on and off as he talked. Indeed I did. My eyes darted from his dimple to the dent. "My ex-girlfriend threw it at my head," he explained. Flash, flash, flash.

Rufus: On a blustery fall morning in 1995, I encountered a beautiful girl who was letting herself in the looming door of my new place of work. It was my first day on the job, so each detail was of great consequence. I asked her name and she said Genevieve as she marched by. A half-second of eye-contact made clear that she was street-smart, pensive, and entirely un-interested in me. She appeared to be one of those rare people who seem not to take the social precautions others do—her presence was unfiltered and raw, to the point of being mildly shocking, as if she were a cerebral streaker. I was helpless.

G: It wasn't long before we were secretly meeting for lunch in nearby Madison Square Park. He talked a lot about his happy childhood, for some reason—homesick, I think. I mourned the impending death of my failing re-lationship of two years, carefully avoiding the subject of what my freedom would surely mean for us. Funny, but just weeks earlier I'd been fighting the good fight to get my boyfriend into couples' therapy. After meeting Rufus, after sharing our fifteenth sandwich, shivering side-by-side in an empty park, I stopped seeing the point in that.

R: When Genevieve went to retrieve laserprints or make photocopies outside my office door, she swayed back and forth on two-inch heels, her curtain of wavy blond hair parted by a pair of '50s librarian glasses. My powers of concentration were feeble. It was clear, however, that I needed to be patient, that this was a long-term project.

Soon our conversations couldn't be contained in our stolen lunch hours and began spilling over into office e-mail. Those exchanges became food for me; their absence, even for a period of minutes, left me fidgety and slightly nauseous. I sometimes made a point of not opening the notes for thirty seconds or even a minute at a time, like a kid trying to ration Halloween candy. I was hers.

G: Every real-life love story has a beginning, middle, and an end, whether it takes a lifetime to travel this arc, a year, a tempestuous couple of months, or a single, lock-eyed moment. When I met Rufus I was enrolled in a writing workshop. "Don't tell your story too soon!" advised the wise elders of the group. "Live first, write later!" But they couldn't stop me—each week I brought in another chapter of our love story, told from that week's perspective. Little did I know those chapters would only add up to the prologue. It's been a couple years since the heady days when we fell in love under the fluorescents; the lighting has improved, and it seems pretty clear that we haven't even reached the middle yet.

Some of the love stories in this chapter begin at the beginning, some at the end of powerful loves. Robert Olen Butler allowed us to excerpt his novel *The Deep Green Sea* months before the book was published. "Mix it up any way you like," he said. "Just don't give away the ending." This was fine with me: explosive as the book's conclusion is, the first love scenes between the heroine and hero, a Vietnamese woman and an American veteran old enough to be her father, move me even more.

While Butler's lovers achingly surrender themselves to one another, Carole Maso writes of a very different kind of ache: that of a woman torn between her desire for a man and her will to escape his bittersweet clutch. Love can be excruciating, and rarely more than for the partner of a talented lover who doesn't love.

R: Historically, the love story has been a kind of fairy-tale, a vessel of eternal youth, unflagging erections, and Teflon infatuations. Love stories have tended to avoid the easing of relationships into familiarity, as well as the sexual misfires, distances, or periods of complacency. It takes a confident writer indeed to begin a love story at its end, to render clearly the nostalgia and excruciating affection that can accompany an act of sex both parties know might be the last. It takes a braver writer still to present the piece as a memoir, as nonfiction, to offer the world one of her most vulnerable moments. Catherine Texier has done this in "A War Journal," one of the first pieces we published, which has since grown into the book *Breakup*.

It takes a brave reader, however, to sympathize with John Hawkes's narrator in "But She Was Not Mirabelle," an older man obsessed with a young girl. This is, nonetheless, one of the greatest passages by one of this country's most talented novelists, which was, criminally, out of print when we published it.

The book's final piece, Jack Murnighan's "Watershed," may appear at first glance to be a tale of lust, and surely it is, but more than that it is a story of emotional appetite, which may be the strongest appetite of all. One of the reasons we have dedicated an entire magazine—and book—to the subject of sex is that we find it the most compelling metaphor for human hunger, for our desire to exist, and exist passionately.

The Deep Green Sea

Robert Olen Butler

Tien

There is a moment now, come suddenly upon us, when the sound of the motorbikes from the street has faded almost to silence, and I can smell, faintly, the incense I have burned, and I am naked at last. He is naked, too, though I still have not let my eyes move beyond his face and his arms and his hands. He is very gentle, very cautious, in this moment, and to my surprise, I say, "I have never done this before."

I am lying on my bed and he is beside me and we are lit by neon from the hotel across the street and he has touched only my shoulders. His hands are moving there when I say these words, and they hesitate. There is also a hesitation in me. I hear what I have said. Some place inside me says these words are true, and some other place says that I am a liar.

I am twenty-six years old and I have been with two men in my life. But I was never with them in this bed, I was never with them in this room where I was a child of my grandmother, this room where I keep the altar to my

216

dead father, and when I removed my clothes with these men, I did not feel I was naked with them, though I wished to be. There was fear in my heart and incomprehension in their eyes, and when we rose from the places where we touched, I felt nothing except that I was alone.

Until this moment with Ben, I have known how to understand that. I am a girl of this new Vietnam. I am not my mother, who is of a different Vietnam and who had her own fear and incomprehension with men, and who is far away from me. I am alone in this world but it is all right, I have always thought, because in a great socialist republic everyone is equal and each of us can find a place in the state that holds us all. There is no aloneness.

But everything is different now. I am suddenly different. I am naked. This is what I wish to tell him with my words. It is what I wish to tell myself.

There is a surge of sound in the room, the motorbikes again, the others going around and around the streets of Ho Chi Minh City on a Saturday night, and I wish it was quiet again. I want to hear the sound of his breathing. I want to hear the faint stretching of him inside his skin as he lifts slightly away from me in thought and turns his head to the window.

His chest is naked and so is mine. I feel my nipples tighten at the thought of him and I want it to be quiet and I want the light to be better too. I want to look at his body, this part at least. No more for now. I want to start with this naked chest of his and also his hands, which I have been able to see for these past days but that I have not yet really looked at. I take one of these hands now in mine as he thinks about what I have said. I take it and in the cold red burning of the neon light I can see his thick hand. He worked once in the steel mills. He told me of their fire. He worked once driving a great truck many thousands of miles across his country, the United States of America, gripping the steering wheel of this truck, and I love the corded veins here as I hold his hand. "It is all right," I say. I lift his hand and put it on my chest. I cover my yearning nipple.

I look at his hand and it is very large and my own hands are small and my fingers are slender and his are not, his are thick and his skin in the light from the moon and the hotel across the street seems pale and mine seems darker. I am Vietnamese. Every Vietnamese child hears the tale of how our country began. Once long ago a dragon who was the ruler of all the oceans lived in his palace in the deep deep bottom of the South China Sea. He grew very lonely, so he rose up from the sea and flew to the land, the rich jungles and mountains and plains that are now our Vietnam. And there he met a fairy princess. A very beautiful princess. And they fell in love. This is the thing that is told to us so easily and no one ever questions her mother or her grandmother or her aunt or her friend hiding with her in the dark roots of a banyan tree, even here in Saigon, the great banyan tree in the park on Dong Khoi that was there a hundred years before the revolution. I heard the story there, on the street, and you never think to ask whoever is telling you, How did this happen? How did this feeling happen between two such different creatures? My friend Diep, who was also the daughter of a prostitute, but one who did not flee, did not give her daughter over to what she saw was a better life, my friend whispered the story to me and a stripe of light lay on her face through the cords of the roots in the banyan and she said that the fairy princess and the dragon fell in love and they married and then she laid a hundred eggs in a beautiful silk bag. And I said only, Yes, like I understood such a thing. I said, Did he love her very much? Yes, Diep said. Very much.

And the princess had one hundred children. And there was no childhood for them. They grew instantly upon birth into very beautiful adults. Diep told me that they were both princes and princesses. Fifty boys and fifty girls. For a while they all lived together and the fairy princess was happy and the children were happy. But the dragon was not. He missed the sea and one day the fairy princess woke and he was gone. He had returned to his palace beneath the water. She understood. She tried to live on without him. But it was very difficult because she was very much in love with him. And so she called him back. I do not know how. I did not think to ask. Somehow he knew to come back and yet he could not stay. He told her that their differences were too great. He could not be happy in the land. He had to return to his palace, though he promised that if she ever knew any danger or terrible hardship he would return to help. So he took fifty of their children with him and he returned to the sea. And she took fifty of their children with her to the mountains. And these children became the people of Vietnam.

It seemed a very beautiful and sad story to me. And I came home to the very room that I lie in with this man. Years ago in this place I came home to my grandmother and I told her the story and she said that it was true.

No. Not my grandmother. She and I lived in this room for most of the time I was a child. But I heard about the dragon and the fairy princess before that. I came to my mother, and that was near to this place but not in this room, and I was perhaps seven years old, and I told her the story and she said it was true. But she corrected one thing. They were all sons. A hundred sons. And the eldest of them became the first king of Vietnam. I did not ask anything more, questions I now have that roll in me and break in me more strongly than the waves of the dragon's precious sea. It is this that I wonder as I hold this man's hand in my bed: How did she look upon her dragon when she first lay with him? Did the princess take the great scaled hand of this creature that she was loving so strongly even then, ready as she was to open her body to him, did she put her tiny, silken hands on his and did she pass her fingers softly over the layers of his hard flesh still smelling of the sea, did she touch the tips of his claws, did she look into his great red eyes and see all the gentleness that she had dreamed for? And surely the answer is yes. Surely that is what she did.

I cannot see Ben's eyes. Not the color of them. Not what might be there on his heart. He turns his face to me when I lead him to touch my breast and there is only shadow where his eyes are and I cannot see. But I feel him through his hand. He is very gentle in this place of steel mills and trucks and I know he likes the touch of me and I know this even though he lifts his hand now. Just the tiniest bit so that he does not touch me with his flesh, but I can still feel the heat of him. "Are you sure?" he says. He believes this thing I have said about myself. I believe it, too. And I am sure of this: with this man, I am naked and I do not feel as if I am alone. "Yes," I say, and he puts his hand on me but not over my nipple. He puts his hand in the center of my chest, between my breasts, and the tip of his middle finger is in the hollow of my throat. It feels as if he touches my whole body with his palm and I do not know what is to come and I tell myself I do not care.

Ben

She tells me I'm the first man she's ever done it with and I stop right off. It wouldn't make a difference in my feelings for her, either way, but when she says she's never made love before, I do feel like I've been given some kind of a second chance. I almost tell her it's the same for me. For Christ's sake, to be able to start again from a place where there's nothing to remember, nothing to ask about, nothing but what's there for both of you right in that moment, without any history at all, that's almost too good to be true. And to my surprise, my face goes hot and I get a feeling in my eyes like when you step in front of a coke oven and you take that first blast of heat before you start shoveling the spill.

Like that maybe, like a feeling at the mill, but that's a little bit of bullshit on my part. In fact, it's like when you're about to cry. This woman lying here in a dim room saying she's a virgin and she wants me to be inside her body and she is who she is, she listens to me talk like she does with those sweet dark eyes never looking away even for a second and she takes me into a room like this and says so easily this is my good luck Buddha and this is my long life Buddha and this is my ancestor shrine and it's like she thinks I'm going to understand these things right off. She just makes me part of them, though a couple of the things should seem silly to me, little ceramic fat guys sitting on the floor, but I don't want to laugh at them, only maybe a quiet laugh in pleasure from her being like this. A Vietnam woman. In a room in goddamn Saigon, after all. Those people out there going around and around all night on their motorcycles, a bunch of them maybe guys who twenty years ago were in the business of killing Americans. And she tells me that there is no past at all and she wants me and I feel like I'm going to goddamn cry.

So I turn my face to the window. And I hope that it will be all right for her. I hope she shouldn't be waiting for the man she's going to marry, though it's not like I've ruled out that the man she could marry is me. If I figured otherwise, I think I'd be strong enough to get up and thank her as sweetly as I could so it wouldn't hurt her and I'd get the hell out of here. But I realize— and this is a shock to me, as a matter of fact—that it could be me. It took me to come back to the fucking Nam to realize that I could be married to somebody again. And just at the moment I come to the little shock of that, Tien says, "It is all right," and she takes my hand and puts it on her breast.

This is the first real touch. The first touch of sex. We're half naked at the moment and we've been kissing, but this is the first touch. I take my hand away but not very far. I can't say that something's warning me. I just want to be sure she isn't making a mistake about what she wants. They think about these things a little different over here. Even if the communists are in control, they still seem to think in some older ways. I don't want her to end up spoiled for some other man, just in case. Though I'm wanting to go on with this very bad now. And it's been a long time since I've felt this way. I don't even try to think of the last time. I lift my hand just a little bit and my palm is burning with the tiny hard spot where the tip of her nipple was and what I do think of is a moment when I was pulling oil on the Cali-

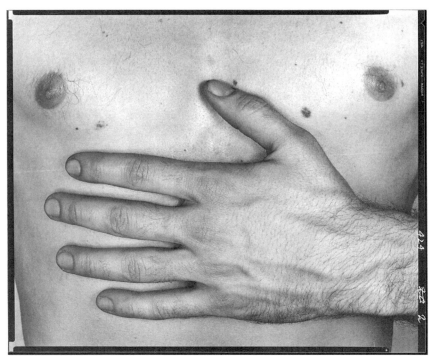

George Platt Lynes

fornia coast, some years ago now, and I stepped out of my rig in a rest stop somewhere in the San Joaquin Valley and it was night and the air was full of the smell of oranges. A couple of Peterbilts had just huffed away and they'd been full of oranges and the smell was everywhere, that and the smell of diesel fuel, and I suddenly wanted a woman bad. I wasn't sure why but it seemed to have something to do with this place. Saigon. These streets are always full of that kind of mix of smells, some sweet something, fruit or flowers or incense, but something else too in the same air, dry rot or old fish or the exhaust from the motorbikes. I got out of my truck, and what passed for a marriage in my life was dead already and I didn't care if my pecker ever saw the light of day again and it was a thing that smelled like Vietnam that made me want a woman once more.

I push Tien a little bit. "Are you sure you want to?" I ask her and I hope the answer is going to be yes. And it is. She says it right away and I put my hand in the center of her chest and I wish my hand was big enough to hold her in it, all of her, just cover her with the palm of my hand and keep her safe and make her happy. I ache in the shoulders from wanting that. And the mix of things is in the air right then. The incense from her ancestor shrine and the smell of all the cheap motors outside and somebody in a room nearby cooking with the fish oil they use.

Soon after I got back here to Vietnam I came to this street I once knew. It was the only one that stuck in my head after all these years. And that was because of a woman. I guess we used the word *love* to each other for a few months, her and me. Whatever love was for me at twenty. And there was something between us for a while. Something. But I didn't come back here looking for her. It was just a street I knew. There were bars along here, in 1966. A clothing shop now. A noodle shop. A place on the sidewalk fixing tires. Just a street with its life out in the open like life in this city always seemed to be and it still is and I walked around here and I sat at a tiny plastic table in the open garage mouth of the noodle shop and I drank a warm Coke, staying away from the ice, and this was all I had to worry about now, the water, and I watched these people moving around and I just held still knowing that I didn't have to be afraid about Vietnam anymore.

The water and the dogs. They always shy away as if every one of them has been beaten since birth, but I don't trust them. They're slick featured, scoop-eared, more like dingoes or hyenas than like American dogs, and while I was sitting on that first day at the noodle shop, one of them sniffed by, stopping at a stain on the sidewalk and then he saw me watching him and he flinched back right away, ducking his head like I'd raised my hand to hit him. I was thinking I shouldn't have this feeling. He'd just had it bad as a pup and I sucked back my nerves and clicked at him a little bit. He stopped at this but he was clearly not going to come to me. "Be careful of all the dogs," a voice said and I looked up into her face.

That first moment I saw her, I flinched a little inside, her face was so beautiful. And like with all these Vietnamese, it surprised me. There's always something floating in a Vietnamese face that you don't expect. There was an old woman with her gums red from chewing betel leaves who'd been crouching for a long while off to my left, drinking her soup with her bowl up at her face the whole time, but once, she'd glanced over to me, just a couple of minutes before I clicked at the dog and started all this, and she smiled her bright red smile and she had a color in her eyes like when the interstate ahead looks like water and is reflecting the sky. Wet and almost blue but dark from concrete. And I thought when I saw the mama-san's eyes that her daddy was French or something. So when there was this beautiful face before me telling me to be careful of the dogs, I wasn't surprised by the things you didn't expect in it. Her eyes were very dark but they weren't so sharply lidded. They looked soft around the edge and her face wasn't so round. She had a squareness to her jaw and a mouth that smiled now a little bit but just on one side and her skin was pale and I just eased back and thought, Holy shit this is a beautiful woman, and she said, "They might be sick." She'd been talking English, too, with not much of an accent at all.

"Thanks," I said, and she was moving off. Just like that. Nothing more. She was through a passageway a couple of storefronts down and gone and I sat there wondering what the hell just happened. I looked over to where the dog was and he'd taken off. I thought about standing up, about walking down to the passageway and at least looking along to where this woman disappeared, but I didn't. The mama-san was gone too. There was the buzz and rush of motorcycles in the street, of course, and people crouching on the sidewalk in either direction, but it was the time of day in Saigon when if you're on foot, you find some shade and stay still and nobody was near me or coming toward me and for a moment I felt absolutely alone. In the midst of this city of all places, I felt invisible, and that was a feeling I realized I wanted to hold on to for awhile and so I didn't get up. I let her face fade and I waited and I even closed my eyes.

Then there was a car horn close by. I opened my eyes and at the curb was a Renault with a Saigontourist decal across its back window and I knew she was going to appear again. And she did. Out of that passageway and across the sidewalk and into the car and she didn't even give me another glance. So I thought, that's the end of it. But a week later I have my hand on her naked chest and she says yes it's okay and I still don't move. This time, it's from sitting there and wondering at the switchback my luck just seemed to take.

Tien

He does not move his hand when I tell him it is okay. I am ready for this moment, but he is waiting. I like this about him. He will be very gentle with me. Very slow. I listen to hear him breathe. There are still too many night sounds and I tell him, "Bring your face close to mine, please."

This makes him cock his head, like he has not understood. "Bring your face close," I say and he does, sliding to me, and he thinks I want him to kiss me and I say, when he is very near, when his breath has touched my cheek, "Just there. For a moment wait please. I want to know that you are real." He waits. He is real. I can feel his breath on me.

On the day I first saw him, I would not look at him a second time. Not straight at him. But I glanced in the rearview mirror as the car pulled away. I am a careful girl. I already acted a different way from who I am by finding some American man sitting almost directly beneath my window and speaking to him, even if it was for his own good. Now I could only see him again in a mirror, like the American legend I read, a story about a man and a woman with snakes for hair who could turn him to stone if he looked at her directly. And his face was turned this way and I wondered if he could see me watch him in this small mirror and so I looked for the dog. I feared this man might try to touch it and he would be hurt. I saw no dog and I thought that I was not really so very interested in where the dog was, and when the car began to move and the man's face was gone, I was a little bit angry with myself for my shyness.

But I am not shy when he brings his face close to mine in my bed. I feel his breath on me and I pull back just a little bit to see him clearly. His eyes are very dark, like a Vietnamese, I think. And I am reminded of the dragon once more. There are many straight lines in the face of a dragon, square corners. Ben's face has much of this in it. At the bottom of his face, at his jaw, there is a squareness that I think is like a dragon's head. I am still trying to understand the story I learned from my friend inside the banyan tree. For a moment I try to see the terribleness of such a face as beautiful. I mean by this, the dragon's face. When I feel Ben's breath and he becomes real and when I know that this real man is about to put his hands on me and his mouth and all the secret parts of him, I do not find him terrible. But I think he can help me understand, because on this night there is something inside me that is afraid, and this is in the same moment with some other thing inside me that wants to reach to him and to put my hand behind his head and pull him to me.

I tell myself, the fairy princess loved the dragon. She loved him. There are things that frighten us for a while and then from the very strong feeling of this fear we find a different strong feeling. I lived sometimes in a room not far from this one. I was still with my mother and it was on the nights when she did not leave me with my grandmother. I know now that these were the times when there was no all-night man from the bar where she worked. Some man may be there in the afternoon, but she did not lie naked with him through the long night till the morning, and it was those times she kept me on a pallet nearby. And when it was the rainy season I woke from the sound of thunder. The storms came in and bellowed in the air and I heard them with my ears but I felt them inside my body also, each cry. And for a few years it was like this. The cry of the thunder would carry me into my mother's bed on the nights when there was no one else and she would hold me in her arms.

Sometimes the bed smelled very strange to me, not the smell of my mother at all, something wet, a little like the rain that was rushing outside but stronger, thicker, a smell more like brine, like the sea. For a while I wondered if she was loved by a dragon. The thunder would beat at my body and this smell was in me and my mother was naked beneath the thin silk robe she wore and she held me close and I dreamed of the dragon rising from the South China Sea and flying to my mother and loving her in some way that I did not understand and then he went up into the sky because his kingdom needed him and he did not want to go but he had no choice and he rose high into the air and he cried out his pain and she felt it in her body and I felt it in my body and the dragon cast the sea down upon us to remind my mother of his love and he flew away. And so I came to love the thunder. On the nights I was with my mother, I went to the window at this call and I opened the shutter and I let the sound take me in its hands and squeeze me until I grew wet from the rain and my mother would draw me away. In jealousy, I thought. And when my mother was gone away and the rockets brought another thunder to Saigon, I would go to the windows and the sky was red and my grandmother would pull me away and tell me that there was something dangerous out there. But I still loved the sound. I loved this thing I once had feared.

I lift my hand now and I put it at the back of Ben's head and he is not wet from the sea and his flesh is not hard scaled. He is soft. His hair is soft and I let my fingers slide inside his hair and I pull him to me and he does not rush, he lets me draw him to me as slow as I wish. Then his breath is on my face and then his lips touch mine.

I have known other kisses. A boy, dim now in my mind, in those dark early years of our socialist republic, and I was sixteen and he was a guard at Reunification Hall, and he wore a uniform the color of a tree gecko, and we tread on each other as lightly as that, like lizards. And there was Mr. Bao, who was a driver for a while at Saigontourist. He asked me one night to go to a theater that plays movies from America. It is in a long room with a distant screen and it is very dark. He asked me to go to this place because Elizabeth Taylor and Paul Newman would be there in a movie called *Cat on a Hot Tin Roof*. He did not speak good English and he wanted me to tell him the meaning of this title. I did not know. It was not an idiom I had studied. I said that it must be some American legend that would be made clear in the movie.

It was so dark we could not see to move once the movie began, but all around us, there were couples kissing. This is the only place in public in our city where this is possible. On the screen was a woman's voice translating all of the speaking in the film into Vietnamese, for all the characters, both men and women. I could hear only a murmur of Elizabeth Taylor and Paul Newman speaking beneath this one female voice. I tried hard to listen to the American voices, but I could make out none of their words. I grew angry at the very sound of my own language. I should have felt shame at this, I think. But I cared only for these Americans on the screen. I grew more ashamed, conscious now of my secret attachment to these people. But Elizabeth Taylor was very beautiful and her husband was very harsh with her and I was concerned. He did not wish to touch her, in spite of her beauty. And he also was very angry at his father. The father wanted very much to please his son. He tried hard, I think. He was there in a great house with his son, alive, and he was trying hard, and I grew very angry at Paul Newman for not understanding.

These thoughts were in me when Mr. Bao's hand came and turned my face to him and he put his lips on mine. At the touch of his lips, I felt only a hard little knot in my chest. I pulled back. He said he was sorry and I said that it was okay and we both looked at the screen. I wanted to jump up from my seat and scream at Paul Newman to go to his father and embrace him. He is your father, I would cry, you should be grateful to have his love. And then I would tell Paul Newman to go to his wife and do what she desires. People should touch when they are in need. And I heard these words in my head and I felt Elizabeth Taylor's pain as my own and I looked toward the darkness where Mr. Bao was sitting, hurting still from my coldness.

And so I took my hand and I turned his face to me once again and we kissed some more, though I wondered at this thing, why people sought it so, and then time went on from that night, and eventually we were in the bed in his rooms, and with each touch between us, the thing I wanted so much to feel murmured beneath our acts like the voices of the American actors in the movie, saying things I wanted to hear but being drowned out by this other, too-familiar voice. And I lay beside Mr. Bao afterwards, and all the voices were silent, and when he coughed softly I was startled, because I had forgotten that he was there.

So I rose up from that bed and left Mr. Bao and after that I have not touched a man. I have been free to do so. But I have chosen not to. I have taken my place in the state, working for Saigontourist to show the truth of how we live to those from other countries that come here. And until this moment, this is how I live. When I do not work, I have some girlfriends and we go to a movie or to a park or to a restaurant or to karaoke or to the show at the theater that was once the French Opera House and was then the national assembly building of the puppet government of the divided Vietnam. Or I sit alone in this room and I read a book or I listen to the radio to the classic Vietnam opera or I say prayers and light incense for the soul of my father.

These prayers I say every night. I am a modern girl of a great socialist state but I am not a communist. Not so very many Vietnamese are communists. I can still pray for the spirits of the dead like my mother and my grandmother taught me. I pray for my grandmother, too, but the ancestor shrine that sits against the wall next to the window has one careful purpose and that is to receive the prayers for the soul of my father, a soul that I have always understood to be suffering terribly in the next life and in great need of these things I offer him.

And when I lie down in my bed and it is night, there is still the smell in the air of the incense I have burned for him. I lie in my bed and sometimes I wear a silk robe and sometimes I am naked. I lie in my bed for all these years that I have been in this room as a woman, and I always lie alone until this night when Ben touches me for the first time. But it was not clear to me how alone this was until Ben came to me. I did not feel how painful all the nights without him had been until he was here. This is a strange thing to me. As Ben kisses me and I feel he is here with me and I feel that no one has ever been here until this moment, I think that perhaps my father has always protected me from that pain. Perhaps what I gave to my father's soul, the company of my prayers, he always gave back to me. This is what I think as Ben kisses me. And I may seem shy still, as I think too much of Mr. Bao and Elizabeth Taylor and my friends who go with me to restaurants and fill the air with empty words, and I do not concentrate on the feeling of his lips on mine. But it is not shyness. There is at this moment the smell of incense in my room. His lips are upon me and I smell the smoke of my father's soul.

I try not to think of my father at this moment. But the smell of the incense of my father's shrine is very clear to me and I try to hold that smell away from me and it is very hard. I have lit the slender tips of the incense a thousand times for him, more, five thousand times perhaps—every night since I was ten years old—and it is not easy to pretend that this smell is not here, that his soul is not here, but I want only to feel the touch of Ben's lips. And little claws of panic are burrowing deep into me in the place between my breasts where his hand touched me moments ago. I think: I am missing my first kiss with Ben. I concentrate on the soft touch of his mouth. I press my mouth harder against him and his lips open mine slightly and he is touching the inside of my lip with his tongue and I am forgetting now, forgetting the past, I am touching Ben and I am not expecting what is next. I feel suddenly his hand on my bare stomach and then it slides down and inside my pantaloons and I yield to him as easily as the silk and his hand goes to that place between my legs.

There are many things that I do not fully understand about my body. I know the ways of understanding from before the revolution: a woman's body was given to a man by her parents and it was to make children for him. I know the ways of my mother: a woman's body was something of such little value to her that it could be sold to any man. But the ways of our leaders now are not very clear. We are to be modest about our bodies because they are to be given to the service of the state. I think in order to make children for our country. Something like that. There were words about these things at first when the country was finally made one. That was in those early years when the streets of Saigon were thick at night with darkness except for a few scraps of fire in a gutter, a kerosene lamp burning down an alleyway. And there was such a terrible quiet. I sometimes wish in this era of our country that the motorbikes would stop outside in the streets, but they are better than the silence. I can wake at three or four in the early mornings now and it is quiet but it is quiet from a sound that was there only a few hours ago and will come again soon, it is still not like those years when the sun went down and there was no electric light and there was the smell of wood fire and kerosene and there was no gasoline and there was only the faint click of bicycle chains and we all whispered to each other. In those years I think a woman's body was intended to make children for our great socialist state, but now I do not know. The lights returned and the sounds, but I do not know where our bodies are.

When I met Ben, before he touched me for the first time, I crouched in my bathroom one night and I sponged my naked body and I began to tremble. It must have been because of him. He had been in the other room that very day and I had served him tea and now he was gone, but something of him remained, like a faint scent of smoke, and I was naked and this part that he would soon touch felt as if it had begun to pout, like a child, pout from being left out of something she wanted very much to do. I stood up and I was still wet from my bath and I was naked. I moved to the little mirror and I could see only my face and my throat and only a little of my chest, not my breasts at all. I was modest still, in this great socialist state, modest even to myself in my own bathroom.

The mirror hung with a cord from a nail and I touched it with my fingertip just at the bottom and it moved and my face disappeared and my breath caught when I saw my own nipples like this, before me, apart from me, and it was because of him. I tipped the mirror farther and I could see the little dark flame of hair coming up from that secret place between my legs and I let the mirror go and my face rushed back and quaked there and I remembered my grandmother's question, and though I saw only me in the mirror, I did not feel alone: I had seen my nipples, my secret place, and he would someday see them, naked before him. And here was my face as he would see it. It tried to smile for him, but the pouting between my legs was very strong, and I had to stop because it was becoming painful now, this pleasure, this yearning.

Ben

She says, "Ben." When I put my hand on that place between Tien's legs, she speaks my name and I think, This is the moment it will all stop. I've gone too fast. And I stop and I'm ready to move my hand away and I'm beginning to curse myself inside because I don't want this to end and I've fucked it up now. Fucked up the most important thing of all, for even that brief touch is different from anything I've ever felt and it is suddenly very important. All up and down the forefinger edge of my left hand is her softness and I'm stunned by that, it's her, it's Tien I touch, and I touch her in a place that seems so entirely part of her and so entirely secret that I am drawn out of myself and it feels as if I've just discovered my hand, I've never had a real feeling there before, but now I do, and I rise to her and I know that I will soon find other parts of me that I never knew I had, never did have. I raise my hand from her and it's flushed and I feel my heart beating there and Tien says something to me in Vietnamese. It's urgent, but it's soft. Then I think she realizes how she has spoken and she repeats it in English. "I didn't mean for you to stop."

"You said my name. I didn't know."

"I said your name because I was happy you touched me there."

"Are you sure?" I ask.

"I told you before that it is all right."

"About your breasts. I didn't know if it applied..."

"It does."

"I'm hearing myself now," I say. "I sound like a damn fool."

"You sound very nice."

"It feels like the first time for me, too."

Her voice grows eager. "Does it really feel like that?"

"Yes."

"Though you have done this many times?"

"Not so very many. I don't remember."

And this is true. I can't remember. I have no past, either, it seems. My hand returns to that place and she opens her legs and I have trouble drawing a breath because of the gentleness of her there and because of all that has gone before, as blurred and sometimes blank as my memory is, I have a sharp sense now of the long road to this touching, this sweet and momentous touching.

Knowing that Tien and I will make love, I flare inside. I am hot in my clothes and blocked in some painful way and her dark eyes are watching me, waiting, and I bend to her and our lips touch again, and very gently I move my hand upon her and she sighs into our kiss, I feel her breath move into me as if I've been dragged dying from the sea and she wants to bring me back to life.

And I'm still hesitant. I must ask her first. I pull my mouth away from hers and say, "Can I take these clothes off?"

"Yours or mine?" she says.

"Both. Though I meant mine."

"Am I ready?"

Tien

I hear how childish I sound. I should know if my own body is ready to take a man into it. It has done this thing before. No. I have spoken a true lie to Ben and I must hear its truth for myself. It is not just a matter of readiness for a man. It is this *one* man. No one else has been Ben.

"Are you ready?" he repeats, completely baffled by the question, and I am embarrassed.

"Yes, I am," I say, pretending that it is his question and I am giving him my answer. This confuses him some more. "Thank you for asking me," I add.

He stares at me, trying to figure all this out.

"Yes you can," I say, trying to move on to the question of our clothes.

"Are you doing this on purpose?" he asks. His voice is gentle and in the neon light I can see his brow knit and his mouth shape a smile. He is enjoying me.

"Yes. I am a great kidder," I say, though if it is true about me, then it has come about only in the past few moments.

"I am very confused now," he says, but there is a playful thing in his voice and there is nothing confusing about what is going on between his hand and that special place on my body. I know this for sure.

I say, "I will help make things clear for you. Yes I am ready. Yes you can remove these clothes. Yours and mine."

He smiles again and he brings his face close and he kisses me on the lips and I like that kiss, but as soon as it is over, I say, "I am not kidding." Because I am ready.

He nods and he says, "Thank you."

"No, thank you," I say.

And he begins with me. He pulls back and I am already naked above the waist and I am very comfortable with that and he puts his hands on the rim of my pantaloons. And I expect things to be floating by in my head, like the bits of the jungle in the Saigon River, I expect the things I live with in my head to just keep on passing through: my mother and my father and my grandmother and my work and the Socialist Republic of Vietnam—what it is and what it expects of me—and even the dragons and the jasmine flowers of our lovely stories.

But when Ben puts his hands inside the top edge of my pants and his knuckles lie warm on my hips, all those things vanish from me and there is only the slip of his hands over my hipbones and down the outer edges of my thighs and past my knees and my calves and my ankles, and as his hands move I feel my nakedness emerging from him in their wake, and then the silk bunches over my feet and then is gone and I close my eyes and all that I am is in my skin, all that I need ever to know opens with my pores into the moist air of this room and I wait with my eyes closed, not because I am afraid but because in this moment I have become my skin and seeing has nothing to do with that, and then Ben's skin falls upon me, his thigh against my thigh, his chest against my chest, I open my eyes and his face is to my side and I turn to him. We touch our lips. He touches my cheek with his lips. I close my eyes again and his lips are on my eyelids, and now there is a new place of touching. A clear, hard spot on my hip and I know what part of him is doing this, and then he shifts and the spot disappears and he is over me and I wait. And in that special place on my body, that place of such strange and sometimes sloppy mystery, that place that sometimes I love and some-times I shun, Ben is beginning to nudge his way in, and I wait for this now, I wait for the rest of my life to begin, and I open a little and a little more and then there is a hard, fleshy wrenching, a bloom of pain that unfolds quick and sharp into my womb and my thighs and I gasp.

"I'm sorry," he says.

"I'm sorry," I say. I do not want him to stop. I open my eyes to Ben. His brow is knit above me. His is not moving. I feel held open. And the pain is blunt now. And then it is tiny. And then it is gone.

"Do you want me to stop?" he asks.

"Go forward for the good for the revolution," I say and this surprises me. It is from some schoolbook from the early days of the liberation. Per-haps I am a great kidder after all. We both laugh and that special part of me clenches with the laughter and his special part moves a little, and the effect, I quickly decide, is very nice and I would like to have that effect with no laughter. "No more questions now," I say.

And now he makes love to me. And I am close to him. I am close to this man. I suddenly understand how far away people are from each other, even passing near in the street, even brushing shoulders, even looking into each other's eyes and speaking each other's names, there is this great empty space between us and now there is no space at all, I clutch Ben's naked back and he is inside me and my body is a blur, the very cells of it are twisted away from each other and perhaps they have always been like that and I am just realizing it and I gather for Ben, everything is twisted apart so that something can find its way out and gather it in me, ready for him, and now suddenly all of this, all these cells of mine, rush into focus, I am pulsating hard where our bodies are joined and everything is suddenly very clear and I am put together again.

And he is still moving and I realize that he has not yet given to me and he says, "I will come out of you now." I know what he means and for him to spill himself outside of me seems a terrible thing. I feel him drawing out.

"No," I say and I hold him tight. "And do not ask if I am sure."

He slides back inside me and I am happy for that.

And on this night of the first time I make love to this man, I hold Benjamin Cole close to me. And we are naked. And we are sweating. And then I know he has given to me. And I am a cup filled to overflowing.

Ben

She does not want me outside her body and I don't question her. What's between us seems to call for this. She knows it and I know it. But still there is a moment just before I am about to run inside her that I think it will be like it always has been, this thing will have its own life and I am clenched tight down there, it is near to time, and I'm waiting for something to snap free, some hitch that will lose a pin and my body will rush on and I'll be left behind in the center of an empty highway wondering where I went.

But I can hear her breathing. Short, quick, soft in my ear, and she clings to me hard and our bodies are slick and I can't sort out one part from another, there's no single place where there's a pin to slip and we'll break apart, not even where I grow leaden with readiness, not even that hard dangling place is separate now, we are fused together, all up and down us, from the stroke of her breath on my face to the press of her insteps on my thighs we are one body with parts long lost, missed only in our dreams, rejoined, and I rush now and she shapes a sound and it moves through me and we open our mouths together and cry out and we press tighter and my face is in her hair and her hair is dark and the darkness smells faintly of soap and of incense and it smells, too, of diesel and of oranges and though I can see nothing of my body I know from the clutch of her and the smell of her that I am complete.

And we do not separate our bodies for a long while. At some moment we turn onto our sides, still joined, a world spinning on its axis, but we neither of us want to let go after what we've done, and we lie without speaking, and whenever she makes some slight movement, the shift of a leg, the slide of an arm, the tiniest adjustment of her face against my chest, it surprises me a little and then it delights me, she is someone other than me but she is me as well, I feel the movement of her body as my own body and I am not only whole, I am multiplied, I am rich with limbs and flesh and voices.

"I love you," I say. I do not expect to say it, though I mean it, and I wait for my other voice to reply.

A War Journal

Catherine Texier

SEPTEMBER 19, 1996

I dreamt last night that you were leaving, but you were not leaving our apartment. We were staying in a suburban house that looked like the one you grew up in on Long Island, and our bed was covered with this flowered yellow bedspread matching the curtains and the wallpaper. I was lying in bed with Juliet, who was about ten in the dream, and all your luggage was spread out in the bedroom and around the house. All over the place, there were these huge clothes bags and duffel bags already packed, old baggage from your college days, baggage that I didn't even know you had, that I had never seen. You didn't leave in my dream. You were still home in the morning, and I was still lying in this flowered bed, surrounded by all your stuff.

Before we went to sleep, you were raging at me: you said that our relationship had turned claustrophobic and that you had wanted to have a separate social life from me, but it didn't mean, then, that you had wanted to leave me, you never even thought it would be a problem. You said I couldn't handle anything and that I was falling apart all the time. I listened to you, lying on my back. You were not looking at me. You were sitting on the side of the bed, your back to me and I could see your muscles tensing, your shoulders hunched, and at one point you got up to go to the bathroom. Our relationship has become sick, you said on your way back, and for some reason I stared at your naked hip and thigh, I didn't want to see your face.

You got back into bed, still not looking at me, still shaking with rage.

I had no idea you had such resentment for me, I said. You kept saying you loved me.

I don't have any patience with this anymore.

Do you think I am falling apart now? I asked you.

You got angry again.

How would *I* know?

Am I falling apart now?

I don't know, you said. I think you're just disguising it.

SEPTEMBER 22, 1996

You told Juliet you were only staying because of her and Lola. Juliet asked you: Do you still love Mom? And you said: I don't know.

This morning you apologized to her. You said you didn't mean to scare her.

SEPTEMBER 23, 1996

We went to a screenplay reading yesterday. Our first public outing together since I came back from France. I didn't know if we were going as a couple or as...as what? Is there a word for what we are? I was sitting on a chair waiting for you to get me a drink. After a while I got up to look for you. You were at the bar, talking to two women, one the producer who had inadvertently provoked our fatal fight in July.

We met at the Bowery Bar, the producer said to me.

Oh, I said, looking into her eyes, yes, and I smiled. I thought life was ironical. What about my beer, I asked you.

Here, you said, and you handed it to me, smiling.

Fabrizio Rainone

You and me smiling those fake, social smiles to cover up the abyss between us. I hung out with you for a while. Then I moved away from the bar, not wanting to intrude, and I saw you lean to kiss the producer on the cheek. Bye, girl, you said. Confident, flirtatious, a player.

And I knew what had terrified me all through last year, why I had clung to you so ferociously, trying to pull you back to me. The fear to lose you to the world. And I understood your rage at me for trying to hold you back to our little world of the two of us, that world that you said had become suffocating. I watched you play the room, nod and kiss and talk about your next projects, with your new soft black hat, your hip-hop/biker cool look. I remembered how shy you had been years ago, hanging back with me. How shy the both of us were. I saw why you needed to take your distance, that you were like a butterfly coming out of your cocoon and trying out your wings, and that I represented the cocoon that you'd come out of. I felt cold and exposed, utterly naked, taking shaky steps into a world where you had already grown confident. And I knew that I was going to dive in, that I wouldn't cling to you anymore, that I didn't have the choice, that there was no turning back.

Later on, in the middle of the night, I felt your hard cock brush against my hand like it does, when you're half asleep—your body wanting me while your mind resists—and you turned your back to me but I could feel you still wanted me and I wasn't sure if I wanted you because I've had to shut down my feelings too to protect myself, but you pulled me to you and sat me on your face and I felt your mouth open my cunt lips like you love to do and I placed your hands on my tits and you started to play with my nipples while you were eating me, sucking me off till I came into your mouth with deep grunts and I slid down your chest and you were soft and I played with you with my mouth and my fingers till you got hard again and I sat on you and flicked your nipples and tried to kiss you, but you pulled your face to the side, not wanting to give me your love, and I said: it's okay, baby, it's okay. And you let go inside of me right away, your come spilling out of me on the inside of my thighs. And I dismounted you and went to pee, and when I came back you'd turned your back to me but I cradled you in my arms and you curled your body inside of mine. And we fell asleep together.

SEPTEMBER 28, 1996

The air is cool now, late September early morning air, pure and light, the summer softening, folding into the ripening of fall, a gentleness to soothe my open wounds, our ailing relationship now wide open, oozing puss and blood on the operating table.

We've been back for a whole month.

Your arms around me, I feel you stir against my thighs. Not only because you are horny, I think because you're letting go of something. Your body tucked inside of mine. Searching mine. My arms encircling you. It wasn't just about sex that time, no overt eroticism. But a deeper need, reaching out through the layers of anger and frustration, our bodies looking for closeness, for each other, like they always have, like fishes underwater in the dark.

I pulled four hamburgers out of the freezer for dinner and laid them on the counter next to three ears of corn we'd just gotten with the box of organic vegetables that gets delivered every Wednesday, and when you came back down from your office upstairs—it was about 6:30 P.M.—and saw the four hamburgers, you said coldly: I'm not having dinner here tonight.

I felt a little twinge but I repressed it because it's our new way: total freedom and no questions asked. So I said, okay, and put one hamburger back in the freezer. And right after that I felt fine: this was the deal, my deal with you anyway, because I don't think you've got a deal with me. What you have is an attitude, I-bet-you-can't-pull-it-off-I'm-waiting-for-my-next-check-and-I'm-outta-here attitude. I lay down on the couch next to the girls who were watching an old rerun of "Blossom" on TV and told them: it's just the three of us having dinner tonight, your dad is going out, are you already hungry, how soon do you want to eat? And Juliet said she was hungry and asked for potatoes and I got up to start them.

Around sevenish, I saw you getting ready, putting your shoes on, a shirt over your T-shirt, preparing your briefcase—so this was going to be a work dinner—and all of a sudden you told me about several film deals that were about to go down. All the details spilled out, and I went to hold you in my arms and kiss you. I was stupidly happy about that, not so much about the film deals, but happy about your opening up to me, that we still had that little thread of a connection. Does that mean we'll be swimming in money? I asked, as if we were still going to be together, you and I, when these deals come through, climbing the social ladder side-by-side. And you said, I don't know about that.

I know you must think I am in total denial. And I am, in a way—not just denying but asserting what I believe, which is that deep down we are still together, and acting accordingly.

You let me hold you but didn't hold me back.

I stepped away and went to prepare dinner. When you were ready to go out you went to the couch to kiss the girls goodnight and on the way out you brushed my waist with your hand and said goodbye.

Maybe you were grateful, amazed even, that I was letting you go, no questions asked, no strings attached. It wasn't entirely self-sacrificing or masochistic on my part. When the door closed behind you, a strange warmth spread inside of me. I felt whole, released. I was glad that you were gone. You were taking the tensions with you. I was happy to be eating dinner alone with Juliet and Lola, just the three of us girls in front of some stupid TV sitcom. I gave a bath to Lola afterwards and took her to bed and went to bed myself.

When I woke up it was 1:30 A.M. and I heard the TV downstairs, which you like to watch when you come back late at night. A little while later you lay down next to me. I said hey to you and you said hey, but I could feel you had closed up again.

OCTOBER 3, 1996

Something's been broken, damaged, you said, and your anger keeps the wound active, and yet on another level our life together is not broken. It's as if you had two lives: outside and inside the house, where we are all together, and sometimes the two intersect when we're both invited somewhere and our relationship goes on. We talk daily about the kids, about work, and sometimes about your overwhelming anger, and about your feelings towards me, or what's left of them, and about my feelings towards you—I cling to my undying love for you—and we cook and eat dinner together (tonight you made a big pot of tomato sauce), and we sleep together naked in the same bed every night and sometimes we make love, tentatively, protectively, and sometimes you hold me in your arms and I can tell that you're not quite there at times, and at other times you let go of your anger or whatever is eating you and your warmth gushes out.

If I asked you again, if I tried to take your emotional temperature, you might—probably would—say that your feelings haven't changed, that you're still shut down. Which is the reason why I will not ask you. And yet life moves imperceptibly like waves lapping at a cliff, every minute of peace making its little dent, leaving its print, every minute of peace soothing the wound.

OCTOBER 7, 1996

You don't seem scared, my shrink said to me.

But I am terrified, I feel like I'm standing at the edge of a cliff staring into the void. Because I've uprooted myself from my country, you are my home, my heart.

When I flew to New York from Montreal a month after giving birth to Juliet, you had prepared the apartment for us. Among the ladders and the two-by-fours and the brick walls of our future bedroom you had laid out an oriental rug and a mattress covered with an Indian bedspread and pillows and you had lit a candle and set a bottle of chilled white wine and two glasses on the floor. I lay Juliet in her basket outside the room on a steamer trunk and you took me into your arms.

To me you were the home I never had, your arms and your chest and the perimeter of the kitchen table with your mug of steaming coffee in front of you.

That night, in March 1981, Juliet was one month old. She had fallen asleep in her little basket. You sat down on the bed next to me and handed me a glass of white wine.

Welcome home, baby, you said. And I melted into your arms.

OCTOBER 10, 1996

This morning at the Union Square greenmarket I had the blues while I was buying eggs and chicken and filling my straw basket with Winesap apples fresh picked upstate. I had stale memories of our Saturday morning trips to the market, boring, boring, boring, and yet reassuring, in hindsight, as if shopping together had been a ritual asserting the reality of this constantly moving and elusive entity: a family.

OCTOBER 12, 1996

A peace seems to have descended on the house. Maybe the peace is in me— lying down on the big white couch with a newspaper or a magazine, sitting at my desk and writing, filling out the space, feeling at home when you're not here, not having a clue who I am at this point in my life, and yet feeling that weird sense of peace, after you called me from Saugerties this afternoon, to tell me you were freezing your butt on your motorcycle, that you were going to stop by somewhere to warm up and would come back later in the night.

It's as if the fever has broken and I can relax, I don't have to prove anything to anyone anymore. I don't have to do anything, except what I want. Excited at the coolness of fall, the prospect of wearing heavy sweaters, winter boots, hats, that a new year has opened up. Feeling free: free to travel, free to think, free to start a new project, free to imagine, free to take chances. Free and scared.

Now that I am letting you go, I am left with myself. Myself, not the mother, not the lover, not the wife, and I am faced with an anonymous, countryless identity.

One of the first things I did, after you told me you wanted to leave, was buy the biggest French-English dictionary I could find at Barnes & Noble, a Larousse, and to stand it on the shelf near my old, college-days Harrap's. Maybe I had an idea that the key to my identity was my ability to translate the two languages into each other. I had been wanting a new dictionary for years. There had never been a sense of urgency. And now there was.

I can't take care of you anymore, you said, I can't be your mirror anymore, I have no patience for your tears, for your anxieties, for your neediness anymore.

No more? No more leaning on your shoulder, no more hearing your voice, so soft, so tender, telling me, as you did so many times: everything's going to be okay, baby, don't worry?

Thanks, baby, for the bitter pill, thanks for the wake-up call.

And I thought I was the most lovable, vulnerable woman.

Yeah right.

New York, tough city.

OCTOBER 13, 1996

Juliet is sleeping over at a friend's in North Salem. I dropped her off at another friend's house on Broadway in the afternoon, they were going to take the train together to Penn Station. Lola is playing Barbies with her friend Claudia upstairs in the guest room. I can hear them laugh at intervals, high-pitched voices rising above the buzz of the steam heat coming up in the radiator. Reassuring sounds that make me feel safe, connected.

The house doesn't seem a trap anymore, the space opens up, it becomes fluid, alive.

With Juliet today we wondered if you feel left out when the three of us girls hang out together. Three French women talking clothes and makeup and tampons and yelling up and down the stairs while you're doing the *New York Times* crossword puzzle or watching the baseball game or a fight on your own. In your own family the women knit and cook and chat away while the men sit sullenly in front of the TV or read the newspaper. Maybe you feel this house has become a replica of your original family life. I don't know. But I can tell that you don't have enough space here. That our office is going to hell, that you talk for hours on the phone in a barely audible voice. The phone, your lifeline to the outside world.

You want to run, to escape.

OCTOBER 16, 1996

Yesterday, Sunday, coming back from your bike trip, you said: I am so troubled right now, the only time I feel okay is when I go on the bike, because of the attention it demands. On the motorcycle, your concentration has to be 100 percent, your eyes always on the road, anticipating what's going to happen, your attention can never waver, it would be too dangerous.

When you said, I am so troubled right now, it felt like a gift to me, a confidence. A tiny moment of openness. A tiny moment of trust. I am living for these little crumbs. And when you came back for dinner later, and we ate around the round table and watched a movie on TV, an atrocious remake of Clouzot's *Les Diaboliques,* it was the four of us together again, this fragile balance, a music that we played. And you were here, not elsewhere. But in bed, no. You kept to yourself, quiet, reading. You let me hold you until you fell asleep. That's all.

And yet, a couple of nights ago, the sex was so hot. I barely touched your thigh and zap, we were in each other's arms. I couldn't have you inside of me because of the surgery I had earlier this week, so you squatted, your back to me, and I took you between my thighs with my hand and rubbed my breasts against your ass, then my mouth, then I stuck my finger in and you came all over my hand. Later, curled inside your arms I whispered: don't take that away from us. Sex is a lot more than sex. You are free, I don't want to hold you back.

You didn't say anything. We hugged each other for a while, and then you turned away.

Robert Stivers

But She Was Not Mirabelle

John Hawkes

Just once, or so it seems, I did experience the full flowering of depression. We were living in Vence, at that time a smallish town in southern France about twenty miles from Nice, where I was expected to write fiction (and where I would begin to write such novels as *Travesty* and *The Blood Oranges*). Our French friends feasted us on Provençal rabbit; the surrounding landscape was yellow with genêt, the heady blossom that Henry Plantagenet always wore on his hat. But I was in the grip of a dark paralysis, for no reason that I knew of, and saw the clear light of the Côte d'Azur as dulled through the waves of my own misery. I could not eat the rabbit, took no walks, could not bear to listen to the soft sounds coming from the dovecote.

Every evening, after a dismal dinner, I fell asleep while Sophie began helping our youngest son with his schoolwork. Every morning I sat benumbed and mindless at a small table of polished cherry wood. Every morning Sophie left a fresh rose on my table, but even these talismans of love and encouragement did no good. All was hopeless, writing was out of the question.

245

Then there came an invitation for lunch in town and Sophie insisted that we accept it. Our hostess, a vivacious Frenchwoman, tried to cheer me up with a lively bit of gossip about a middle-aged man who went to pick up his young daughter at a school in Nice, only to discover accidentally from one of the young girl's classmates that his daughter was an energetic prostitute who had already gone, that day, from the playground to a sexual assignation. As I listened to that story, my interest quickened; I drank a glass of wine, and I saw myself walking jauntily toward a lone girl near some empty swings. At that moment I was distracted but no longer depressed. When we finished our meal (a specialty of cod and boiled potatoes served with aïoli, a lovely rich garlic sauce) and parted outside the restaurant, I kissed our French friend as happily as did Sophie, yet I was sorely impatient to get to our car.

In the hours and days to come the fresh roses sparkled on my table and I took for granted that I was close to beginning my novel for that year. Obviously Colette (not the writer but rather our friend) was if anything sympathetic to the father in her anecdote, whom she considered morally injured by his wayward daughter. From the beginning I was convinced that the father was in fact an odious man, while I was curiously pleased that his daughter was able to enjoy her after-school hours in a way generally considered a most serious transgression. (Here I should say that I too disapprove of child prostitution or pornography. But in fiction I have always been an immoralist of sorts, and was already thinking of Colette's story as fiction. I should say too that I have always been committed to eroticism in fiction, and convinced that there is nothing less erotic than the usual slang terms we often hear, even in the work of today's fiction writers, who somehow think they are being liberated because they write "cunt," a truly ugly word when compared to the erotics of "vulva," a word that resonates with the depths of the female sexual organ, or "cunny," the seventeenth-century term, which I believe is related to "bunny," suggesting a lighter view of the matter).

At any rate my distaste for the father grew. And within a week, two essential memories came to mind, one of a critic and one of a story my father once told me about a riot in a women's prison. The critic was a Marxist, who at a conference in a small college for women caused me considerable embarrassment, while making clear, I thought, his own contempt for the imagination. As soon as that memory returned, I knew that this figure, in his black suit and humorless face, was my protagonist (the novel would eventually be called *The Passion Artist,* ironically, of course). My father's story was this: at a young age, and as a member of the National Guard, he had helped to quell a riot in a nearby women's prison. My father and the other guardsmen had beaten the women with barrel staves. As good a man as he was, my father was apparently unaware of the horror of what they had done.

The Passion Artist, then, centers around a women's prison, a riot in which the women defeat the male intruders, and a doctor in the prison—Dr. Slovotkin—who performed tests on the imprisoned women in order to develop his theory of gender. It's an oddly compelling theory—namely "that men and women are both the same and the opposite." (No doubt the reader might dismiss this contradiction entirely, or disagree with both halves of it individually, but it does become meaningful when elaborated on.)

By the end of *The Passion Artist,* we learn that Mirabelle, Konrad Vost's daughter, is living happily with her boyfriend, that both Vost and Dr. Slovotkin have died, and that, after the successful liberation of the women's prison, it has become a home for transient Eastern European women.

The Passion Artist is a study of severe sexual repression (mostly affect-ing the men in the novel) and of the power of women. Paradoxically, it is a novel filled with highly erotic—even sexual—scenes, reflecting, in part, a collection of books I found hidden in one of the massive bookcases in that old house we were renting in Vence.

One of the most erotic of those scenes comes early in the novel, when Konrad Vost both betrays his daughter and yet succumbs to a prolonged afternoon of oral sex with the nameless girl who met him in the school yard.

"But She Was Not Mirabelle," which follows, is an example of the ex-tent to which a mere anecdote may be transformed into fiction. Also, I must add that this same piece appeared under the same title in 1978 in *Penthouse;* it is the only prose of mine ever to appear in such a popular magazine. I keep my only copy of that issue, as I have kept it for nearly twenty years, in a calf-skin binder made for me by my daughter.

———

Barbara Vaughn

In retrospect he was not able to discover the source of the well-being he felt that day or of the realization, upon him once more, that again the day had arrived when, as many times in the past, he would devote his entire afternoon to Mirabelle. But there it was: the good feeling, the benevolence, the exhilaration of seeing the day through a sheet of ice, and the determination that he would refuse the ordinary demands of his daily life in the pharmacy and undertake the long familiar walk in order to greet Mirabelle at the end of her day at school. The satisfaction attendant on this decision was immense: the students would emerge from the several gray buildings behind the wall on the top of which were strung the long strands of protective wire. The students would fill the sandy compound with the life of their bodies; the moving students would remind him of Gagnon's birds. He would see Mirabelle; he would stand still and wave; Mirabelle would return his greeting, surprised, happily understanding that once again her father was taking the trouble to walk home with her from school. Arm in arm they would set off together as they had done less and less frequently in these five surprisingly bearable years since the death of Claire.

He was breathing exactly the same clear cold air as would soon fill the lungs of the dispersing students. He was alone and walking eastward into the shadows of exactly the same street he would be traversing westward into the pale fading light with Mirabelle. It was the route of the small infrequent trolley cars, those doorless vehicles of gray riveted metal, and the sight of the narrow rails embedded in a field partly of cobblestones, partly of concrete, and the sagging overhead cable and the tin-roofed shelters where waited no passengers, no parents with children in hand: the sight of this thoroughfare on which he alone was proceeding could only evoke, as he strode along, the sound of Mirabelle's voice at his side and the vision of the entire schoolful of students swarming toward him suddenly with arms in the air and shoes and boots clattering on the empty stones.

He reached the landmark of the fountain, an amateurish replica in concrete of a dolphin from the mouth of which trickled not a drop of water. He turned the familiar corner where now, as always, he was both vindicated and offended by the smell of sewage pumping upward through an iron grate in the stones; he approached within sight and hearing distance of the low darkening school. But he heard nothing. He saw no one. He quickened his pace. With misgivings, with the utmost of disappointment, he entered the sandy square intended for recreation and calisthenics. But it was empty, except for a single girl who was walking listlessly in his direction and who was not Mirabelle. The impossible had happened. He was too late. He who was always correct, precise, punctual, was now, too late. Nevertheless, he decided to speak to the girl, who evidently meant to speak a few words to him.

"I am looking for Mirabelle," he said, "the daughter of Konrad Vost. Is she here?"

He inclined himself slightly from the waist, he relaxed his face, he assumed a pleasant quizzical expression, all in order to put at ease this girl who, except for her clothes, was strikingly similar to the girl he was seeking. The same rather large size, the same dark hair cut to shoulder length in imitation of an adult style, the same unformed quality of the face that still belonged to a child. Of course, instead of wearing skirt, blouse, shoes tied with the laces, this girl was dressed in pants of faded blue denim and, clinging to her torso, a thin white collarless and sleeveless shirt that was like a sweater. Across the front of the shirt and conforming the shape of this child's womanly bosom was printed in black letters the message WE AIM TO PLEASE. He noted the boldness of the letters but did not understand the pathos of the double meaning, since the message on the shirt was couched in that language he had never learned to read. He noted too the wooden sandals, on the bare feet, the goose flesh on the arms and upper chest. Mirabelle would not approve of such a costume. And she was perhaps too shy to stand this close to a stranger in the lengthening shadows of an empty school yard. But the incongruity of the lone girl was appealing as was the directness with which she was looking up at his face, so that he found himself bending again from the waist and attempting to disregard the tightness of the pant, the shirt.

"Well," he repeated, knowing the uselessness of the question, "and Mirabelle? Is she here?"

"No, she's already gone," said the girl, inclining her shoulder vaguely and drawing still closer. "If you want Mirabelle you must come earlier. But I'm available. And I can give you more than she could. And for less."

He waited. She said nothing more. He listened intently. And was someone else, someone very much like himself though with briefcase, topcoat, cane, face in the shadows, now approaching this same empty place to pause at the gate, to draw back, to stand quietly watching a tall middle-aged man already conversing with the obscured figure of the very person he, the imaginary stranger, had come to find? Had he visited this same school yard weeks in the past? Had this same girl been waiting? For a moment longer, he, the actual man, the living father, he who had come on his innocent mission, stood darkly within the institutional enclosure creating a dream, clinging as best he could to incomprehension. But then his entire world fell on him, like a facing of ice from an immense cliff, so that he was left with only defeat instead of disbelief, with the intolerable pain of sight after blindness, with the feelings of young fingers on the sleeve of his coat. So the school was in fact visited by men who were not at all the fathers of the concerned students; so she who was now waiting beside him meant what she had said and did not know or care who he was; so in an instant he had discovered the true uselessness of inquiry about Mirabelle who was already the genie who knew how to escape from the bottle. He was cold. He felt annulled. He was able to think of nothing but an armful of corsets. He was inflamed. He was annulled.

"Now," said the girl at his side, recalling him to the young fingers and the voice he would never forget. "Now, are you coming?"

He nodded. She requested his billfold. He complied. After she had transacted her business, alone, impervious to the fading light, oddly considerate of the man who possessed a steel tooth and who had made her friend her competitor, she stepped around his rigid figure and led the way out of the sandy enclosure and through the cold streets toward the building that concealed the shuttered room in which he knew she would again confront him with what he had hardly thought of since Claire's voice faded and the deathbed contained only her still form.

Between the school yard and the shuttered room there were only the determined clattering sounds of the wooden sandals and the cold blanketing knowledge of himself as a single anonymous older man in pursuit of the illicit services of a girl who was still in fact a child. Within the caverns that were now himself, even this knowledge was a form of oblivion. The girl made no attempt to conceal their passage together. He found that he was neither alarmed nor dismayed at the loudness of the sandals that protected the bare feet from the stones.

But it was precisely the sandals that she removed first in that small room with its single shuttered window and its empty walls of whitewashed concrete. One narrow door opened into the cubicle that was the toilet, which the girl now used, while the other opened into the cubicle containing the stove, the iron bottle of gas, the meager tins of food, the outmoded refrigerator on the top of which rested the radio of blackened Bakelite. In one corner of the room stood a table and two upright chairs; along one wall was the sparsely padded couch that obviously folded out into a bed for both mother and daughter; from the corner opposite the table and the chairs, and positioned so that it bisected the corner exactly, there protruded the shockingly incongruous sight of a gaunt narrow chaise lounge which, with its gilded lion's feet, its gilded frame, its upholstering material stitched with the enormous brown heads of flowers in the bloom, might have been dragged from an abandoned chateau that existed only in the pages of a moldy volume bound in green leather. Clearly this shabby, overly rich piece of furniture, situated in concrete and emptiness, represented the unattainable taste and vision of the mother; here she rested whenever she returned from working in the bakery, dry goods shop, laundry, rested in poor splendor while the girl, no doubt, played the radio in the cubicle that was filling with the smell of meat boiling in a steel pot on the stove.

No sooner had the toilet flushed than the girl reappeared, zipping her trousers, disregarding him where he stood fully clothed between the chaise lounge, the bare table, the couch. Through the slats in the shutters the light entered the room as if through the skeletal ribs of an animal long dead. He had not moved since entering this place of nakedness, and when the girl returned from the cubicle in the kitchen bearing a small glass filled to the brim with a clear liquor, he found it difficult to raise his arm, extend his hand, seize the glass. But he did so, while the girl stood watching him, and at the precise moment he coughed on the last of the liquor, the girl, in an easy gesture, and with both hands, pulled the white shirt over her head and free from her body. He coughed, he felt the burning in his nose and throat, the wetness in his eyes, and in the midst of this condition induced deliberately by the girl as preparation for the sight of her nakedness, he attempted not to think of Claire but instead gave himself the full benefit of what in his lifetime he had never seen: the thick and womanly breasts of a young girl.

She took the glass from him and replaced it not in the kitchen but on the bare table, so as to keep him in sight. The room smelled faintly of garlic and bottled gas; in the puckering of the naked waist he saw a scar that might have been inflicted in the fury of some childhood beating. Through the open door he could see the black-and-white toilet stark and waiting like an instrument of execution, and still wet and noisy from the girl's use. Around her neck was a thin chain bearing a small golden heart for a pendant.

Then, taking his hand in hers, she directed him, as if he were a walking invalid, not to the couch as he had expected but instead to the anomaly of the chaise lounge that extended into the room like an ornate tongue, like the narrow prow of an entombed boat, like the reclining place of a courtesan with feathers and painted skin. He could hardly bear to stretch himself out on it. But he did so, as she directed, allowing her to straighten his legs and, with her hand in his brow, to push his head gently backward into the cushion. She did not remove his shoes or spectacles; against his forehead her hand was as dry and naked as the bare feet, the bare breasts.

She remained at the head of his half-seated, half-prostate form, retaining the single childish hand on his brow, until patient, unhurried, staring down at him, she extended the other hand and touched him behind the ear,

Barbara Vaughn

on the back of the neck, and then inserted two fingers between the collar of the turtleneck shirt and the skin of his neck and slowly, in gestures that were now circular, now probing, worked the fingers downward as far as she could comfortably reach. He felt that those fingers were exalting his bones and flesh and buried spine. Fully clothed, hands at his sides, he felt himself imperceptibly reaching upward with the top part of his body toward the upright heaviness of the girl at his side. Her breathing deepened: the fingers probed, he allowed his head to incline gently to the right so that through half-closed eyes he could see the armpit, the surprising hair, the shape of the ribs like curves of light beneath the skin, the rounded bottom of one large breast. Hearing the girl's breath and his own, he allowed himself to raise and maneuver his right arm and hand so that his forearm was extended between her legs and the hand was clutching to himself the tightly denimed weight of the girl's leg and thigh. The zipper was half open, the thigh in its skin of cloth was hot.

He felt the fingers withdrawing from the neck of his shirt, he felt the bareness of the girl as she leaned over him and, with the fingers that only moments before were on the pulse of his neck, began to massage his chest and abdomen through the black shirt. He was not moving, and yet in his entire upper body, from his hips to his head, he felt himself straining to arch his back. Without looking he was aware that the girl's trinket, the small golden heart, was sliding in little fits and starts down the black expanse of his shirt, and knew that the girl's spread fingers were working insistently into the secret of his hard chest.

Slowly she dislodged his hand and arm and momentarily disappeared from the darkness in which he lay. He waited; on the chaise lounge he felt like a man fallen to the narrow ledge; never had he known what he now recognized as the beginning of the state of ecstasy. Then with relief, with anxiety, he realized that the girl was kneeling at the foot of the chaise lounge and was gripping his ankles in her two hands and pulling apart his legs so that he had no recourse but to comply, to bend his spread legs at the knees and to allow both feet to drop to the floor on either side of the flat narrow bedlike portion of the chaise lounge. The position, that of lying backward with legs wide apart and feet on the floor, like a survivor upside down on his back and awkwardly straddling in reverse some enormous wet black beam of a ship, exposed him suddenly, unmistakably, to the total mercy of the nameless young half-naked girl who was herself now straddling the flat narrow portion of the chaise lounge where his outstretched legs had lain.

For a moment he looked down the partial length of himself and into the eyes of the girl. He confronted the steady eyes, the hanging hair, the naked breasts, the tight fat triangular area where the strain on the girl's spread thighs was causing the zipper to creep increasingly open of its own accord. Then, as she moved closer and leaned forward and reached for him with her two hands, the small golden heart swinging free of her naked chest like a plumb line, then his entire person underwent a moment of brief spasmodic revulsion which, in the next instant, collapsed and gave way to a wave of trust and desire. Even before he closed his eyes he felt the girl's fingers flicking loose the tongue of his leather belt and unzipping and pulling wide the mouth of his trousers.

His eyes were shut, he gripped the edges of the chaise lounge; his breath was short and helpless in his mouth. The girl's fingers were inside the now invaded clothing of his loins which were flat, rigid, tumultuous in both concealment and accessibility. In his darkness he could feel the belt no longer buckled, the shirt pulled free from the trousers, the sensation of unexpected air. He could not have felt more naked if she had removed altogether the black trousers and the severe and modest underpants. But he was clothed and unclothed at the same time, and the girl's fingers—seemed to be multiplying inside his clothing and next to his skin. Somehow he was aware of the fingers all together and individually, detecting now the careful circumvention of the tight seam, now a smooth endless tickling or caressing sensation in the most vulnerable portion of his anatomy, now a rushing of all her fingers together inside the private tangle of his groin. In the midst of this pleasure, suddenly he became aware of the girl pushing one of her fingers into his rectum, and he gasped in a silent cry of joy and humiliation. How could he have been so ignorant of this experience? How could the girl have the knowledge and daring to do what she's doing?

But then, as he knew by the sudden pressure and profusion of hair, then the girl's face was buried in his disheveled groin. It was as if her head had become suddenly the head of a young lioness nuzzling at the wound it had made in the side of a tawny and still-warm fallen animal. Her face, her head, her mouth, her tongue, and suddenly he was confronted with his own unmistakable flesh—flaccid, engorged, he could not tell—aroused and moving in the depths of his clothes, in the mouth of his trousers, in the mouth of the girl. Bright blood, golden hair, and now the girl's head swerved once in a large circle of violence, tenderness, and then abruptly stopped, became fixed and rigid so that all her determination was now concentrated in the now fierce sucking activity of the hot mouth. The rectal pressure was increasing, the sound of breathing ceased, in the midst of his shock and pleasure he was not refusing what he knew was inevitable inside himself, fighting the greedy mouth as the child fights his bladder in the night. But then it began, in darkness and in the midst of what sounded like distant shouting, that long uncoiling of the thick white thread from the bloody pump, that immense and fading constriction of white light inside the flesh. Whom could he thank? How could he admit what had happened? He wanted to breathe, his head had fallen to one side, for a moment he did not even know whether he, like the poor child, had soaked his clothes in the futility and brightness of that emission that was now, finally, at an end.

He could not move. His eyes were closed. But then—after how long? and how soon before the mother would turn the corner and approach the silent building that housed this room?—then he felt the girl stirring and lifting her head from his lap. But she continued to move, not climbing indifferently to her feet, as he expected, but moving forward, keeping her body close to his own, until suddenly he felt her two hands pressed gently to the sides of his head, turning it, straightening it, and felt her mouth pressed against his own in a kind of protracted youthful kiss he could not have expected and had never known. Then as she continued kissing him with lips, tongue, jaw, slowly into his exhaustion, his joy, his mortification, there came the realization that now the girl was returning him the gift, the taste, of his own seminal secretions, his own psychic slime.

When he finally reached the doorway, adjusting his clothes, attempting to stand at ease, he could think of nothing except that the discoloration between the girl's buttocks had reminded him shockingly of a blown rose, and that the girl had in fact removed his spectacles and hidden them safely in the right-hand pocket of his black coat, where now he found them.

In the doorway and clothed again in pants and shirt, the girl spoke to him at last:

"I've done it before with an older man," she said, as his age and station came thundering down upon him once again. "But this is just the beginning. I promise you, just the beginning."

In the dark street there was no sign of the returning woman, the deceived mother, as rapidly and with set face he turned his back on the scene of his awakening, his degrading, at the hand of a dissolute child, and walked away into the night. The streets were empty yet everywhere he heard the sound of clattering sandals.

Can't

Carole Maso

Her pale blue scarf loose in the wind and her hair...

Objectively she can watch the descent, until she can't anymore.

His mouth at her neck. And it's not fear she's feeling but surrender and dread, a floating feeling and the full head of curls. The mouth...*Oh...*

And he stops at her breast and lingers there in a kind of stranding, stranded, surrender, beached there, can't, circling, lapsing, oh, not altogether pleasurable, anymore...Wings beating. Useless against. *I can't, Francesco.*

Shhh, he begs. And what world there is blurs. And time slips.

The room: intermingling of dark and light. On the night table four anisette biscotti on a gold plate. A point of reference. Before and after the descent. Something for the return—should they make it back. A decanter of amber. Strange drugged beacon.

Just outside the window sorrow, the sound of bells ringing. *Pius is dead. Paul is dead. John Paul is dead after only months.*

He'd brought her back a black bra from Sicily. *I love you.*

She tries to—*I can't anymore*—but he puts a finger to her lips.

I'm thirsty.

The night nurses.

She says to him, *Please Francesco, I can't.*

He licks the hair under her arms. Precious, most precious. Reading from the *Book of Saints*. He doesn't skip a single one. Saint Agatha. Saint Jerome in the desert. Most precious...

And she can't help but think of Antonioni in the slowness, in the excruciating heat, just how much time he takes. She tries to move herself, down, arches her back in an attempt to get to that mouth now. But then gives into it—the slow.

She is a passenger, she thinks, passive without control of where they are going—across the desert then? His slow devotion. She watches a black cat licking its hind paw at the window's ledge. Outside the smoke. Waiting. Crazy. A small thrashing. *Don't move.*

She tries to squirm to meet him. Scratching beard. *Pazienza, Ava.* She is caught in the lapsing, in the promise of, that eerie otherworldly place he takes her to.

And those cries and chortles—the babbling—is that she or just some worldly reverberation? Bristle of cat and slow and milk flowing. Somewhere a cyclone. A vortex of birds. Oasis. Hallucination.

Stalled now at the left breast. *Francesco.* In this downward...sucking on a rib, desiring...

Read to me from the Book of Saints. Their bleary, suffered, bleeding— *Oh God...*

And she is caught in this for years and falling as he descends.

Far from the place of God, and no God, *Francesco don't start,* but it's already too late, already far too late of course.

He whispers at her belly, *My mouth is already there.*

Having put down the book some time ago now, *I can't...*

And she is falling, undeniably. And the room darkens with his first touch. And the world blurs as she tries to fight it, only—*Francesco, I can't.* Having put down the film ledger, the small light out. The humming choir for a moment. And her breathing more and more shallow and he unlocks the black bra and smiles, *Can't what?*

I can't...

He lifts her striped dress. To reveal garter belt, silk stockings, as he has requested, her heels already digging into his back. *I can't.* She holds her dress in her hand, clenched, as he unbuttons her sweater. Cashmere. The black Sicilian bra.

The feel of his curls on her cheek, then neck, then clavicle. The sound of bells.

Striped dress. And the stripes of that extraordinary room—stanza, dark and light—the Venetian blinds. Her hand in his hair, *Can't anymore,* but pressing his head down, wanting, falling. Undeniably. *Oh...*

How did she suppose she'd ever resist this extraordinary, and now total, giving in? *Do what you like, whatever you want, forever, like that.*

Drained, the wall away, the cat dragging a mutilated bird across the room, passionate wreckage, shred of bells and—what she had wanted to say—this slayed and begging, partially destroyed...Pressing his shoulders down, *Please.*

Hanging only slightly out of reach. *I can't live.* Her head thrashing back and forth, blindfolded, now. He holds her hands down. *I can't.*

Don't. With his brute force now.

In the end, a pale blue scarf...removed from the eyes or the wrists.

What pulses, waiting there, glistening in the dark. The cat transfixed.

I can't live like this.

Ava Klein, how are you feeling?

And she watches the Roman sun in winter traverse *can't* and *live.*

We're falling.

Outside the transfiguration. Outside the mourning. Nailed to the wall, she screams. The collage of cardinals draped in red. The ballots cast once more. All the burnt offerings. Their grave task. Black smoke. From the cut throat—smoke. From the most precious blood—smoke. A somber electorate. As they go down. Outside a pope has died. *Oh*...After only months. An unnatural event. And she weeps.

Incense floats above the bed. She's floating off in its wafting, the perfume, pleasure, drifting passenger. The world comes and goes, amplified and then diminishing into an incredible calm. Once more. Beautiful last stanza, Francesco. Bathed in radiance. Just once more.

And oh how the mouth will seem fused to that spot, barely moving for a while.

What now begins to throb...the fingertips throb and the ends of her hair throb and all thought: *I want, I thought, fuck, love, take, now—without care for safety or—the flames. Look.* In the room. And then a kind of vacuum...

Live, he whispers and takes and opens, well practiced—and in love with this. An expert. *Live.*

He brings her knees to her head. Takes the pale scarf...

The odd angle at which we are suddenly positioned. Via Dante Alighieri—the right road lost. Tourists coming and going. American Express. *Francesco, I can't.*

God his head. His mouth now...

Almost, almost...

The way she writhed against his giant hands, mouth, erect. *Close up, you are like...*

And isn't it all just a little much? All the small tortures, her little half protests and signs and his insistence, swelling, the music bordering now on the film-scorish. He takes out his light meter. *Francesco...*

He stares at her, adjusts the blinds slightly. He is so absorbed that he barely sees her, looking up. Like one blinded. Now on her breast. Gorging himself. And she whispers, caught off guard—and how can she be off guard? But she is, always, still. The words sound strange to her: *Up close you are like a statue.*

Her dress. Blurring stripe, fading stripe in her bliss-filled eye. As he goes down. *I can taste you already.*

Each time it is something of the same: *Up close you are...You are...*

Falling. Sound of the breath, of the heart beating. *I can feel your heart. I can feel.* And the bells burn.

They're falling.

It's hopeless. Holding her as if in music or in prayer. *Bellissima,* he whispers.

It's hopeless.

As if in prayer. His lips parting, *Dear Ava.*

Morning and the nurses.

Into that slowed-up backward beating time, where the heart is yet to be broken once again, where the heart is yet to be mended, again and again. *You know Francesco, I think it is hopeless.* Her heart and dress ballooning in the room. Sad last stanza.

Tiny white parachutes. *Someone help me...*

He moves his mouth as if in prayer down her silken leg now slow. *Oh...*

Why did she think if she loved him, she'd be safe?
And she straddles the question, mystery, body, the absence of
God, in its perfection. Shudders and the praying one looks up
frightened all of a sudden whispering into that radiant center.
The great convulsive, floating, contracting—

Madonna, he gasps now, having...

It's hopeless. One scarcely, scarcely knows what else there is to be done. She smiles, as if there is some relief to be had.

Shall she tell you about relief once more? Refreshment? Once more? *Up close.*

A kind of whispering, motion of the tongue between teeth, lips. Whispering, coaxing, then harder almost devouring. *Yes, like that.* Holding his curls in her hands, forcing slightly the head. *What do you want?* And then he sucks hard—her fingers in his mouth, she can touch his tongue on her. He wraps his hands around her neck, then breasts, then holds her waist, encircles her waist with his arm, for a better angle, *There.* Clasped like that. All the points and ways of entry. *There.*

This is the Francesco she loves—the one she met when just a girl really, a student of comparative literature in Rome. She was just cantering, seventeen, then. Idealistic girl in a blue scarf looking into the endlessness of ocean and future. *Fuck me again,* she begs.

From the cut throat, birds. From the severed neck—rough this time—birds fly.

Striped wall—the light filtered through the blinds. Bells. The way his mouth...Source of heat, source of all inspiration. Those patterned operatic—How many afternoons did we spend like that? A lifetime ago.

She drenched and swollen and—

Live, Francesco says more to the nurses than directly to her. And then, *Get some rest.*

From the severed neck, a flock of birds fly. And outside the window now, bells.

Making love all night. What does she see when she closes her eyes? Bells turning sorrow into a song.

An anisette biscuit. A drained decanter of amber.

His favorite striped dress.

And across the wall.

It was at the beach at Rimini when he first took her hand. She wore a pale blue scarf. Hair escaping in the wind. Dark glasses. A glittering sea.

Tumbling to or toward this: a hospital bed. Even then. The destroyed bird on the window ledge. Feathers in the mouth of the cat.

He gets up to leave. He's an F-stop away. He's in the dark.

Twenty-four years old at the end. Already past her prime. One last time. Having come from another woman's body. She tastes her all over him. *I can't...*Fluttering on his open, his most expert...*I can't live like this.* And she watches light travel across the wall. Utterly dizzied. Such sadness and pleasure and beauty. *I can't live.* A square opens behind her eyes where mourners slowly enter one by one in black, waiting. And as more and more populate the beautiful piazza bordered by palaces and saints and extraordinary trees something opens like a rose, *Oh...*Such spaciousness, or hopefulness—never having experienced such option, such possibility, and perhaps never to again. But was this not everything and enough? Certainly enough. From the sexual bath of light promise comes. In that extravagantly striped afternoon room.

A woman weeps and turns her face away. The veiled afternoon. Outside a pope. Mournful bells. Birds in their bunting. A black flock swoops. People gather in the square. Witness gladiola and rosary.

Outside in bright light: milk, birds, smoke pouring from the cut throat. Blood flow and sorrow. Left at the edge of the bed: a pale blue scarf. *It shall blow in that breeze at Rimini forever Francesco.* As he leaves once more, as he goes off again for some months at a time with the most beautiful woman in the world again.

She reaches for him through smoke. *I love you,* he says, and he is off.

A nun holds a black bouquet. An extraordinary space opens in her.

Francesco, I can't live like this anymore.

Watershed

Jack Murnighan

That afternoon I had decided to stop kissing everybody. That was my master plan. To stop kissing Eleanor because it was starting to matter to her too much, to stop kissing Simone until she trusted me and wanted me back, and to stop secretly kissing her housemate Anna, too. Then it happened: a group of English Lolitas who together could form the cast of any number of one-acts of the id, pranced into my life and asked me to give them poetry tutorials. There I was, Hylas leaning towards the depths, nymphs beckoning...sometimes, you know, we just don't have a choice.

I proposed we read Milton. Eva wasn't part of the original group, but she'd heard about it through the grapevine and showed up for the first meeting. And despite the multitude of diversions, I noticed her immediately when she walked into the room. She was dressed more for a Russ Meyer casting than a poetry class: platinum blond bob, two trapped glacial lagoons for eyes, eyelashes like a pair of flexing tarantulas, her mouth a blood red drooping orchid. I, ingenuous to the end, didn't catch on at all. Every seam seemed ready to burst, the few buttoned buttons on her babydoll blouse

263

aching with the strain, her black mini a skin graft on racehorse thighs. She had come from Oxford and wanted to find out about this young American who had the hubris to propose to teach the English their own poetry. Her plan was to bury me.

Only later when we had drenched the sheets and closed the blinds to the sun, did I know the future is contained in the present as sure as in amber.

Piety

Now I have been fucked nearly to death. There are large tracts of skinless meat on my knees, elbows, and the tops of my feet; I have purple-black bite rings on my shoulders, around my neck, and down my arms; I've thrown a muscle in my lower back; my neck and shoulders are stiff as hell; and every time I touch her or even think about her I get so erect I think my penis is going to split like a pole bean along its seam.

It's never been like this and it does little good to use the word happiness to try to describe it. I feel more like a laboratory rat pressing the pleasure bar, ignoring food, ignoring water, ignoring society...We dream only of enclosure, to be phoneless and walled up like an amontillado, paired but anchoritic in endless white-knuckle worship.

The Sex Scene

I wake her with dirty fingers. Fresh stained with Vespa grease, I slowly run thumb and index along her sleeping brow, following the arcing line with mothwing-tender kisses. The parabola widens down past her clavicle, running my tongue along its slow ridge till my fingertips catch the edge of the duvet. In a steady tug I pull it off her body and there she lies golden and tousled in the late-morning sun. The touch recommences below her left breast, tracing kisses down to the gentle swell where snow white down first turns dark. She trembles, but does not wake. I unbutton my jeans and gently part her knees with the back of my hands. As she begins to stir, I lean my naked torso long out across her body, place my lips to hers, and slide myself into the warm and familiar aperture. Now she is awake and aware and kissing me back between a smile and arching her back and raising her knees. I tuck my hands under her ass, stand up slowly and pull her to the edge of the bed. She arches a bit to the left, guiding my movement with her left hand on my stomach, feeling each groove and ushering forth the long steady thrusts. My zipper is digging into her thigh and she'll have bruises from my belt buckle and button marks on her shanks, but she keeps biting her other thumb and circling faster and faster movements on my stomach. I lift her gently, pushing her legs back with my shoulders, and her left hand moves from my stomach to reach between her legs. She grinds, loses the composure of her expression, stroking herself with fore and middle fingers paired. Her breath comes heavy, and in an instant she is glazed with sweat. The pace quickens to the breaking point, my strokes are tight pulses, her ringlets replaced by a side-to-side mania, and then she gasps, pitches hard against me, does a long last grind, opens her eyes and unfurls a slow smile. She looks deep into my eyes and I just laugh, release her legs and kiss her full and wet on the lips. We know we've only just begun.

I try not to pull out after the first orgasm, just pause, drink a bit of water, bite her on the curve of her neck, and then recommence in delicate, attenuated circles. Her come glues me to her walls; I can barely pull backwards. It feels like fucking a stalled cement truck. Then I slip my shoulder round and roll her on top of me. She takes my hands and puts them high on her hips, then starts working in tight circles, leaning back little by little to take in ever more of me. She bites her lower lip, her hard high breasts are shining with sweat, her mouth opens, eyes close, and she smiles the smile of a fallen, defiant angel. Eva, my sweet Eva. Of my sugarplums, my deep-drives, my hemoglobin.

Toccata

"Lift it for me. Show it to me. Lift it for me slow. Speak to me with it baby, lift it, tell me you love me you know I love it. Show it to me, oh yes, show it to me honey, do that thing you do. I gotta have you baby, gotta touch you, let me rub my face all over it. Take the pillow, yeah, use the pillow honey you'll be more comfortable, I gotta rub my face all over it, gotta touch you. Fuck I love you baby. Shit I'm trembling all over. I'm losing it baby, I'm gonna split or fall apart or something. No don't do this to me baby, don't, don't. Oh don't fucking do this to me baby. No you can't possibly move it that way, you can't baby, no please don't. Oh just let me just let me touch, oh shit, oh shit. Oh yeah, oh yes, yes baby yes, oh you can't be doing that you can't. Oh jesus, holy fuck, oh baby please. Yeah shake it, oh yes move it, oh yes, oh I can't take it baby I just can't. No you've gotta be kidding, you have got to fucking be kidding, oh let me, let me let me let me. Move it baby, show me how you can move it. Holy fucking shit, oh I like that baby, fuck that's good, that is so fucking good. Oh yeah honey, go baby, fucking christ, I'm gonna fucking lose it, I'm gonna fucking explode, I'm just gonna fucking die. A little fucking more baby, oh yeah, a little, just a little more, oh shit, oh shit, oh my fucking god, oh..."

Fugue

Butterfly your arms to their furthest extension, arch your scapulae pinioned beneath your lover's weight, then rotate your palms and bury nail and knuckle through the sheets and deep into the foam; then pull, pull, squeeze, stretch, buckle; then, when you're about to snap, when you hear yourself scream and feel the sweat run in rivulets down your face, you will begin to have an idea of what I'm talking about.

She tells me that when I die she'll have me cremated, put my dust in a douche and run me through one last time.

I, however, remain a bit stymied. The closest phrase I've found is "I love the shit out of you." These seven words, as I halt the millionth time from repeating them, emerge again as the final frontier, the last outpost of language on the range. In my dreams I see the hordes of bison, the unmassacred millions of bison, the massive, sanguine, mindless triple-hearted bison ever charging the further field and each thundering footfall the mute's testimony of my singular truth.

Beneath a footprint, below a gopher hole, under an oil well, deeper, deeper than the blackest sea abyss where the transparent fish traded eyes for malice and kill not for sustenance but to syncopate the monotony, that is where my echo sounds.

I have died but that doesn't keep me from dying again and again. A whisper—death. Two minutes late—death. A hemline—death. Like a field of sorghum, the folly of identity has been surrendered to the lilt, whistle, and push of an eternal wind.

She seems to feel likewise.

Contributors

JOHN PERRY BARLOW is a Wyoming-based rancher, a lyricist who composed for the Grateful Dead, a contributing editor at *Wired*, a member of the WELL board of directors, and a cyberrights activist who penned the Declaration of Cyber Independence. He is also a nomad and the father (tour guide) of three girls. **DEBRA BOXER** has been writing erotica since her Spanish class in high school, where it was a technique to stay awake. For the last four years she has written book reviews for *Publishers Weekly*. She hopes to publish her first novel and have sex before she turns thirty. **POPPY Z. BRITE** has worked as an artist's model, a mouse caretaker, a stripper, and (since 1991) a full-time writer. She has published three novels, *Lost Souls, Drawing Blood,* and *Exquisite Corpse,* as well as a short story collection, *Wormwood,* and the biography *Courtney Love: The Real Story.* **ROBERT OLEN BUTLER** is the author of seven novels, including *The Deep Green Sea.* Butler's short story collection, *A Good Scent from a Strange Mountain,* was awarded the 1993 Pulitzer Prize for Fiction and nominated for the PEN/Faulkner Award. He is also the winner of the 1993 Guggenheim Fellowship for Fiction. He teaches creative writing at McNeese State University in Lake Charles, Louisiana. **LISA CARVER** is the author of *Dancing Queen* and publisher of the magazine *Rollerderby.* She hates it when sensualists try to lick her face. **QUENTIN CRISP** has made a living as a commercial artist, an artist's model, and an author. Crisp is best known for his autobiographies, *The Naked Civil Servant, How to Become a Virgin,* and most recently, *Resident Alien.* He has appeared in the films *Orlando, The Bride, Philadelphia,* and *To Wong Fu, Thanks for Everything, Julie Newmar.* He believes that "sex is a mistake." **M. JOYCELYN ELDERS, M.D.,** entered the United States army as a first lieutenant at the age of eighteen. She attended the University of Arkansas Medical School on the G.I. Bill, and later joined the UAMS faculty as a professor of pediatrics. In 1987 Dr. Elders was appointed Director of the Arkansas Department of Health. She was sworn in as Surgeon General of the U.S. Public Health Service by President Clinton on September 8, 1993. Dr. Elders stepped down from this post in December 1994 to continue her professional career at UAMS. **LARS EIGHNER** is the author of *Pawn to Queen Four: A Novel, Gay Cosmos,* and *Travels with Lizbeth,* among other works of fiction and nonfiction. He lives in Austin, Texas, with his dog Lizbeth. **COURTNEY ELDRIDGE** lives in New York. "Anonymous" is her first published short story. **GREG FRIEDLER** was born in 1970 and grew up in New Orleans, Louisiana. He received a Master of Fine Arts in photography from the School of Visual Arts in New York City. **CHARLES GATEWOOD**'s photography has been supported by three fellowships from the New York State Council on the Arts, awards from the American Institute of Graphic Arts, the Art Directors' Club, and *Photographer's Forum,* as well as the Leica Medal of Excellence for Outstanding Humanistic Photojournalism. His books include *Charles Gatewood, Sidetripping* (with William S. Burroughs), *Wall Street, Primitives,* and *True*

Blood. **FIONA GILES** was born and raised in Australia and educated at Oxford, where she specialized in nineteenth-century literature. She is the editor of *Dick for a Day: What Would You Do If You Had One?* **AL GOLDSTEIN** is the publisher of *Screw* magazine and producer of the cable television show *Midnight Blue.* He is a photographer, gadget collector, film buff, cigar aficionado, and writer whose work has appeared in the *New York Times,* the *Los Angeles Times, Harper's,* and *Playboy.* He is also a contributing editor at *Penthouse* and a columnist for the London-based *Arena* magazine. He holds an honorary doctorate from the Institute for the Advanced Study of Sexuality. **PETER J. GORMAN**'s obsession with photographing nudes began when he bought his first camera at age sixteen and began shooting his girlfriend. Peter has worked since college as a photographer and contributes regularly to *Black Book* magazine. **LUCY GREALY** is a poet and the author of *Autobiography of a Face.* She attended the Iowa Writers' Workshop and has been a fellow at the Bunting Institute of Radcliffe and the Fine Arts Work Center in Provincetown. **AMANDA GRISCOM** is a writer and assistant editor at *Feed.* She writes regularly for *Newsday, Wired News, Blue,* and *Time Out.* **MATT HARNETT** has published photos in *People, Newsweek, Time Out, New York Magazine,* and the *Village Voice.* He holds a Master of Fine Arts in Photography and Related Media from the School of Visual Arts in New York City. His street portraits of New York City's East Village inhabitants are included in the book *New York: An Illustrated History of the People,* edited by Allon Schoener. **JOHN HAWKES** wrote sixteen books of fiction, including *An Irish Eye, Sweet William, Adventures in the Alaskan Skin Trade, The Blood Oranges,* and, most recently, *The Frog.* He was T. B. Stowell University Professor Emeritus at Brown University, and a member of the American Academy of Arts and Letters. He passed away in May 1998. **EVANS D. HOPKINS** has written for *The New Yorker,* the *Washington Post,* and *Slate,* among other publications. He is currently at work on a prison memoir, as well as other fiction and film projects. **AARON JAMES** is the pseudonym of a writer who moved to New York from the Midwest nine years ago. He has written for the *New York Times Book Review* and the *New York Observer.* His first novel, *Assuming the Position,* will be published in fall 1999. When he is not writing or hustling, he tends bar. **THOM JONES** is the author of two short story collections, *The Pugilist at Rest* (a National Book Award finalist) and *Cold Snap.* His stories have appeared in *The New Yorker, Playboy, Esquire, Harper's,* and *GQ,* and have been widely anthologized. **RICHARD KERN** studied art and philosophy at the University of North Carolina at Chapel Hill. His films have been shown at the Whitney Museum of American Art and his photographs are collected in the book *New York Girls.* **BARBARA KILGORE** is a United Methodist clergyperson, teacher, counselor, and author. With Dr. M. Joycelyn Elders, she has written for the *Los Angeles Times, Playboy, POZ,* and *Encyclopedia Brittanica.* She is at work, with Dr. Elders, on a book about masturbation. **NORMAN MAILER** was born in 1923 in Long Beach, New Jersey, and grew up in Brooklyn, New York. He published his first book, *The Naked and the Dead* in 1948. *The Gospel According to the Son* is his thirtieth book. Mailer won the National Book Award and the Pulitzer Prize in 1968 for *The Armies of the Night* and was awarded the Pulitzer Prize again in 1980 for *The Executioner's Song.* He has directed four feature-length films, was a cofounder of the *Village Voice* in 1955, ran unsuccessfully for mayor of New York in 1969, and was president of the

American PEN from 1984 to 1986. **VIVIENNE MARICEVIC**'s work has been exhibited at the International Center of Photography, the Houston Center for Photography, and Nikon House, New York. She is the recipient of a New York Foundation for the Arts Fellowship. Her book of photographs of transvestites and male-to-female transsexuals is entitled *Male to Female: La Cage aux Folles.* **CAROLE MASO** is the author of *Defiance, Aureole, Ghost Dance, The Art Lover, Ava,* and *The American Woman in the Chinese Hat.* **GLORIA MITCHELL** has written for Lycos and Yahoo! *Internet Life.* She thinks all the awful things people say about the Internet are true but likes it anyway. **RICK MOODY** is the author of *The Ice Storm* and *Purple America,* among other works of fiction and nonfiction. He is presently at work on a genealogical narrative, *The Black Veil.* **JACK MURNIGHAN** is the senior editor at *Nerve* as well as a doctoral candidate in Literature at Duke University. He is at work on a dissertation on medieval allegory entitled "Beatrice's Smile." **BEN NEIHART** received his Master of Arts from Johns Hopkins University in 1994. He is the author of *Hey Joe,* and his stories have appeared in *The New Yorker.* **DIANORA NICCOLINI** was born in Florence, Italy. She has been a fine art photographer, specializing in male nudes, for twenty-five years. Her work has appeared in ten anthologies of photography on the body and hangs in the collections of the International Center of Photography, the Museum of Fine Arts, Texas, and the Alternative Museum in New York City, among others. **DALE PECK** is the author of the novels *Now It's Time to Say Goodbye, The Law of Enclosures,* and *Martin and John.* His work has appeared in *Out, QW,* the *Nation,* the *Village Voice,* and *Men on Men 4: Best New Gay Fiction.* **SYLVIA PLACHY** is staff photographer for the *Village Voice.* Her first book, *Unguided Tour,* won the International Center of Photography Infinity Award for Best Publication of 1990. Her photographs have appeared in *Newsweek, Artforum,* the *New York Times Magazine, Grand Street, Wired, Doubletake,* and *Tatler.* Her work is in the collections of the Museum of Modern Art, the Metropolitan Museum of Art, the San Francisco Museum of Modern Art, and the *Bibliothèque Nationale.* She has had solo exhibitions at the Whitney Museum of American Art and other venues. Her weekly photographic column, "Unguided Tour," appeared in the *Village Voice* from 1982 to 1993. She is at work on a new book. **FABRIZIO RAINONE** is an Italian-born fashion photographer with a degree in filmmaking. His photographs have appeared internationally in *Vogue, Harper's Bazaar, Marie Claire,* and *Cosmopolitan,* among others. **ADAM ROGERS** is a reporter for *Newsweek* magazine, where he covers science, technology, and medicine. He has also written about science fiction, animation, comic books, and various other topics on the geek beat. **ANDRES SERRANO** studied photography at the Brooklyn Museum Art School in New York. He has received grants from the New York State Council on the Arts, the National Endowment for the Arts, and other foundations. His photography has been exhibited at museums around the world, including the Whitney Museum of American Art, the Museum of Contemporary Art, and the National Museum of Photography. **RUTH SHALIT** writes regularly on politics and culture for the *New Republic,* where she is Associate Editor. Her articles have also appeared in the *New York Times Magazine, Gentleman's Quarterly,* and the *New York Observer.* **TARYN SIMON** is a recent graduate of Brown University with a Bachelor of Arts in Art Semiotics. She has studied photography at the Rhode Island School of Design and

Spéos Photographic Institute, Paris, France. **MEREDITH F. SMALL** is a professor of anthropology at Cornell University where she is teaching biological anthropology and primate behavior. She spent many years studying the mating behavior of macaque monkeys in captivity and in the field. Her latest book is *Our Babies, Ourselves: The Biology and Culture of Parenting*. **ROBERT STIVERS** has shown his work extensively in the United States and Europe. His photographs are in the collections of the Los Angeles County Museum of Art, the Museum Ludwig, and the Victoria and Albert Museum of Art. **DAVID TEAGUE** studied literature at Hendrix College in Arkansas and at the University of Virginia. His short stories have won the Redneck Review of Literature Western Fiction Prize and the Delaware Division of the Arts Fellowship in Fiction. He is currently completing a novel, *William Norton's Death*, and a screenplay, *Singletree*. **CATHERINE TEXIER** was born and raised in France and now lives in New York City. She wrote her first novel, *Chloé l'Atlantique*, in French, and is the author of a memoir, *Breakup*, and two novels in English, *Love Me Tender* and *Panic Blood*. Her work has been translated into nine languages. She was coeditor, with Joel Rose, of *Between C and D*. She is the recipient of a National Endowment for the Arts Award and a New York Foundation for the Arts Fellowship. **SALLIE TISDALE** is the author of five nonfiction books, including *Stepping Westward* and *Talk Dirty to Me: An Intimate Philosophy of Sex*. She is a contributing editor at *Harper's* and *Tricycle*, and a columnist for *Salon*. Her work has appeared in the *New Republic, The New Yorker, Spin, Traveler,* and *Antioch Review*. She is currently at work on a new book entitled *Pigs in Blankets*. **CAMMIE TOLOUI**'s photographs have appeared at the New Museum of Contemporary Art in New York City, P.S. 122 in New York City, and the Camerawork Gallery in San Francisco. She has been published in *Elle, See, Surface, Vi Menn* (Norway), and *Visual Communications Quarterly*. Cammie is the recipient of the *New York Times* Award for Excellence in Photojournalism and the Greg Robinson Memorial Photojournalism Scholarship. She holds a degree in photojournalism from San Francisco State University. **BARBARA VAUGHN** is a New York-based portrait photographer whose clothed clients include celebrities, corporate executives, rock bands, authors, artists, and families. Her nude clients include women in all the aforementioned categories and more. A former competitive figure skater, she spent several years in the corporate world before pursuing her passion for photography as a career. **WILLIAM T. VOLLMANN**'s books include *You Bright and Risen Angels, The Rainbow Stories, Whores for Gloria, An Afghanistan Picture Show, Thirteen Stories and Thirteen Epitaphs, Butterfly Stories,* and three of the projected seven novels in his "Seven Dreams" series: *The Ice-Shirt, Fathers and Crows,* and *The Rifles*. He is the recipient of a Whiting Foundation Award. His most recent book is a collection of stories called *The Atlas*. **ELISSA WALD** studied writing at Columbia University. She has worked in the circus, on Indian reservations, as a phone sex operator, a stripper, and as an outreach counselor to prostitutes. She is the author of *Meeting the Master*, a collection of short stories. **KIM WESTON** started taking pictures at age six. He learned the craft from his father, Cole Weston, son of Edward Weston. Kim has exhibited his work in Europe and the United States. **BARRY YOURGRAU** is the author of *The Sadness of Sex* and the star of the movie comedy version of the book. He has presented his tales on MTV, NPR, and Comedy Central. He is at work on a new book, *Haunted Traveller*.

You've just had a small taste of *Nerve*. **If the stories, essays,** and photographs you've seen here leave you wanting more, please visit www.nerve.com. We hope you will share your thoughts, confessions, har-rumphs, or hallelujahs with us and other *Nerve* readers in the Nerve°Center community space. We also welcome e-mail feedback at info@nerve.com.

nerve°

LITERATE SMUT